SAVED BY DARKNESS

Katie Reus

Cover art: Jaycee of Sweet 'N Spicy Designs
Editor: Julia Ganis
Author website: www.katiereus.com

Saved by Darkness/Katie Reus. -- 1st ed.
ISBN-10: 1635560047
ISBN-13: 9781635560046

eISBN: 9781635560039

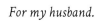
For my husband.

CHAPTER ONE

52 years ago

I an instinctively scanned the attendees as well as the exits as he and his friend Mason stepped into the huge hotel courtyard.

"Why are we even here?" Mason asked Ian, tugging at the collar of his tuxedo shirt. Mason LaCour was a New Orleans native, unlike Ian, and had a Cajun accent that got thicker when he was annoyed.

Ian lifted a shoulder. He hadn't been in the city long, just a couple weeks. "We were asked." And when the vampire running the supernatural fights Ian participated in asked for something, Ian wasn't going to say no unless the request was offensive. Coming to a glitzy party wasn't his idea of fun, but there had been no reason to decline.

Mason grumbled, but snagged two glasses of champagne off the tray of a passing waitress. The hotel had been around since the late eighteen hundreds and the courtyard was just as lush as the interior. Star-shaped oil lanterns hung from trees in addition to the string of lights crisscrossing above them. Ian's dragon frowned at the lights, annoyed that they would tangle in his wings if he needed to make an escape.

But he could just burn them to ash if necessary.

All the women had big hair that seemed to define the style for this decade, smoky eyes and, to his appreciation, all their glittery dresses were ultra-short. He'd seen a lot of changes in style over the last few decades and this was by far his favorite. A jazz band played in one corner, the music upbeat, while some people danced on a small wooden dance floor. The majority of the all-supernatural partygoers were in clusters, talking, laughing, smoking and drinking.

Instead of offering Ian the other glass, Mason downed both of them, one after the other, making Ian snort. "Try and act somewhat civilized."

Ian didn't fit in with these rich people either, but he knew how to act as if he did.

Mason set the glasses down on a nearby table. "Easy for you to say."

Ian frowned, not sure what his friend meant, and decided not respond. Ian was part demon and part dragon. He didn't even know any other dragons, but they had to be out there. His mother had once told him that dragons formed clans—though he'd never been part of one. She'd been tight-lipped about that part of his heritage and he'd never pushed. Hell, she'd been quiet about all of his heritage, though he knew her mating with his sperm donor had been forced.

And if he ever found the full-blooded demon male, he'd kill him for it. All he had was a name. It wasn't much, but it was something. One day that male was going to feel Ian's wrath.

Shaking off those dark thoughts, he picked up a drink from another passing waiter, mainly to blend in better.

"Let's head to the bar," Mason muttered, veering off in that direction before Ian could respond.

There were three bars, but his pseudo-friend was heading to the nearest one—a wood and glass rolling cart filled with bottles of liquor. Sidestepping a female who he was certain was a vampire given her flash of fangs, he fell in step with Mason. Before they'd gone far, Bruneau, the vampire who'd asked them both here tonight, appeared from seemingly out of nowhere.

Or more likely he'd just dropped from one of the many live oak trees in the courtyard. The male could be creepy when he wanted to. And that seemed to be often.

"Mason, leave us." Bruneau flicked his wrist once, dismissing Mason—who didn't grumble, simply did as he was ordered.

Ian's dragon and demon both rankled at the tone from the other male but that was something he'd learned to keep under control over the years. For the most part, he knew he was the strongest male in any room. Or damn near close to it.

He'd had to be strong from the time he was a child. As a mixed breed whose mother had been alone in the world, he'd made it clear to any supernatural—or human—predators that if they tried to mess with his family, they would die. The first time he'd killed someone while protecting his mother, he'd been eight. It had been an accident.

The first time he'd killed with intent, he'd been ten. And he felt no guilt over it.

As if the vampire had read Ian's mind, he said, "If I'd ordered you to leave like that, you'd have taken my head off."

Ian softly snorted. Not true. He didn't care enough and he wasn't psychotic enough to attack someone for something like that. But most supernaturals in New Orleans who attended the fights seemed to think he was an animal. His nickname in the fighting ring was "Beast."

Not that he'd ever shown his other form—either of them—to anyone here tonight. Certainly not in the ring. But he fought like an animal.

"Or maybe not," the male murmured, his greenish-gray eyes intense as he stared at Ian. As if he wanted to see through to Ian's soul. "I'm surprised you came tonight."

He nodded. "Thank you for the invitation."

The male just stared for a long moment in that creepy way of his. Ian held his gaze, unable to stop himself. It was the Alpha dragon in him. Waves of strength rolled off the vampire, but Ian's dragon sneered at the male, arrogant in his own power, even though he'd be no match for Ian's. He wondered if Bruneau realized it.

Bruneau finally cleared his throat, glancing away as a female headed their way. Another vampire. Her approach gave the vampire the excuse needed to break eye contact. Petite with dark hair, ebony skin and a skintight gold, sparkly dress, the female gave Ian a wide smile. Instead of introducing them, Bruneau simply whispered in the female's ear, telling her politely to go away.

Ian didn't audibly sigh in relief, but he was grateful Bruneau didn't try to push another female at him. He liked females. But every supernatural being he'd met so far through Bruneau just wanted to "fuck the Beast." He rolled his shoulders at the thought. He wouldn't let anyone use him.

"One day I will find a female to your liking."

"Or you could just find me a worthy opponent." He was tired of winning all the fights he engaged in, ready to move on from New Orleans. The scents could be overwhelming during the day, especially the garbage warming under the sun in the Quarter. But he'd learned that he could live with just about anything, and managed to tune out some things. He hadn't been here long, and while he liked the atmosphere of the city, it was time to leave. Lately all his opponents hadn't been remotely strong enough to be in the ring with him. He didn't like pummeling the weak. He wanted a challenge. So he'd been holding back as not to completely maim or kill his newest opponents. And Bruneau knew it.

"I believe I've found one." Bruneau jerked his chin behind Ian, his eyes glittering with excitement.

Half-turning, Ian felt his heart stop in his chest as he locked gazes with a striking female. Her vivid blue eyes reminded him of the ocean. Tall, though still a head shorter than him, the woman had dark hair looped over one breast in a long braid. Her ivory skin seemed to glow against the bright pink of her fringe dress. And her legs went on for miles.

At a growling sound, his gaze snapped to her male companion—who Ian hadn't noticed until now. The male also had dark hair and blue eyes—and looked as if he wanted to kill Ian. For a moment he wondered if they were siblings.

He fully turned to face the couple.

Bruneau stepped forward so that he was in between Ian and the newcomers. "Ian, this is Colm O'Riley. He's in the city for a few weeks on business—and is also undefeated. He'd like to fight you."

At the moment, Ian didn't care about the male's name or fighting. He wanted an introduction to the female next to Colm. Ignoring the two males, he held out a hand to the female. "I'm Ian."

The other male growled again, but Ian ignored that as well.

The female blinked in surprise and something that looked a lot like amusement quirked her full lips up as she held out a hand. "Ah, I'm Fiona."

The scent of her was wild, like the ocean itself. He wondered if the taste of her would be as wild, exotic.

Before he could take her hand, touch her, Colm stepped forward, shoving Fiona behind him. Ian growled low in his throat, letting the leash on his most primal side slip a fraction. That was when he realized everything had gone quiet, even the music. There was a nervous energy in the air and everyone was staring at them.

"You don't look at her, don't touch her." The male's voice was low, a deadly razor's edge to it.

Ian's dragon reared up and he barely managed to keep him contained. His back and arms rippled under the force of holding his beast in check. He'd never experienced this lack of control before, but her scent and closeness was making him edgy. He wasn't sure why, wasn't sure he liked it. He'd analyze it later. "Name the place and we fight," he growled.

Next to them, Bruneau cleared his throat. "Is three hours soon enough?"

Ian nodded once and so did the male, though neither of them backed down. It was taking all of his strength not to attack the newcomer, to rip his head from his body for standing between him and the female whose scent was embedded in his brain forever now. He inhaled again—and not subtly—wanting to drink her in. Didn't matter that the male was blocking her from Ian; Colm couldn't hide her scent. As if the other male knew what Ian was doing, he growled even louder, flashed his canines.

"Break it up," Bruneau murmured.

They weren't even touching each other, but Ian nodded once, keeping his gaze pinned to Colm's. He wouldn't be taking his eyes off the male. No animal looked back at him, but he scented the wildness in the other man as well. He was a shifter of sorts, though Ian wasn't sure which kind. He was huge, just like Ian. Maybe…bear or wolf.

Didn't matter. He'd be taking care of this male in the ring. Then he would talk to the female. He didn't understand the primitive part of him that had flared to life so suddenly, but he wasn't going to ignore it. To do that would be to ignore an intrinsic part of himself.

Finally, the other male stepped back, but only, Ian noticed, because the female tugged on his upper arm. Hard.

He frowned at the sight of her touching the male. Ian didn't know her, had no claim on her, but…he didn't like that one bit.

Once Colm and Fiona blended back into the crowd, the music started up once again and people resumed talking as if nothing had happened.

"At least now I know your type," Bruneau muttered. "But I advise you to make yourself scarce until the fight. He has two brothers."

Ian nodded and handed him the champagne glass he was still holding. No further response was necessary. He caught Mason's eye across the courtyard and the male waved him off since he was talking to a female. Nodding again, Ian started up a stone path in the courtyard, heading to the hotel.

He wasn't sure if they were aware of it, but everyone carved a path for him, automatically stepping back and giving him room. It had been like that for as long as he could remember.

No one was in the hotel lobby other than staff and he hadn't checked a coat so he didn't need to make any stops. Energy hummed through him as he thought about the upcoming fight. He might have no idea who the male was, but he didn't like him for the mere fact he'd been acting so territorial with Fiona.

Fiona. He let her name roll around in his head, savored it.

"Wait!"

Everything inside him stilled at *her* voice. He'd only heard her say a few words but her voice was already etched into his mind.

He turned to the right and saw Fiona standing half behind an oversized palm tree. If she thought she was hiding, she was doing a terrible job.

Tall and sexy, in that bright pink dress she couldn't blend in anywhere. After looking around the lobby nervously, she motioned with her hand for him to follow then turned on her heel.

He didn't even think to question if it was a trap, just trailed after her as she hurried down a short hallway and ducked into a small room right off the main lobby. It turned out to be a walk-in coat closet.

"Shut the door," she whispered as he stepped in after her. Wrapping her arms around herself, she stared at him expectantly until he did as she'd said.

Her wild ocean smell overwhelmed him, surpassing the perfumes, colognes and the faint scent of cigars clinging to some of the coats and jackets.

His dragon rippled under the surface again as he looked at her, breathed her in. Lust and a need to claim overwhelmed him. He wasn't complaining that she'd called him in here, but... "Why do you wish to speak to me in a coat closet?" He felt awkward as he talked to her.

She took a small step forward. "I know you're supposed to fight my brother later, so I'm just warning you...he's never lost. He's very, very strong."

His heart stopped beating at the word brother. The male wasn't her lover.

She continued, her brow knitted together. "I know you haven't lost either, according to Bruneau, but...you will this time. And my brother is angry at you for the mere fact that you spoke to me. Just walk away. Please." There was a desperation in her voice.

He frowned, surprised by her concern even as his dragon and demon rejoiced that the male was her brother. "Are you mated?"

She blinked those startling blue eyes. "Did you hear what I said?"

"Yes. Are you?" He would have scented another male on her, but he wanted to hear her say the words. He needed the confirmation.

She let out an exasperated sound. "No, I'm not."

He nodded once and closed the distance between them. Not bothering to hide what he was doing, he leaned in and *almost* touched her jaw with his nose as he inhaled again. It took all the restraint he had not to reach out and touch her. But he didn't want to scare her and she hadn't invited his touch so he kept his hands to himself. He might be a mixed breed and undesirable to many shifter females, but he wasn't an animal. Not like his father. He would never be like that sorry excuse for a male.

She didn't back away, just stared at him with a mix of emotions, confusion being the main one. But there was a hint of lust, one she couldn't hide.

"I won't kill the male since he's your brother." It was the only concession he could give her. He tried not to kill in the fighting ring but it wasn't always avoidable. Sometimes his opponents pushed and pushed, refusing to yield until death for them was the only option.

Her eyes widened even more before she just shook her head. "Foolish male."

Foolish? She was truly concerned about his well-being even if she appeared to think *he* was weak. That thought rankled him. He would have to show her he was a worthy male—strong enough for her. "Will you have dinner with me tomorrow night?"

"If you get in the ring with my brother in a few hours, you won't be around to have dinner with me tomorrow," she snapped, her hands going to her curvy hips.

His dragon blazed to life at her words. She truly thought he was weak. He didn't much care what other supernaturals thought about him, but her words... He needed to show her how strong he was. Something primitive and dark flared inside him at the challenge. "If I survive, you'll have dinner with me."

"That doesn't sound like a question."

He didn't respond, just watched her and breathed her in. Her scent was addictive and was making it hard to think clearly, much less talk. His demon side didn't like the lack of control, but his dragon side didn't care. At all. He could roll around in her scent; wanted to bathe in it, live in it.

She huffed out an impatient sigh. "Fine. If you manage to survive, I'll go to dinner with you. Just...reconsider what I said."

He snorted. Her brother was the one who should walk away. "Meet me at Mandina's tomorrow night. Six o'clock?" He wanted to lock down a time and place. Because this was a female he couldn't let walk away. He'd be a fool to do so.

She hesitated for a moment, blew out another frustrated breath, then nodded. "I'll be there."

That was all he needed to hear.

Because her scent was starting to make his dragon get edgy, he turned and left the closet without another word.

He'd fight her brother tonight, then see her tomorrow. He just hoped he didn't have to hurt her brother too badly in the ring.

Because he planned to show this captivating female that he was a worthy mate. Killing her brother wouldn't do him any favors.

CHAPTER TWO

Present day

"Hey, man." Ian shook Malloy's hand once at the front of Bo's supernatural-only club. His half-brother Bo was off on his honeymoon right now but he'd kept the club open, letting his family run it while he was gone. On the outside the place appeared nothing more than a warehouse. Since it was located near a marina and well away from prying eyes, any human who stumbled on it probably assumed it was for boat storage. "Busy tonight?"

The ghoul lifted a shoulder. As head of security Malloy had a pulse on every aspect of the club. "Not bad for a Wednesday. Your brother and Liberty are in the office."

"Thanks." He'd received a strange call from Rory, telling him he needed to talk to Ian about something important. Ian couldn't imagine what, but wanted to get it out of the way. His brother had been acting a little strange since a couple days before Christmas.

Inside the club, Ian immediately scanned the main bar, saw his half-sister Cynara bartending. She smiled at him, flashing her fangs before returning to her customers.

Muted music filtered in from well-hidden speakers. Half the roped-off booths across the main dance floor already had the heavy curtains closed, giving the supernaturals inside privacy. There were no windows anywhere in the two-story building in case nosy humans stumbled on the property.

The scent of sweat and sex filled the air, intermingling with the various perfumes. Men and women were on the half-dozen platforms, dancing and groping each other. Instead of moving through the throng of high-top tables near the bar, he skirted the edge of the club and only stopped when he reached a plain white door.

It was unlocked, no doubt because Malloy had let Rory know he was here already. Once he was in the hallway, the music dimmed even more thanks to incredible soundproofing.

The door to Bo's office was already open, and inside he found Liberty sitting on Rory's lap on a chair in front of the desk, curled into him like she belonged there. Which she did.

Seeing them together and happily mated made him smile. His brother deserved a sweet female like her, someone who made him happy and who would do anything for him.

The blond female smiled when she saw him, but didn't move from Rory's lap. Rory didn't make a move to get up either. Since they had different mothers there weren't as many familial markers between them—at least in human form. They both had darker hair, but Rory had a slight Scottish accent whereas Ian had a faint Irish one. And Rory's eyes were green, or "mossy green" as Liberty had once told him. Whatever the hell that meant.

"Wondering when you'd get here," Rory murmured. "Traffic bad?"

"Not really." Biloxi could be busy, especially around five o'clock, but it hadn't been worse than normal. Probably because things had slowed down after Christmas. People were tired of shopping and wanted to relax. Ian sat on the chair closest to them and propped his feet up on the desk. "So what's up?"

At his question Liberty shifted nervously in Rory's lap before pushing to her feet. She moved to one of the bookshelves in the small office and started straightening books that didn't need straightening. The female was mostly human and young by their standards. In her twenties, she'd been through the worst kind of hell so age didn't really matter versus her shitty life experience. He respected the hell out of her for all she'd survived. She didn't do well hiding her emotions, however.

Rory's body tensed slightly as he leaned forward. "Finn came to me with something right before Christmas. I didn't want to ruin the holidays, so..." He cleared his throat, looking nervous, which was out of character for his brother.

Ian and Rory had discovered each other decades ago and lived in a Hell realm for most of that time. There was no one he was closer to. His brother's tension agitated Ian's demon side. "Just say it."

Rory flipped open a thin manila file on the desk and revealed an 8x10 glossy of...

Fiona.

Ian blinked once. Twice.

He stared at the picture, feeling his entire body heat up. It had been years since he'd seen her. He had a picture of Fiona, but it was from decades ago and it was in one of his safes—along with other treasures. That was not a myth about dragons—they loved treasure. Given her modern style of dress, this was taken fairly recently. "What is this?" His voice was always raspy, but even more so now.

Rory flicked a glance at Liberty before looking back at Ian. "This is what I wanted to talk to you about. Finn wants to speak to this female. She lives on the outskirts of his territory. Not in it, but close enough. And we needed to know if she is a trustworthy female. I know you *know* who she is, but I don't know the nature of your relationship." He stared at Ian questioningly.

Ian stood abruptly. He'd shared almost every part of his life and history with Rory. Fiona was the only thing he'd left out of that narrative. He simply couldn't talk about her. It hurt too bad. Made his dragon want to take over, to burn everything and everyone to ash. "She's trustworthy." Without saying anything further he strode from the room. He heard his brother curse softly behind him, but ignored him.

Rory was lucky he hadn't burned a hole in the ceiling and just flown out of there. Which yes, was insane, but Ian wasn't in control now. He needed to get to the Stavros estate as soon as possible. The Alpha wolf who ran this territory wouldn't be happy to see him since he didn't plan to call first, but the male could just deal with it. Seeing Fiona's picture again had his most primal nature clawing to the surface.

He couldn't even convince himself that he'd buried memories of her because it was a lie. He thought of her every damn day. The woman lived inside him, was his mate. It didn't matter that they'd never crossed that final line and mated. That he'd never marked her—that she was mated to another. Another female would never do for him. Now to know that she was somehow nearby, close to Finn's territory... He was going to find out everything from the Alpha.

Then he was going to see her. He knew he shouldn't. She was mated, taken. She'd broken his heart into a thousand shards and gone off with another male. Another male her family deemed worthy. Too late he realized she'd done it to protect him, that she'd sacrificed her own happiness to keep him alive. Or it had been an attempt to—but he didn't need anyone's protection. He would have kept them safe, alive. He just wished she'd known that, trusted him enough.

Now there was no logical reason to go to her. Still, he would see her. He had to.

* * *

"Did that go as well as you thought it would?" Liberty frowned at the open doorway, her dark eyes filled with worry.

Rory stood, debating if he should go after his brother. "Yeah, just about." He scrubbed a hand over his face.

Liberty was in front of him in seconds, wrapping her arms around his waist.

He loved how affectionate she was. Ever since they'd mated, there were no walls between them. She still struggled at night sometimes, but at least she didn't try to hide the fact that she had nightmares, and he did everything he could to comfort her, to assure her that she was safe. "I feel almost guilty that I withheld the information about that female from him."

Liberty squeezed him tight. "You didn't withhold anything. You just waited a couple days because your Alpha asked you to."

And that was the crux of the problem. Since he'd joined with a new pack, his wolf had divided loyalties.

As if she'd read his mind, Liberty tilted her head back to look at him but still kept her arms around him. "You feel torn between your new pack and Ian?"

"Sort of." He'd never been beholden to anyone before. For decades it had just been him and Ian. Them against the Hell realm that had been their world. They'd occasionally retreated into the human realm to check on their investments and ensure that they were still making money, but that had been about it. And for all Rory knew, Ian had never searched out female company when he'd come to the human realm. He wondered if it was because of the female from the picture. "I knew she meant something to him. I just hated sitting on the information the last few days."

"Do you regret joining Finn's pack?" Liberty's voice was carefully neutral.

His brow drew together as he read between the lines. "No. I could never regret that." When he'd made the decision to settle down in Finn's territory it had made sense to join the Stavros pack. Because it protected the female he loved more than anything. No one would ever mess with her again. And if they were stupid enough to try, they would have the entire Stavros pack to deal with, not just him. That kind of backup... Yeah, he'd do anything for his mate.

"Do you think we should go after him?"

He shook his head even as he pulled his cell phone out. He needed to call Finn and let him know that Ian was on his way. Because knowing his brother, Ian wasn't going to call and ask to enter the male's estate. No, he would probably do something rash and demand entrance.

Ian was half demon, half dragon. He didn't like to ask for permission for anything. It simply wasn't part of his nature. When you were at the top of the food chain, what else could you expect?

Rory could relate, to an extent. But he was still a wolf and a basic part of him liked being a member of a pack. His demon side didn't give much of a fuck, but his wolf liked having an Alpha, liked that chain of command.

"I'm going to call Finn," he murmured to Liberty, who simply nodded.

Finn picked up on the second ring. "What's up?"

"Ian's on his way to see you." Rory just hoped that his brother kept his shit together.

* * *

Ian snapped his wings out, gliding in for the final descent even as he knew what he was doing was stupid and likely to get him attacked by wolf shifters. But he needed to talk to Finn Stavros, Alpha of one of the most powerful shifter packs in the South—and he wasn't waiting one second longer than necessary.

Not after seeing Fiona's picture.

Hell, getting clawed up by some wolves might distract him from the pain in his chest. Wind rushed over his scales and wings as he dove down toward the cluster of trees. The compound was in a historic part of Biloxi on acres of private land. Gated, expensive and very private, considering the pack owned most of the neighborhood, it was enclosed by a huge iron fence and thick trees. The Greek revival mansion was about two hundred yards from his landing point.

As he landed, he let his camouflage fall, revealing his huge dragon form to anyone on patrol. Some members of the pack had seen him before when he'd helped them defeat a crazy shifter who'd thought he could take over Finn's territory. His act of loyalty to them was the only thing that might stop the wolves from attacking him right now.

A dragon's coloring was always unique to their clan. Unfortunately for him, he had no idea who his clan was. Or if he even had one.

He snapped his wings in. His dragon body was a waterfall of colors, starting with gold, violet, and shifting into a pale lavender. The colors were constantly moving as his beast moved, making him appear to be almost liquid. It was a handy part of his camouflage.

The scent of wolves nearby filled his nostrils. Yeah, he was definitely going to be attacked. It would be worth it because he was about to find out where Fiona was.

He'd tried to put her out of his mind for the last five decades. Even now, knowing she was mated to another didn't matter. Neither his dragon nor demon side would be appeased until he saw her with his own eyes. And the truth was, he wouldn't even be appeased then. But he had to see her. *Right. Fucking. Now.*

Shifters were notoriously obsessive when it came to their mates. So were demons, for that matter. And he was a mix of the two. It was no wonder his control was on a razor's edge right now.

The size of a small house, his dragon couldn't be hidden. So he wasn't surprised when a dozen snarling wolves appeared out of the trees, seemingly out of thin air, moments after his feet touched the ground.

Taking a deep breath, he let the shift overcome him, let his human side take over in a burst of light and magic. The pain of the shift quickly faded as he stood up.

"The only reason you're not dead is because your brother called ahead of time." Finn's voice carried through the trees a moment before the tall male with midnight black hair stepped out wearing jeans and a T-shirt. His ice blue eyes had a faint glow to them as he approached.

Ian's dragon side sneered at the words. A bunch of wolves couldn't kill him. They could rip his flesh to shreds but he was a dragon and could incinerate them with a single stream of fire. The Alpha wolf, on the other hand, Ian wasn't so sure about. The male had a lot of power rolling off him and Ian's senses told him that Finn could withstand dragon fire. He wondered if the Alpha was even aware of it. Ian sure as hell wasn't going to tell him. "I should have called first."

"Is that your idea of an apology?"

Ian lifted a shoulder. "Yes."

Finn sighed, looking more annoyed than angry. From what Ian had come to know of the male, he was always fair. "You get a pass this once because you helped my pack." He shoved a bundle of clothes at Ian. Which if Ian had been thinking clearly, he'd have remembered to bring his own. "Put this shit on. And come on. We'll talk in my office."

Nodding, he fell in step with Finn, the other wolves watching him warily as they followed close behind. Inside he quickly dressed. They were both quiet as they ascended the winding staircase to the next floor. Everything was all dark, polished wood. And everything smelled like wolf. It wasn't unpleasant and reminded him of his brother. Though Rory's scent wasn't just wolf.

The second they were inside Finn's office, Ian turned to the Alpha. "I will have her location now."

Finn blinked once then rubbed a hand over his face. "You're just like Bo."

Ian frowned. That didn't sound like a compliment. "You have a problem with my brother?" After recently discovering that he had another brother as well as a sister, he'd become very protective of them.

Finn just snorted. "You know I don't. Bo's a good guy. But you both seem to have a problem with asking and not demanding."

Even though it went against his nature, Ian sat on one of the chairs across from Finn's desk. He tried to appear civil and passive. If he had to pretend to be civilized, he would. Anything to find out more information on Fiona. Since moving back to the human realm semi-permanently, he hadn't looked her up. He could have hired someone to do so or started searching himself, but he'd restrained himself.

She was supposed to be mated now. With another male for the rest of her very long life. He hadn't wanted to see who she'd ended up with, hadn't wanted to learn that she had children—children that should have been his. But now that he knew she was on the border of Finn's territory? He couldn't show any restraint. Something dark had risen inside him and he couldn't control it.

He *would* see her.

From his desk, Finn picked up a manila file similar to the one Rory had and handed it to Ian. This one had more than a simple picture inside it. He quickly scanned the two pages detailing information on Fiona O'Riley. They didn't have much on her.

But reading about her somehow made him feel closer to her. Which sounded stupid. He frowned. "There's nothing mentioned about her clan or her mate." He nearly choked on the last word.

Finn leaned against the desk, arms crossed over his chest. "We've been watching her for a little while and so far, haven't seen any dragon activity."

"You wouldn't. They're very private." All dragons were, but her clan especially.

Finn shook his head. "I don't have any indication that she's had any interaction with males whatsoever. Not at work, and she lives alone."

Ian frowned again. That didn't make sense. Anyone mated to Fiona would never let her out of his sight. Maybe for work, but nothing else. If she was Ian's... *Nope.* No sense going down that road. She wasn't his. And she never would be. "She has three older brothers. And her parents. They are all very overprotective."

"My trackers are very good. They know how to blend. There's been no evidence of any family in her life. Not even her phone calls."

Ian's eyebrows rose. "You tapped her line?"

Finn didn't respond one way or another. "What else can you tell me about her? She's apparently been bordering my territory for a while and I know nothing about her other than she runs a shelter for abused supernatural women."

Ian's mouth pulled into a thin line. He didn't like talking about her. It felt like a betrayal. And he wasn't surprised by what she was doing with her life. His Fiona had always had a big heart. "I haven't seen her for a very long time. I don't know what I could tell you."

"Liberty's volunteered to set up a meeting with her and act as a go-between. My question is, is she trustworthy enough to allow someone as untrained as Liberty to go in and talk to her? She helped relocate all the females we saved weeks ago."

"Does she know your pack saved them?"

Finn shook his head. "No. They approached her alone. So far all I hear is that she is very powerful. From what I can tell she's trustworthy, but that kind of power..." He lifted a shoulder. "I can't put blind trust in her before sending in one of my own."

"She would never hurt an innocent female. She would never go out of her way to hurt *anyone*, regardless of species or gender. Unless provoked." If Ian thought otherwise he'd never allow his sister-in-law to go see Fiona. It didn't matter that decades had passed—some things about an individual simply didn't change. Fiona wouldn't hurt Liberty.

"That's all I need to know."

"When will Liberty be going to meet her?"

Finn didn't respond, just took the file back and set it on his desk.

"How long has she run the shelter?" Finn had redacted some of the information in the file, but Ian had been able to read between the lines.

"About five decades."

Ian frowned again at the time frame. He needed to see her for himself, needed to see if she had gotten mated. She'd told him she would be moving back to Ireland after she mated with a male from an allied dragon clan. And he'd seen her mating manifestation from her family's estate, had known she was with another male. His dragon rippled beneath the surface, pushing, pushing, wanting to burst free at the memory of that night.

But if she'd been living here during all that time, running a shelter... Abruptly, he stood. "Thank you."

Finn just watched him carefully, his body tense. "Don't go see her before I've had a chance to talk to her."

Ian stiffened and looked back over his shoulder at the male. "My brother might be part of your pack, but I am not."

The Alpha's blue eyes turned to chips of ice. "Fine, I'm asking you not to go see her. I don't want anything to affect Liberty's meeting with her."

Ian didn't respond, but he would never do anything to endanger his brother's mate. Something Finn no doubt knew. Still, just because Ian wasn't going to go talk to Fiona didn't mean he couldn't get a visual, and his camouflage would give him the perfect opportunity.

Just one look. That was all he wanted. He couldn't believe his own lie, but it didn't matter. He was going to see her. No one would stop him.

CHAPTER THREE

52 years ago

Fiona's heart felt as if it would jump through her chest. She couldn't believe she'd snuck out of her family's compound, but…she wanted to see Ian. She didn't even know his last name. And there was no way she could have asked her family who he was. Especially not after last night.

They kept her out of anything they deemed "important." She was to be seen and not heard, as far as they were concerned. And most of the time, not even seen. They had no use for her because she was female. So lately she'd made herself as invisible as possible.

Waiting for her chance to break out on her own, leave the clan behind. She loved her family, but…she couldn't live like a prisoner anymore.

Nerves jagging through her, she glanced around the busy street, looking for any sign of the tall, impossibly sexy male with dark hair and bright amber eyes. He had a sexy, brooding quality that she couldn't deny she found fascinating. It was crisp out, with hints of fried seafood carrying on the air. The New Orleans restaurant looked more like a house than anything. Two stories, right on the corner of an actual residential neighborhood and painted a bright pink, it was a beacon of warmth and welcoming in the area. Not the kind of place her family would frequent, which was good for her.

When she turned back toward the door of the restaurant, *he* was standing there. As if he'd been there the whole time. And he was watching her.

A thrill shot up her spine at the sight of him.

Wearing jeans and a simple T-shirt, Ian stepped forward, closing the distance between them. "I wasn't sure you'd come." His voice had just the hint of an Irish accent, and it made her insides melt just a bit.

It was hard not to be affected by it. Ireland was her home and though she hadn't lived there since she was a little girl, it was part of her soul. She cleared her throat. "I made a promise."

He nodded once, his gaze traveling over her. But not in a creepy way that made her feel uncomfortable. No, he watched her as if she was special, precious. She didn't know what to make of it. Or him, and the way he made her feel. "I have a table reserved for us."

She blinked, then nodded and stepped forward when he stiffly held the door open for her. He seemed almost nervous, which was at odds with the confident male she'd met last night—the one who'd dominated everyone in Bruneau's fighting ring, including Colm.

Once they were inside, she slipped off her coat. As a dragon shifter, she was warmer by nature, though she wore appropriate clothing to blend in with humans when necessary.

It didn't take long for a smiling human waiter to seat them and take their drink order. Feeling out of sorts because she was on her own, she scanned the place, subtly inhaling to scent if other supernatural beings were here. She scented a couple wolves, or what she thought was wolf, but that was it. Other than Ian, of course. And his scent was unique. It reminded her of pine needles and the forest in autumn, but there was an underlying cedar scent as well.

"Thank you for not killing my brother," she murmured, turning to face him. To think she'd been worried that her brother would kill Ian. Now the thought was laughable. She hadn't been at last night's fight, but she'd heard her other brothers talking and Ian had apparently destroyed Colm.

Ian was sitting stock-still, a huge, immovable force as he watched her. He was big in the way dragons were. She'd thought that last night when they'd first met. When he'd so boldly ignored the introduction to her brother and simply introduced himself to her. No one had ever done that. Maybe because they were too afraid of her clan's reaction. Or more likely because she didn't matter to her family.

Because she wielded absolutely no power among her clan other than her ability to reproduce. She was simply a pawn to them, something to be used. For so long she'd accepted it. Until recently. The world was changing and she refused to fall into the subservient role that her mother so easily had. Fiona was a dragon, the same as the rest of her family, and she deserved the same respect.

"He fought well." A non-answer if she'd ever heard one.

"Until the end," she added. Because her brother had almost gone dragon when it had been clear he would lose the fight. He'd actually released his fire out of rage and frustration—a great shame to her family right now. They went to incredible lengths to keep what they were private. Now all her brothers and parents were livid at Colm.

Ian lifted one big shoulder. "I don't want to talk about your brother. I want to talk about you." For just an instant his gaze dipped to her mouth before his eyes locked with hers.

It was hard to think, much less speak around him. "What are you?" she blurted, knowing exactly how rude she sounded. "I mean…" She cleared her throat, feeling her cheeks heat up. "Your scent is unique. I like it," she tacked on. She liked it a whole lot. More than she'd admit.

He watched her for a long moment, his amber eyes searching hers. He looked at her as if he saw her as a person of worth. She wondered what it would be like to feel his lips on hers, especially when he looked at her as if he could devour her.

"Does it matter what I am?" he finally asked.

"No. I was just curious. I think you probably know what I am after last night?" The place was loud, with none of the patrons paying any attention to them, but she kept her voice low regardless, for his ears only. When her brother had released his fire, Ian had dodged the blow almost as if he'd been expecting the attack. But even so, Colm's stream of fire had been wide and raging hot according to her other brothers… And they'd said that Ian had seemed almost immune to it. Which meant pretty much one thing—he had to be a dragon.

Ian nodded and for the briefest moment his gaze flicked to his animal. Her breath caught in her throat to see his dragon looking back at her.

"So we're the same." The truth was, she wouldn't care what the male was. The connection she felt to him defied logic or sanity. Her dragon wanted to preen in front of him. When she'd pulled him into that coat closet last night she'd been concerned for him because...she didn't even know why. All she knew was that her dragon had become very, very interested when they'd met. But she couldn't get rid of the feeling that there was more to him.

He shrugged, not exactly answering. "You're from Ireland. Are you just visiting New Orleans?"

Okay, he didn't want to talk about their shifter nature. That was okay with her. "Yes and sort of. I was born near Galway but my clan has holdings everywhere. For now, we've settled in New Orleans, but I don't know how long we'll stay. My father has business here with some vampires."

He nodded and it was clear he was listening intently. Honest to God listening to what *she* had to say. And her words weren't even important. It rattled her that this felt foreign to her. On the deepest level she knew that wasn't how things should be with her clan. That she should matter.

"What about you?" she asked, then paused as the waiter returned with their drinks. After they both ordered one of the specials, she looked back at him expectantly. "What part of Ireland are you from?"

"Just outside of Cork."

"And…are you with a clan?"

He shifted slightly in his seat. "I have no one." His tone was neutral.

The way he said it made something shift inside her. She wanted to reach out and take his hand in hers, to somehow comfort him, but didn't think he'd welcome it.

She also wondered how old he was, but wasn't going to ask. It was impossible to tell a supernatural being's true age. She could guess based on how much power someone put off, but this male was too hard to read.

"I would like to fly after we eat," he said before she could think of a response. "Will you fly with me?"

The question was so abrupt and unexpected. She knew nothing about this male, but the most intrinsic part of her knew he wouldn't hurt her. She should say no. Should definitely say no… But she found herself nodding as excitement flooded her. Something told her that with him she could experience true freedom, if only for a short while. "I'd like that."

* * *

Present day

Fiona stared up at the blue sky, scanning it for a male she knew wasn't there. A handful of white clouds were scattered around, but it was a clear, cold day.

All her dragon senses wanted to take to the skies, to spread her wings and soar. It was the only time she felt truly free. When her animal took over, she could shelve everything else in her life. At least for a little while.

"The new female is here," a familiar voice said from behind her.

Fiona had scented Ava approaching before she heard her. The vampire could be a ghost when she wanted. Turning, she smiled at her friend and business partner. "After I talk to her, I'm going flying."

"I figured as much. Listen, her scent is different. I don't know how to explain it. I believe what she told me about being abused, but...her responses seemed carefully chosen. I couldn't discern any lies, but I might not have been asking the right questions."

Fiona simply nodded, keeping the information in mind. The female's responses could be based on her own history. She could be used to speaking or answering a certain way so as not to anger her abuser. An abuser who was likely someone close to her.

Many supernatural clans, packs and covens were highly patriarchal and didn't want that to change. Fiona knew that from firsthand experience.

After one last look at the sky, she headed inside. She and Ava ran a center for supernatural women in need of help escaping their abusers. Referrals were all by word of mouth and they took the safety of their clients very seriously. Unlike humans, supernaturals had no one to turn to for help. At least no national or international system. In that, humans sadly had a leg up on the supernatural communities—and that wasn't saying much, considering how lacking the various human systems were.

Which was why Fiona and Ava had started their organization. Their main intake center, where every woman who wanted help came to meet them first, was a big house in the country. It was a comfortable setting away from any prying eyes, human or supernatural. If she or Ava deemed the woman was indeed in trouble and telling the truth, they'd move to the next step, which usually meant relocating her to a safe pack—or clan or coven, depending on what type of being she was. Often the women, and sometimes their children, if they had any, would stay at the house while Fiona and Ava made arrangements. Right now they had no one staying with them, which was fairly unusual, but they'd just relocated a dozen females.

Inside the Colonial-style home, she found the blond female sitting on a love seat in one of the sitting rooms. The room was decorated in natural, soothing tones and the scents were lavender and chamomile. Women who came to her for help were already stressed out enough, either from physical or emotional abuse. Usually both. She wanted to put them at ease as much as she could.

The woman gave her a nervous smile and stood. Her long, golden hair was pulled back into a ponytail. She had a slender build, was almost fragile-looking, and was stunningly beautiful. "Hi. Thank you for meeting with me." She smoothed a hand down her gray pants, clearly nervous.

"Of course. I'm Fiona." She motioned for the female to sit back down as she did the same, sitting across from her in a cushy chair.

The female cleared her throat. "Liberty."

Ava had been right. The woman had a strange sent to her. Not unpleasant. The opposite, like fresh spring rain and cinnamon—with a hint of wolf underlying it all. She seemed mostly human though. Fiona was good at discerning what supernatural beings were. It was one of her gifts. It was rude to ask what a supernatural being's race was, but sometimes she had to. For safety reasons.

"I'm going to ask you something that is impolite."

The female smiled, her expression softening. "You want to know what I am."

Fiona nodded. "Normally I can get a feel for what someone is. But you have a mated sent to you." It wasn't necessarily abnormal; many females who came to her were mated to abusers. That was a bit rarer, since mates tended to shower their females with adoration. But abuse happened.

Liberty ran her fingers over the platinum charm on her necklace—a little wolf. "My mate is half wolf. And I'm afraid I'm here on partially false premises. I'm a member of the Stavros pack. My Alpha, Finn, would like a meeting with you. He didn't want to approach you in your territory. He thought it might be wiser if I spoke to you first."

Fiona was silent as she watched the other woman. She knew exactly who Finn Stavros was. She'd done research before settling down in the area. Decades ago, Finn hadn't been the Alpha of Biloxi. Hadn't been an Alpha of a pack until he'd killed his uncle. And from what she knew, his uncle had deserved it. She'd never had any females from Finn's pack come to her for help either. So by all accounts he was a good and fair leader. Something she had never personally experienced.

But that wasn't the issue right now anyway. "Why didn't he just call me on the phone?"

Liberty lifted her shoulders and Fiona was under the impression she truly was confused. "I don't pretend to understand shifter politics. I've only recently mated to a half-wolf shifter. And we are very new members of the Stavros pack."

"You had to go through an interview process before meeting with me. And Ava is good at detecting lies." Fiona didn't come out and ask what she wanted to. But the question was in the air all the same.

"If you're asking if I was abused in the past, then the answer is yes." Liberty took a deep breath and Fiona watched as her fists clenched in her lap, her knuckles turning white. "I was stuck in a Hell realm for months. I was thrown into the realm before I knew about the supernatural world. *That* was my introduction to it."

Fiona inwardly winced. She went to Hell realms often, helping to save those who needed it. She used her dragon essence to infiltrate those realms. If Liberty had been a human when she'd been sucked into one... Fiona gritted her teeth. She'd witnessed what happened to females in those places. It was something out of anyone's worst nightmare. "I'm so sorry for whatever you've been through. I've been to those realms before."

Liberty simply nodded. "I met the male who is now my mate there. He and some others saved me. And the Stavros pack has taken me in like one of their own. Finn truly just wants to meet you. He was unaware of your presence until recently and he doesn't like unknowns near his territory. At least I think that's why he's so insistent on meeting you."

Fiona guessed that it also had something to do with the level of power she projected. It wasn't something she could contain. She did to an extent, but her power always leaked out. The truth was, she was surprised it had taken the male this long to find out about her. She knew for a fact his pack had recently sent some abused females they'd saved her way, but he'd never approached her or introduced himself. She hadn't been certain he would make contact. Still...he should have made the first contact himself, not sent someone on his behalf. It was improper and she didn't appreciate it.

"My territory might technically be neutral, but it is my territory." Power and anger infused her words. If the Alpha thought she'd ever let him onto her sacred territory, he would find out how powerful she was. Instinct took over and her dragon blazed in her eyes. To her surprise the female didn't seem taken aback by her show of power. Or maybe she shouldn't be surprised. Instantly Fiona felt shame. She knew this woman had been abused. She shouldn't reveal her shifter side at all. "I... should not have done that."

Liberty's head tilted to the side slightly. "Done what?"

She swallowed hard. "I wasn't trying to intimidate you."

"I know. I've seen enough Alpha shifters to know the difference. You're pissed at Finn." A slight smile tugged at the female's lips. "I've seen his own mate give him that same look before."

"The male is mated now?" Apparently she needed to get up to date.

Liberty nodded. "Yes. To a bloodborn vampire."

That was interesting. Shifters could be very rigid in their ideas about mating. All supernatural beings could be, to an extent. "If you'll leave his contact information, I will get in touch with him." She actually had it, but figured it would be more polite this way. She paused for a long moment. "Have you talked to anyone about what happened to you when you were in that Hell realm?"

A tense silence passed before Liberty nodded. "Yes. The healer of my pack has been incredible. And so has my mate."

The fact that she was mated at all, after going through what Fiona knew she must have, said a hell of a lot for how strong Liberty was. "If you ever need someone to talk to, either I or Ava are here for you. And I know of other supernatural trained professionals as well." No matter what, Fiona would help any female she could. She'd escaped her prison on her own, but after that she'd had to rely on the kindness of strangers until she'd met Ava. She'd never forgotten how giving people could be. Her life was so different than it could have been because of simple acts of kindness.

"Thank you."

"You never told me what you are. Because the scent on you is more than just your mate and more than human."

Liberty shook her head slightly. "You wouldn't believe me if I told you. And I'm not going to tell you. Not yet anyway. If we become friends I will."

Even though her curiosity was piqued, Fiona nodded and stood as Liberty did.

"This has all his contact information on it," she said, handing Fiona a card.

"Tell him I'll be in touch—but that he shouldn't venture into my territory uninvited. I won't take kindly to he or any of his pack members showing up on my land." She'd learned many years ago that she had to show serious force against any supernatural beings who thought they could impede on her private property.

They'd learned very quickly that she was not someone to be messed with.

CHAPTER FOUR

From far above the big country home, Ian watched Liberty walk toward the driveway. Against Rory's wishes, she'd driven to Fiona's place alone.

The male could be obsessive about his mate. Something Ian understood. He might not be mated, but Fiona had once been his obsession.

No, she still was.

Only once Liberty had gotten into her vehicle did Ian slowly swoop away. But he didn't go far. Rory and Finn were waiting for Liberty a couple miles away in an SUV. Rory would be getting in the truck with her once they met up again.

Ian could see for miles and miles and didn't need to leave his aerial recon position. He should leave, however. He was in Fiona's territory, and while she hadn't carved out actual territory in the way that Alpha shifters did, this was still her property. She owned it. And she wouldn't take kindly to another dragon flying in her airspace. Dragons were very particular about their property and space.

Right about now he didn't much care. He desperately wanted another glimpse of her. Earlier he'd watched as she tilted her face up to the sky and he had sensed her need to fly.

Because he felt that same need every single day. It was inborn, part of who he was, and not something a dragon could bottle up forever. Once upon a time they'd flown together. To say he missed those days of freedom with her would be an understatement. It had been one of the few times in his life he felt truly free, content. It had just been the two of them in their dragon form, flying high above everything, all the bullshit of the world.

When Fiona stepped out into the backyard, a huge expanse of land that connected to the forest she owned, he tracked her movements. Her steps were sure, steady, confident.

She paused as she was walking. The movement was subtle but he noticed it. He'd always noticed everything about her. As she continued, she looked upward, as if searching for something. He was camouflaged so she couldn't see him. Still...he wondered if she was aware of his presence.

He could cloak his scent to an extent but whenever he was in her vicinity he lost his control. Neither his dragon nor his demon side *wanted* to listen or hide. It was because all he wanted to do was *claim, claim, claim.*

Claim what was his. It was his mating instinct.

There was no doubt for him. His own mating manifestations had been crystal clear decades ago with her. But that was before Fiona had kicked him out of her life and mated with a male her family deemed worthy. Something he did *not* want to think about.

But it was impossible not to, when he was staring down at the only woman he'd ever loved. The woman who'd broken his heart. His chest ached at the thought, and the urge to release a raging stream of fire was almost too great. Almost.

He reined it in just barely but the grief in his chest never went away. Decades had muted it, but it was there all the same.

When she disappeared into the line of trees, he forced himself to fly westward and head back home. He had no doubt that she'd headed into the trees so she could change to her animal form, camouflage herself and go flying.

Much as he longed to see her that way again, he didn't want to be in her airspace when that happened. Soon, however, he planned to see her, talk to her in person.

That probably made him a masochist since she was mated, but he didn't care. Now that he knew where she was, that she was living so damn close to him—he had to see her. Just a glimpse. Then he'd walk away.

* * *

"You sure this is smart?" Ava frowned up at the warehouse building that Fiona knew was a club.

She'd never been to the half-demon Bo Broussard's place, but she'd heard of him and his club. It was considered neutral territory even though it was in the middle of Finn Stavros's own territory.

She and Ava had done more research on the Stavros pack in the last twenty-four hours and while her information on them was still limited, what she did know made her lean toward trusting the male. "I'd rather meet him here as opposed to somewhere humans might over-hear us." It wasn't as if she was worried about being able to defend herself.

"I guess," muttered Ava. Her friend had escaped an abusive relationship with a male into BDSM.

"It would probably be better if you waited outside. You could keep a lookout for anything strange." Fiona had already tried to convince Ava not to come with her because of the location of her meeting. She never wanted to make her friend relive anything she'd gone through and wasn't sure if the sights or sounds here would trigger something.

Ava snorted. "I know what you're trying to do. And I'm a big girl. I'll stay at one of the bars while you two talk, but I'm not letting you out of my sight."

"We're an hour early. You could just wait outside until the Alpha arrives."

"Girl, you know my answer will be no. Don't even bother trying to convince me."

Smiling at her friend, Fiona wrapped her arm around Ava's shoulders for a brief hug as they reached what she assumed was the entrance. A big man who she thought might be a ghoul nodded politely at them, even if his gaze did skate over Ava with interest. They didn't even have to speak, he simply opened the door for them and allowed them entrance.

She wondered if Finn had let the owner know to ex-pect her. She'd come early because she wanted to scout out the place, get a feel for her surroundings. It was part of her predator nature.

Considering it was ten o'clock in the morning on a Friday she was surprised to see about fifty people inside. The music pumping through what had to be hidden speakers was at a normal decibel, not deafening "human club" level. Supernaturals had sensitive hearing so she was glad this place reflected that.

A big open dance floor was ringed by high-top tables. And private booths with thick, plush-looking curtains drawn back lined one of the walls. She also spotted a red door, and knew what was behind it from her research. Private rooms for sex.

On the dance floor it was mainly females dancing with each other. There were a few males sitting at the nearest bar but there were open spots so she made her way there with Ava.

As soon as they sat down, the female with shockingly purple hair behind the bar flashed her fangs at the males in a fairly aggressive way. Immediately the males got up and headed to a high-top table. Fiona shot Ava a surprised glance but didn't comment. That was certainly interesting, but Fiona wasn't sure what to make of it.

The bartender smiled at the two of them and Fiona didn't think it was her imagination when the female gave her a curious look. Very curious. Fiona shifted in her seat slightly. She was tall for a female, but not so tall that she should stand out. Not among supernaturals.

"What can I get for the two of you?" the female asked.

"Blood. O positive," Ava said.

The bartender didn't bat an eye, which told Fiona the request was normal and this place was exactly as she'd heard it was. Supernaturals only.

"Bottled water for me is fine," Fiona said.

The female nodded and set a bottle of water in front of Fiona before pulling out a blood bag from a cooler and fixing Ava's drink. They both murmured their thanks.

Fiona took her time scanning the interior. A familiar autumn forest and cedar scent lingered in the air, but she squashed the hope that Ian could have possibly ever been in here. Over the years she'd had to force herself not to look for him. The thought of seeing him again, touching him, kissing him… *Nope.*

She'd kicked him out of her life long ago for his own safety. So hunting him down after that would have been stupid. Even if she'd wanted to with every fiber of her being. But she loved him too much to get him killed for her own needs. And she didn't doubt for one second that if she started something up with him, her family would murder him. They'd once put her in chains for daring to want to be with him. They'd do worse to him.

Fiona straightened when she spotted Liberty and a big male stepping out from a white door on the far side of the open club.

Ava noticed the change in her, and swiveled in her chair.

The male with Liberty had his hand protectively placed at the small of her back as they made their way through the tabletops and across the bar.

Fiona stood when the two of them neared. She'd expected to see Liberty, but not so early. She'd assumed the woman would come with her Alpha.

Before she could say anything Liberty smiled. "This is my mate, Rory. His brother owns this club but he's out of town on his honeymoon right now. So we're helping watch the place. I'm surprised you're here so early."

Fiona simply smiled back and held out a hand toward Rory, who took her hand in a quick, firm shake. She hadn't realized Bo Broussard had a brother. Or any relatives. Granted, she hadn't done intensive research on the male, but she'd done enough that it should have come up.

Something about Rory's scent was oddly familiar, even though she knew she'd never met him before. Tall in the way shifters were, he was broad and had a brooding look to him. "It's a pleasure to meet you."

"Likewise." He kept his hand firmly on Liberty and from the way he looked at his mate it was clear he adored her.

She'd been around enough females who'd been abused and terrified by their mates to know that Liberty was not one of them. The female leaned into him, probably a subconscious thing. But she seemed to naturally gravitate to her mate. Which was a very good thing.

"Finn is on his way." Rory glanced in the direction they'd come from and something about his body language set off a warning bell inside her. He seemed almost tense.

Ava picked up on it as well. Fiona could see it in the way her friend shifted against the stool slightly, ready to move into action if necessary.

"Would you guys like to get a booth?" Liberty asked.

"I'll stay here." Ava's voice was polite, but neutral. She'd be Fiona's backup if she needed it. They always worked like that. If they had to get a female out of a hot situation, they worked as a team.

"I'll wait for Finn in a booth," Fiona said.

"Would you like company, or to wait alone?" Liberty asked.

"Ah, company would be nice." The truth was, she'd rather be alone. Fiona wanted to meet with the Alpha and be done with it. He could meet her, then hopefully ascertain she was no threat to his territory, and they would have no further contact with each other. She'd actually been in his territory before. It was so close to her own, and she'd never checked in with him as she knew she likely should have.

But she was a dragon and she played by her own rules. She'd spent the first few decades of her life being kept in check by her own clan leader and family, and she wouldn't be subjected to another's authority ever again.

The three of them made their way over to a booth. Fiona slid in opposite them and gave herself plenty of room to get out quickly if need be. The existence of dragons was mostly a secret, and while she didn't relish the idea of revealing what she was, if she had to make an escape she wouldn't hesitate to shift to her animal form in front of witnesses.

Rory stayed on the outside of Liberty, and still had that uncomfortable, tense look about him.

"Is there something I need to be aware of right now?" Fiona asked. She was never one to hold her tongue. At least not anymore.

The male looked at her and didn't pretend to misunderstand her question. He shook his head. "No. I'm just concerned that a certain patron of ours might be arriving soon. With my brother away I'm in control of his club and I want to make sure everything runs smoothly."

Though she didn't sense any deceit in his words, something about his tone was still off. So his words were true, but he could be leaving something out. It wasn't her concern, however. She didn't sense any ill will from these two, and she was very good at sensing danger from others. While the male Rory was definitely a dangerous individual, she didn't think he meant her any harm.

That could always change if the situation altered, but for now, she let herself relax a fraction.

After this meeting she had things to get to—namely another meeting with a male she'd helped get out of a bad situation when he was just a boy on the run with his mom. Now a grown man, the wolf shifter had stumbled on something in a Hell realm and wanted to run some things by her.

"How did you come to settle in this area?" Liberty asked.

"Ah...timing, I guess." She let out a short laugh. "Ava and I had just met." The story was a lot more complicated than that. They'd both just escaped different versions of hell. "We were in the process of helping some female jaguar shifters move out of the area when a lot of land went up for sale. I bought it so we'd have a base of operations and...from there we just started helping people on a referral basis." It was mostly pro bono too, but considering the investments she'd made over the years and the money that Ava had taken when she'd escaped her tormenter, they could afford it.

"It's good what you're doing. I know a d— shifter out west who's started something similar," Liberty said.

Fiona nodded once. "That's good to hear. We work with other small organizations like our own." But they were very careful who they trusted. It was why just the two of them ran things. "I wish there was a way to link all of us better, but I fear it would erode the privacy factor of what we do." She and Ava were lucky that in the fifty or so years they'd been doing this, they'd only been confronted and attacked by angry individuals a handful of times.

And all of them had died by dragon fire.

Liberty started to respond, but turned around when her mate let out a short, colorful curse.

Fiona followed the male's line of sight. Finn—who she easily recognized from the small file she had on him—was moving across the dance floor, his strides purposeful. She frowned, not sure why it was a bad thing that he was here, but froze when she spotted a male she hadn't seen in decades.

Ian McCabe.

Just like that his scent overwhelmed her, seemed to surround her, *drown* her as if there was nothing else in the near vicinity but him.

Half dragon shifter, half demon. The only male she'd ever loved. Still loved. He was a few feet behind Finn, his expression fierce and determined as he made his way to her. There was no doubt in her mind he was headed for her either.

Not when those beautiful amber eyes had locked onto hers.

Her breath caught in her throat, her heart beating triple time as she stared at the male she'd never moved on from. So long ago her heart had ripped into pieces when she lost him and it had never mended. Moving on from a male like Ian? Impossible.

That old, familiar fear rose quickly inside her that her brothers would leap out of the shadows and try to kill Ian simply for daring to want to make her happy, to claim her as his.

A deep-rooted terror made her look around, scanning for her brothers just in case. It didn't matter that she hadn't seen them in decades, that she'd cut them out of her life and burned one of their family homes to ash, that she knew it was crazy to be afraid of them. She still had to look.

To make sure that Ian was safe from them.

CHAPTER FIVE

"I swear to all that is holy," Finn growled in front of Ian as he stalked across the dance floor. "You and I are coming to blows later."

Ian ignored the Alpha. Ignored everything but Fiona, who was staring at him from across the room in shock and maybe a little horror. The knife in his chest twisted at the sight.

He'd come to Bo's club to find a spot so he could simply get another glimpse of Fiona without being seen. He'd known she was meeting Finn here in a couple hours. Apparently she'd arrived early.

When Finn had actually told him to leave, tried to order *him* away? Yeah…he might have burned a few cars in the parking lot to ash. No one was going to keep him from Fiona.

He was aware that his behavior was insane. He didn't care. He'd committed to this and wouldn't back down now. His demon half could be such an asshole and there was no way in hell he'd been able to simply not show up when he'd learned Fiona would be here.

Out of the corner of his eye, he saw Rory and Liberty stand. When Fiona broke his gaze, as if she was looking for someone—her mate?— he glanced at his brother. Whatever Ian's expression was, it was clear enough that no one better mess with him now. Rory took Liberty's hand and moved away from the booth, his expression grim.

Ian tuned them both out as he and Finn reached Fiona—who was looking a lot like a dragon caught in headlights.

Finn cleared his throat. "Fiona O'Riley, I'm Finn Stavros. Officially." The Alpha held out a hand, his actions perfectly polite.

Ian still growled low in his throat. He'd never liked anyone touching Fiona. Not even a happily mated male like Finn. Right now he wanted to slice off the Alpha's hand. Fiona looked the same, but different. It was…strange. Still incredibly tall and beautiful, her dark hair was longer than he remembered and was free of any restraints as it flowed down over her unfortunately covered breasts. Not that he wanted another male to see her, but he remembered what she looked like naked. Remembered every single inch. The way her pale brown nipples hardened when he kissed and licked them.

"I believe you know Ian," Finn continued, as if Ian hadn't just growled at him.

Those blue eyes moved from him to Finn and back again. "I…do. Ah, you two know each other?" Her voice was slightly unsteady.

"We do. And Ian was just leaving." Finn shot him a hard look.

Ian ignored it, his focus on Fiona. "I'm staying. You're not mated?" Because he couldn't scent it on her and now he was close enough that he should be able to. If she wasn't mated—he wasn't walking away again. Period. To hell with the consequences. He wasn't even sure how it was possible that she wasn't. He'd *seen* that mating manifestation, *read* the marriage announcement in the newspaper her mother had gleefully given him. For so damn long he'd assumed she sacrificed her happiness in an attempt to save him.

"No." Her bright blue eyes swept over him as if she couldn't believe he was standing there in the flesh. "You look great, Ian." Her voice was soft and as sweet as he remembered.

"So do you. More beautiful than ever," he murmured, his heart pounding out of control. And she wasn't mated, he told himself. Wasn't taken. Now Finn's files on her made sense. If she'd left her clan she wouldn't have any contact with them and that lined up with the research Finn had on her. Her clan would have cut her out of their lives. Why hadn't she come to him then? Maybe she'd still been trying to keep him safe all these years. Joy and rage pumped through him in equal measures. She wasn't mated and they'd lost so many damn years.

He wasn't sure how long he stood there staring at her—how long they stood staring at each other—but eventually he was aware of a bunch of Stavros packmates, his brother, Liberty, and even his sister Cynara all watching them.

"Let's sit." Finn motioned to the booth she'd been sitting at and much to Finn's annoyance, Ian was certain, he slid in with them, sitting right next to Fiona. He was dying to touch her, but kept his distance.

"You're part of the Stavros pack now?" she asked, scooting to the middle of the circular booth so that she was sitting in the middle of them but had a foot and a half of space between both him and Finn.

Though the most primal part of him wanted to shift closer, to drink in her scent, he managed to retain some of his civility. Barely. All he could think about was that she wasn't mated. That she was his, and would officially be soon. *Mine, mine, mine.* He was like those seagulls from that cartoon movie Liberty had made them all watch.

"Not yet. I'm still trying to convince him to join us. But there's a clan up north who want him as well. He's got options." Finn's voice was butter smooth, with no hint of the anger he must be feeling right now.

And his words stunned Ian. He wasn't sure what the Alpha was playing at, but he wasn't being sarcastic. Finn made him sound like a worthy shifter, someone others wanted around. What the hell was the sneaky wolf up to? He'd find out later.

Ian cleared his throat. "My brother—"

Her eyes widened. "You have a brother?"

"Ah, I met some family members after we..." *Nope, not going down that road right now.* "I have two half-brothers and a half-sister." Well, that he knew of. He could have more, considering what an asshole his father was. He motioned to Rory, who was sitting at the bar and pretending not to pay attention to them, and to Cynara, who was avidly watching them.

Fiona's lips curved into a soft smile. "I'm so glad you found family. Where's your other brother?"

"On his honeymoon."

She blinked once. "Bo Broussard?"

He nodded, watching her digesting the new information. He'd been alone when they'd met, wandering with no purpose. Still felt like he was, some days. Because without Fiona in his life, it was as if he was missing a vital part of who he was.

Finn cleared his throat again, drawing their attention to him. "Look, I appreciate you meeting me here. And I really appreciate what you did a few weeks ago by helping all those traumatized shifters. I sent them to you. One of my packmates discovered who you are and what you do. I should have contacted you personally but we thought it was best if they approached you by themselves. I didn't want to do anything to jeopardize you helping them."

As the Alpha wolf talked, Fiona struggled to wrap her mind around Ian being right next to her. Barely two feet away. What the hell was going on?

Somehow she managed to nod at Finn's words, force herself to focus on him. A dozen shifter females had come to her and Ava in desperate need of help. They'd all told her the same thing: that a crazed shifter had captured them and tried to force them to be part of his pack. Some had been sexually abused, others not. But all of them had been ripped from their lives and most had been too terrified to return. So she and Ava had found them all new packs they knew would take care of them and help them integrate back into society. She also knew—from one of the females—that Finn's pack had saved them from a hellish situation.

"I knew you sent them to me," she murmured.

He didn't seem too surprised by that or maybe he was just good at covering his reactions. She was more stunned that Ian was sitting so close to her, watching her with an unparalleled intensity, smelling sexy and wonderful—like he was hers. He was watching her as if he could take her, right here and now, regardless of where they were and who was watching. And the truth was, she'd probably let him. Where he was involved she was so damn weak. Kicking him out of her life, lying to him, had taken all of her willpower. Her entire body ached being in his presence. She'd never thought she'd see him again, get to look into those beautiful amber eyes. Yet here he was, perfect as ever.

Clearing her throat, she forced herself to remain focused on the topic at hand. "Why didn't you allow them to remain part of your pack?"

"I offered. More than once. I think most of the females wanted to start over somewhere new—where their pack-mates hadn't seen them at their weakest."

Fiona nodded. She'd figured that was the case, but was glad to confirm it. "So…now you know who I am. Where do we go from here?"

"I just wanted to introduce myself and let you know that our pack is available for assistance if you ever need anything."

It was a generous offer, though she wasn't certain she'd ever take it. "Thank you." She cleared her throat, glanced between Finn and Ian. "I take it you know what I am?" she asked Finn. He'd used the word "clan" before and he knew Ian, so it was a fair assumption.

He nodded.

"I appreciate your offer of assistance, and I mean this respectfully…but I'm not looking for an Alpha, a pack or a clan. I'm good at what I do and my partner and I have a good system in place. We operate alone by choice."

"Fair enough. I might ask *you* for advice if you're open to it. My mate and I have been discussing doing something similar to what you do. After Ian and his brothers rescued Liberty, we all realized that there needs to be something in place to help shifters with nowhere to go. I'm…ashamed I didn't think of it sooner."

She glanced at Ian, who looked like a sexy statue as he watched her, then back at Finn. She wished she could get a read on Ian but he wasn't giving her anything other than heat and hunger. It was playing havoc with her system. Her dragon side wanted to jump the male, to kiss him senseless and never let go. *Damn it, focus.* "I'm open to that."

"Good. You're welcome in my territory without having to contact me."

She blinked once. Even though she'd been in his territory before, it was incredibly generous of an Alpha to make that offer. "Ah, thank you." She stiffened slightly, wondering what was behind the offer.

The male must have read her expression or scent because he gave her a wry smile. "No strings attached. Ian vouches for you, and even if he didn't, what you did to help those women tells me all I need to know. As long as you follow my rules when you're in my territory, we won't have a problem."

"Okay."

He slid out of the booth then, gave her a nod, and left. And that was that.

Now that she was alone with the man she'd loved for more than half a century, Fiona wasn't sure what to say or where to look. She wanted to just keep staring at Ian, to drink in the beauty of him. Even his raspy voice was sexy. And he made her think of her homeland. Made her think of home, period. Because at one time, he'd been her home.

"So you've been in the area for a while?" he asked, his voice even despite the heat in his eyes.

She wasn't sure how he sounded so calm when she felt as if she could crawl out of her own skin. "Yes since... About fifty years." There had been a year where she'd been held prisoner by her own family, but that was behind her now. And she didn't want to tell him about that.

He didn't look surprised by the revelation, which meant he'd probably already known, if Finn had done research on her. Which obviously the Alpha had.

"Are your siblings like you?" she asked when he didn't say anything else, wanting to fill the pause between them. She assumed they must be. Rory had smelled like a wolf, but he must be a half-demon like Ian. Ian was one of the only beings she'd never been able to get a solid read on when scenting. She glanced out at the dance floor and found his brother and sister—and Liberty—staring at them. They quickly glanced away.

"That's not something I want to talk about in public."

She nodded, understanding.

"Where's your clan?" he asked.

"Ah, well, that's not something I want to talk about in public either." She gave him a small smile. They could rot in hell for all she cared. Once she'd escaped, she'd destroyed one of her clan's homes and she'd do a lot more if they ever came after her again. She'd never given them a reason to, and she planned to keep it that way.

"Fine. Have dinner with me. We can talk then." His words were brusque, demanding. So very Ian. He'd always been like that.

"I don't think that's a good idea." In fact, she knew it wasn't a good idea. She'd kept her distance from him for decades because she was terrified her family would keep their promise and murder him. She'd angered her whole clan with the way she'd left. She'd destroyed their property, embarrassed and shamed them by rejecting everything they were—daring to have an opinion while being female. And dragons were ancient. They could hold grudges for a very long time. The best way to get at her would be to hurt Ian. She'd never gone after him, never looked for him all this time. For all she knew her clan assumed he'd meant nothing more than a way to escape them back then. It was what she'd told them anyway and they'd believed her.

His amber eyes went heavy-lidded, bringing up all sorts of memories. "I think it's a very good idea. You're not mated. Before I left New Orleans, you made it clear you were taking up with another male." There was something else in his words that indicated he'd truly *believed* she'd been mated. And Ian wasn't the type of male to settle for just words.

"That didn't happen." Clearly. After she'd kicked Ian out of her life to protect him, lied to him about her new mating, her clan had locked her up in chains, tried to force her to "see reason." It had taken her a while to escape but once she had, she'd never looked back. They knew where she was. Once or twice over the decades she'd scented her family in her territory. She knew they'd been checking on her, probably wanting to make sure she wasn't mated or with anyone they deemed unworthy. They might have even wanted to remind her that they were out there, always a danger, by leaving their scent behind. Probably wanted to keep her afraid of them.

His frown deepened. But surprisingly he didn't ask more questions. "Why not have dinner with me? Catch up on old times?"

She let out a short laugh. "Because I think if we spend time together we'll both end up naked." There was no sense denying the truth. Unless...he had a female? But no, she couldn't scent anyone on him, thankfully. She didn't know how her dragon side would react to that. Not well, anyway.

His gaze heated at her words and he didn't deny what she said. "I can't promise that won't happen. But I truly want to know what you've been up to. I've missed you."

Her throat tightened at his admission. And she wished things could be different between them. She'd missed him too, but she couldn't tell him that. She couldn't give him any sort of opening. She'd never given her family a reason to come after her, had never shown interest in a male for that very reason.

Well, because her heart already did—and always would—belong to Ian.

It didn't matter that she'd walked away from her clan; they would never let her mate with someone like him.

Someone they deemed unworthy. And according to Finn, Ian didn't even have a pack or clan. He might have found family, and in a way that was even worse. It was good for him, but she wouldn't put him and his family in danger by sleeping with him. Because her clan would go completely scorched earth on his family. Not only that, she knew that if they slept together he would eventually mate with her. His control around her was so thin. Or it had been in the past. She understood that quite well, because she was the same around him. He brought out her most primal instincts and she always felt on edge around him.

No, she would not risk his life for her own wants. She slid out of the booth.

"I really have to go, Ian. I'm truly glad you found family." He'd been so alone when she'd met him. She'd thought they'd create their own family one day, that they'd have children… Her throat tightened and that familiar ache filled her chest, making it hard to breathe. She shoved those stupid fantasies away. That was never going to be her life. No sense in pretending otherwise.

He was out of the booth and standing next to her in the blink of an eye. He moved with a liquid grace, especially for someone his size. Even for a dragon he was huge. "This isn't over," he murmured.

Not trusting her voice, she simply turned away from him—even though it was impossibly hard—and met Ava at the bar. Tears burned her eyes but she refused to let them fall. Not yet anyway. Her friend wordlessly fell in step with her as they headed for the exit, thankfully understanding that she couldn't talk just yet.

Only once they were outside in the fresh, cool air did she take a deep, shuddering breath and swipe at the rapidly falling tears. The surprisingly icy air cut against her lungs. "Will you drive?" Fiona rasped out, handing Ava her keys before her friend had even answered.

Once they were safely in Fiona's truck, Ava glanced at Fiona as she started the engine. "So I'm guessing that's the male you loved—still love, it looks like?"

Fiona nodded but couldn't force the words out. Seeing Ian had rocked her to her core. She simply hadn't expected to see him ever again. She'd resigned herself to a life without him. Seeing him now, clearly unmated and wanting to be with her... It was too much to handle. She hadn't been with anyone since him. The thought of another male touching her—she simply couldn't do it. Her dragon nature wouldn't allow it even if she'd wanted to. They might not have officially mated, but her dragon had claimed Ian for her own.

All she wanted to do was head home, to decompress and wrap her mind around what had just happened, but she still had another meeting to get to. If it wasn't with a friend, she'd cancel. "Let's just get to this meeting," she murmured as Ava steered out of the parking lot.

She wanted to get it over with and then maybe start day drinking to try and drown her misery.

* * *

Finn lay stretched out on his back in the pack's training room, watching his mate practice with her wooden sparring sticks. Watching her was one of his favorite pastimes. "I really think you need to do that without a shirt on," he murmured.

Lyra laughed, her long, blond braid whipping behind her as she completed an attack on the heavy bag. "You think I should do everything shirtless. And I'm not practicing without my top on." She snorted softly as she swiveled away from the bag, going through one of her many routines. "The thought is utterly ridiculous," she muttered before ducking low and avoiding an imaginary attacker.

Some days they sparred together, but she'd wanted to work alone today. Fine by him. He slid his hands under his head, just watching the woman he loved. As a bloodborn vampire she was already incredibly powerful. But she'd been practicing with weapons for years—after being kicked out of her coven by her brother right before sunrise. She'd wanted to learn how to take care of herself if she ever came up against stronger supernaturals. While Finn hated that she'd been put in the position to have to learn to defend herself because he hadn't been there for her, he loved watching her work. No one else was in the gym right now. It was such a rare occurrence for them to have alone time since he was the Alpha.

"I don't know what I'm going to do about Ian," he said as she set her sticks down and began stretching. "His disrespect today isn't exactly uncommon for someone of his power, but I still don't know what to do. He literally burned three cars to ash in the parking lot when I told him he wasn't allowed entrance to the club."

Lyra let out a small, unexpected giggle. "Sorry, I'm not laughing at what we have to deal with. But it's still a little funny. Was he challenging you?"

No doubt his mate already knew the answer because if Ian *had* challenged Finn, things would have gotten bloody really fast. "No. And that's part of the problem. He has no desire to take over my pack, but doesn't want to join it either. I just have this powerful being living in my territory who won't listen to me." And that could be a huge problem long term. If he allowed someone to publicly disrespect him it could undermine all the hard work he'd done to unify his pack, to carve out this prime territory and keep everyone under his authority safe.

"I was wondering how long it would take for something like this to come up. Do you think if it had to do with anything other than a female he would have disrespected you?"

Finn thought for a long moment. Ian hadn't actually done it in front of anyone. They'd been the only two beings in the parking lot when the male had lost his shit. "No. He's a good male and he helped out our pack when we needed it. And his own brother is in our pack. I don't think he would ever jeopardize his brother's safety." Not that the pack would take out anything on Rory because of something that Ian had done, but still, the dragon shifter was loyal to his brother. "It's just a frustrating situation right now." And he didn't want to overreact and come down hard on Ian when he wasn't certain the situation actually warranted it. Being Alpha sucked sometimes.

Before either of them could say anything more, their eighteen-year-old daughter Vega came running into the gym with a big smile on her face. Her inky-black hair was down today and she wore a violet-colored sweater that matched her vivid eyes. She was the perfect mix of him and Lyra.

He still was coming to terms with the fact that he had a grown daughter. He loved her so much it scared him. Hell, he loved both of them to the point he knew he'd do anything for them. He stood as his daughter raced over the padded mats of the gym. Lyra stopped stretching as Vega threw herself at Finn.

"I heard what you did for Ian. That was so sweet!" She gave him a huge hug, taking him off guard. Shifters needed touch, but he was still getting used to the open sweetness of his daughter. She could be insanely emotional sometimes, but according to his mate that was just because of her age.

"What did I do?" He couldn't think of anything that deserved a tackle-hug, but hell, he'd take it.

"Cynara told me that you told that woman who Ian is in love with that you wanted him as part of your pack. Basically you made him look wanted, *worthy*. That's such a big deal, Dad! And Ian is such a sweet guy. He deserves what his brothers have."

"You didn't tell me you did that." Lyra gave him a huge smile and a tackle-hug as well.

He grabbed both of his girls into a tight embrace and thanked whoever was up in heaven or wherever that he'd been given this incredible family. He wasn't sure he'd done anything to deserve them but for the rest of his life he was going to make sure he treasured and protected them.

He cleared his throat as they stepped back. He'd been beyond pissed at Ian when the male had just sat down at the booth with him, refusing to leave. But the way the male had watched Fiona… "He looked at the female like… Well, like I look at you," he said to Lyra. "I wanted to make him look respectable, wanted." Ian had appeared so damn desperate as he stared at Fiona, as if he'd slay monsters for her or give her the damn world if she asked.

Finn knew exactly how that felt.

Lyra and Vega hugged him again with a fierceness he felt all the way to his soul. Yep. Never letting them go. They were his world, now and always.

CHAPTER SIX

Even though Fiona wasn't feeling remotely like her-self, she put her game face on as they pulled up to the stretch of land right on the water. Or she tried to. Seeing Ian had been a sucker punch right to her heart. She couldn't believe she'd just been sitting next to the only man she'd ever loved, had thought she'd never see again, less than an hour ago.

Focus, she chided herself.

It was almost impossible when she kept picturing him, remembering how talented he'd been with his hands, mouth and everything else. God, that male. The first time they'd met he'd watched her like a predator watched prey. But not in a scary way, because she'd wanted to be caught by him. It was as if she'd woken up the first time they'd locked eyes. At least her dragon half had. She always thought of her life as cut into halves. Before Ian and after Ian. And despite the heartache that had followed, the dulled pain she lived with on a daily basis, she'd never change meeting him, having him, even for such a short time.

She wasn't sure who owned this land, but her long-time friend Gray had wanted to meet here. And it wasn't quite on Finn's territory. Right on the edge and bordering the ocean, it was maybe a mile or two outside his designated domain. Not that she would have told him about the meeting regardless.

"I see part of a vehicle." Ava pointed toward a ramshackle building as Fiona's truck rumbled over the makeshift, gravelly road. The back of a truck came into view as Ava steered around the winding road.

Fiona smiled when she saw Gray leaning against a beat-up old truck, his arms crossed over his chest. The truck was parked next to what had probably once been a bait shack but was now a pile of falling down aluminum siding. He lifted a hand in the air and half waved at them before glancing around, his body tense.

The first time Fiona had met him he'd just been a scared pup. His mother had been in an abusive relationship. Though *relationship* wasn't even the right word for it. After Gray's father had died his uncle had decided that Gray and his mother would become his new family. Fiona had put an end to that situation real fast. And it had been very bloody. But the male was long dead, and Gray and his mom had gone on to have good lives. Ever since then, she'd stayed in touch with the two of them. Gray's mother had re-mated and was living out west, but Gray had remained in the area and was an internationally recognized sculptor.

He actually lived in Finn's territory—with Finn's permission—even though Gray was definitely an Alpha with a capital A. Fiona guessed the only reason Finn was okay with the male living in the territory was because he kept to himself and rarely ventured out in public.

Ava parked a few car lengths away from Gray's truck and they both got out.

Gray was striding toward them before they'd taken a step. He was a big male with broad shoulders and had clear power rolling off him. The sleeves of his flannel shirt were shoved up to his elbows. "It's good to see you. Though I wish it was under different circumstances." Gray pulled her into a hug and lifted her off her feet. Even though he was a wolf he was still slightly taller than her.

She patted him on the back and found herself smiling as she stepped back to get a good look at him. His dark hair was a little shaggy and he'd decided to grow a beard since the last time she'd seen him. She ran her hands up and down his arms and took in his appearance. She squeezed his arms once, frowning. He was incredibly muscular but something seemed off. "Are you eating enough? You're looking a little thin."

The normally surly shifter actually blushed as he shook his head. "I'm fine. I was working on a deadline and then got pulled into some shit. It's a long story. So no, technically I actually haven't been eating well." He nodded once at Ava, who murmured that she was going to head around the perimeter of the area.

There weren't many places to hide on this open stretch of land, which was likely why Gray had picked it. Still, when Fiona and Ava met up with anyone, they always did a check of the immediate area. As a day walker, Ava was powerful in her own right as a vampire.

Gray was a sculptor so the deadline reference was clear, but she wanted to know what else was going on.

"What did you get pulled into?" Fiona asked, getting right to the point.

"A friend of mine was hearing rumors of some bad stuff going down in a Hell realm. Well, worse than the normal shit that goes on in some of them. So he went to check it out. Once he discovered that the rumors were true, he came to get me. He wanted to go straight to Finn, but I wanted to see for myself first. So we made the trek into the realm." He shut his eyes and ran a hand over his face. There was self-recrimination in his expression when he met her gaze again.

Fiona knew without him having to say a word that his friend must have died.

"My friend was murdered and I barely escaped alive. It was such an overwhelming force of half-demons. I hadn't expected them to be so organized."

"I'm sorry."

He nodded once. "I don't know who's behind the whole operation, but I know what entrance they're using to enter the Hell realm. And...there are dragons involved."

Her blood chilled at his words. "How do you know?"

"Because I saw one of them use their fire to open the gate."

Dragons were more secretive than other shifters by nature—and since they lived in clans they were powerful. She had a lot of questions regarding the dragon he'd seen but first she wanted to know what else he'd found out. "What are they into? Kidnapping? Skin trade?" She'd been in enough Hell realms to know what happened in some of them. In many, if not most, the supernatural beings, namely half-demons, lived there because they'd rejected the human realm for whatever reason and simply wanted to be left alone. But bad shit happened in some of them. She knew because she'd helped rescue more than one person.

"Kidnapping humans for their blood. It's not sex trade. Not that I know of. They're draining the humans they take and mixing their blood with a half-demon. I don't know what type of half-demon though."

There were many different types of half-demons. Half-demon/half-human, or half-demon/half-dragon as in Ian's case—the possibilities were endless. She wouldn't let herself think about Ian right now, however. "Why are they mixing the blood?"

"According to my friend, they've been selling the concoction in the human realm. It gives the user an incredible high and has seemingly no side-effects. At first anyway."

She frowned. "So...they're drug running?"

"Not exactly. Technically yes, they are. But this drug kills. A one hundred percent rate. Without fail, any user is dead within four days of use. From heart problems. No matter that the users have mostly been healthy and in their twenties and thirties."

"That seems like a stupid way to do business if they're not going to get any repeat customers."

Gray shrugged. "They don't want repeat customers. They want to start killing humans in mass quantities. This is just their testing ground. From what my friend gathered, they want to either eliminate humans altogether or make them servants."

She knew dragons who thought that way. That humans were vermin that needed to be exterminated. "Your friend found all this out?"

"Yeah. He'd been watching these guys for about a month—but they've been at this a lot longer. He kept pretty good notes and I know when to ask for help. From what I can tell, their operation is pretty big and organized. I don't know what else to do at this point. I'll go back and kick ass with a team but...I can't do it by myself."

She was silent for a long moment as she digested his words. "Why not go to Finn Stavros? You're in his territory."

The male shrugged. "You're a... You're you. I know you. Know how powerful you are. And I know you've helped a lot of people in the past. I figured you might have contacts who could deal with this kind of thing. Finn's all right I guess, but...I trust you."

It warmed something inside her. "I just met with Finn for the first time today."

Gray's green eyes widened slightly. "How'd that go?"

She lifted a shoulder. Thinking of Finn made her think of Ian. Something she didn't need to do right now. "It was interesting. I think he's a good male."

"Yeah, he is," Gray said almost grudgingly.

"Where's the gate?"

"Border of his territory."

She rubbed the back of her neck, glanced out at the glistening water. Ava had her sunglasses on and was scanning the water, her body language tense. At her friend's posture Fiona started scanning the water as well.

Some supernatural beings could camouflage themselves—specifically dragons. She inhaled deeply, scenting Gray, Ava in the distance and...it almost scented like Ian.

Had he followed her, or was that wishful thinking? No telling with that male. She should have expected it, but she'd been so damn anxious to get out of that club.

"I scent others," Gray murmured. "We need to get the hell out of here—"

A burst of fire rained down from the sky, reds and oranges showering them in heat.

Fiona sprang into action on pure instinct, throwing herself over Gray. She must have taken him off guard because he fell backward under the weight of her tackle, grunting as they slammed to the ground.

"Stay under me!" As a dragon shifter she had a natural immunity to dragon fire. It was part of her survival skills. Heat licked all around her so she covered Gray with her dragon essence. She'd saved him as a pup; she wouldn't let him die now. She desperately wished she could see Ava, but didn't want to move until the threat had passed—she arched her back as something pricked her spine.

Blackness swam before her eyes as a spiderweb of agony burst through her entire body, sucking her under in a sharp tidal wave. Her chest tightened as she struggled to breathe, to keep her eyes open.

The last thing she heard was Gray screaming at her to stay awake.

* * *

Terror slammed through Ian as he saw Fiona fall, struggling to protect that male. She'd been hit with something.

Rage like he'd never known welled inside him as he unleashed a stream of blistering hot fire at the unknown dragon who'd dared to unleash its fire on her. Even from hundreds of yards higher than the camouflaged threat, he could see something sticking out of Fiona's back. His dragon senses were beyond acute.

Darts, maybe. He didn't really care what. Whoever had hurt her was going to die.

He barely kept his camouflage in place as he dove down, wings plastered back against his body as he raced toward her. He spotted two giant SUVs spraying up gravel as they raced down the road toward Fiona and the male. He released another stream of fire, blasting the first vehicle.

It toppled on its side before he sent out another surge, incinerating it. Whoever was inside had just ceased to exist.

The other SUV jerked to a halt, quickly reversed. He slowed his descent, needing more control before he landed. He wanted to give chase, but had to get to Fiona.

Suddenly a geyser of ocean water shot upward like a volcano exploding. Fiona's business partner screamed as an unknown force gripped her tight and picked her off the ground. Though he couldn't see what held her, it had to be a dragon clasping her in its talons.

Her body suddenly shot forward in the direction of the quickly retreating SUV. He flew hard, chasing after them. He needed to check on Fiona but he knew how powerful she was, and he also needed to save her friend. Because it would kill Fiona if her friend was taken. That was just the kind of person she was.

He had only a small window of time where he could rescue the vampire. He had no idea who these attackers were or what they wanted, but he wouldn't leave Fiona for longer than a minute. Not even that long. He pushed himself harder, his wings straining under his flight.

Suddenly the vehicle and a screaming Ava disappeared into thin air.

He slowed his flight, not sure he was seeing right. But it wasn't the sun playing tricks on him, and in his dragon form he had exceptional sight. He flew in the same path the vehicle had been going, and then released a long stream of smoke instead of fire in the hopes that it would show the form of someone trying to camouflage themselves.

But even the scent trail had disappeared. He didn't want to give up on finding her friend but there was no question which female he would choose now. *Fiona.*

He would choose her every single time.

Fear for Fiona licked up his spine as he raced back the way he'd come. The sun beat down on his back and tail as he flew. Fiona was breathing steadily, two darts sticking out of her spine as she lay on top of the unconscious male.

Ian landed gently beside her, pulled the darts out of her with a sharp precision then quickly scooped her up into his claws, gentle with her as he tucked her against his chest. The male Fiona had been talking to lay still on the ground, a dagger through his chest, but he was also breathing. Ian didn't want to open up the wound, but this shifter was a wolf, so if the dagger was silver it would continue to poison him as long as it was embedded in his chest. Making the decision, Ian pulled it out and picked up the male as well even as blood poured from the wound.

Ian tucked him against his chest. The flight would be more difficult carrying two people but he had to get them to the Stavros estate as quickly as possible. It was the only way to save Fiona. She was breathing and her heart rate was steady, but she was unconscious. He tried to shove his terror back, to keep thinking rationally, but he was raging inside, desperate to save her.

He hated how rough this flight would be and didn't like jostling their bodies, but there was no choice. It was too far to drive to Finn's and there was a healer at the Stavros estate. It was the only place he knew of where he could get help.

It took twenty minutes at the pace he flew, far too long for his liking, to make it to the estate. Lungs burning, he made a hard landing on the roof of the mansion. There were only two guards on it. He knew they would have only seconds to make a decision on whether to attack him. He let his camouflage fall almost simultaneously as he placed Fiona and the unknown shifter on the ground. Just as quickly he shifted to his human form and raised his hands in the air to find two shifters holding crossbows on him.

"I'm not disrespecting your Alpha. I have two injured friends." He might not know the unconscious male on the ground, but if the guy was a friend of Fiona's, he was a friend of Ian's. "I had nowhere else to go and I know Ophelia can help them. I'll stay here until Finn needs to talk to me. Please help the female." He'd only brought the male because he'd been with Fiona but the truth was, all he cared about was saving her. "Help her!" He'd beg on his knees if that was what it took. He'd shelve all his pride to save Fiona.

CHAPTER SEVEN

Ian paced outside the waiting room while Ophelia did her healing magic on Fiona and the male he now knew was named Gray.

The only people left in the waiting room were his brother Rory and of course, Liberty. Everyone else had left because he couldn't seem to stop snarling at, well, *everyone.*

Even Finn had given him a frustrated growl and left not too long ago.

Ian jerked when the door opened and Ophelia stepped out. She gave him a hopeful smile. "They're both awake. I don't know what was shot into Fiona, but I'm currently running her blood work as well as doing tests on the contents of the darts. Gray's healing from his wound as well. Overall they're healing like shifters should. The male's wound actually punctured his heart so he's lucky to be alive. With Fiona...like I said, she appears to be healing but I want to know what's in those darts."

Ophelia had barely finished speaking when Ian strode past her—or attempted to. She quickly blocked his path and put her hands on her slim hips as she glared up at him.

"Where do you think you're going?" Her dark curly hair was pulled up into a ponytail and she had on no makeup, making her look as if she was in college. Still,

87

there was a fierce edge to the petite wolf. Right now she was directing all of her attitude at him.

"To see my…" His instinct was to say mate, and he didn't care how insane that was. Fiona *would* be his. Now that he knew she wasn't mated and she wasn't even involved with her family anymore. Yep, he'd be claiming her soon enough. He'd already lived without her for over five decades. He would be patient a little longer.

Ophelia's expression softened somewhat. "You can see Fiona. But not if you're going to grill her about what happened. She needs to talk to Finn—who I'm going to get right now."

"I don't give a shit about anything else other than making sure she's okay." He needed to see with his own eyes that she was alive and healing. She'd been so damn still when he'd brought her here. Even if her heartbeat had remained strong, she'd looked…dead. He fought off a shudder at the thought. For so long he'd lived with the knowledge—false as it was—she was with someone else, always out of his reach. To lose her after finding her again?

Unthinkable.

Ophelia stepped back and let him head down the short hallway. Following Fiona's scent, he stopped at the second door on the left and found her sitting up in a comfortable-looking king-sized bed. The room was set up similar to a hospital room, but there were no windows and it had a more welcoming feel to it. His brother had told him that this area was underground, heavily secured and insulated. It had been built for all types of supernatural beings, including vampires—most of whom couldn't walk in the sun.

Relief filled Fiona's eyes as she gave him a tired smile. "I was told that you saved me and Gray. Thank you so much, Ian."

She didn't mention Ava so he assumed she knew her friend had been taken. "I tried to go after your friend. I'm not sure what happened, but they vanished into thin air." He was still racking his brain, trying to think of what might be powerful enough to do something like that.

Fiona gave a slight nod, her mouth pulling into a tight line. "Ophelia filled me in a little, but said you'd be able to tell me the rest. We need to talk to Gray and go after her."

He moved to her side immediately, sitting on the small chair next to her bed. Even though he knew he shouldn't touch her, he took her hand in his to feel the warmth of her. She curled her fingers into his.

It reassured every single part of his being that she was okay. "We'll get your friend back, I swear it. And I will kill every single person involved in whatever this is."

She gave another nod. "We need to talk to Gray. He was telling me about some bad stuff going on in one of the Hell realms and there has to be a connection to what happened to us. But first..." She paled slightly and rubbed a hand over her face. "My dragon is sleeping," she whispered, so low he didn't think anyone else could hear even if they were standing outside the door. Unexpected tears glistened in her blue eyes as she said the words, then spilled down her cheeks.

The tears pierced him. He wasn't sure what she meant by sleeping, but he reached out on instinct and swiped away the wetness, cupping her cheeks in both his hands. "What do you mean?" he murmured.

She blinked rapidly to stave off more tears. He let his hands drop from her face, but grasped her hands in his. He simply couldn't stop touching her, not when it was clear she needed the comfort.

"I can feel her, but she's sleeping. It's the only way I can think of to describe it. I can't shift right now. I've called on my power and...she doesn't respond to me." Stark terror flashed in her eyes for a moment before she masked it.

But he understood her fear. If he couldn't shift, couldn't fly... It would be like losing part of his soul. Not only that, not being able to connect to her dragon would make her more vulnerable, less able to defend herself. *Hell no.*

It had to be whatever was in those darts. Something she would already know so he didn't state the obvious. "We'll figure out how to counteract whatever drug is in your system." He'd sell everything he had, including his soul, to make sure she got her dragon back.

"Why were you there?" she asked. "Not that I'm not grateful, but did you follow me?" She let out a short laugh before he could respond. "I mean, obviously you did."

He didn't bother to deny it because what would be the point? "I did follow you." And he wasn't going to offer any other explanation than that. He'd done it and he wasn't sorry. He'd follow this female into Hell itself.

"Ah, okay, but we're going to go back to that later. For now, I want to talk to Gray and I know we need to talk to Finn. I don't care if his pack will help me. I'm going after Ava once Gray tells me where he thinks she's been taken."

Ian only realized he was growling when Fiona's eyes widened slightly. As if she read his mind, she tightened her fingers in his.

"Gray is just a friend. I've known him since he was a pup. I helped him and his mother a long time ago. There never has been and never will be anything between us."

Something about her tone seemed almost motherly. Combined with the pure scent of truth rolling off her, it instantly eased the tension growing inside him. Ian had saved the male only because he knew it would matter to her. Now he was truly glad that he had. "I swear I'll get Ava back."

"And I'm going to help you." There was a fierce determination in her voice and expression.

He didn't argue, knowing it would be pointless. "Do you want me to get Gray in here?"

Fiona swung her legs over the side of the bed. "I can go to him. Ophelia didn't say how badly he was injured."

As she stood, he held out an arm. To his surprise, she slipped her arm through his. She was wearing what amounted to hospital scrubs, but they were a bright pink. He wondered if that was Ophelia's choice. Probably, considering what he knew of the doctor's taste and humor. She likely made the males wear them as well.

As they stepped out into the hall, he realized how quiet it was. He couldn't even hear his brother or Liberty in the waiting room. This place had to have some serious insulation. A faint scent of lust was trailing down the hallway, however, and Fiona must have scented it too because she shot him a surprised look. Gray was the only other patient here right now. When they reached his door, it was closed.

Fiona knocked on the door once and Ophelia's voice called out.

"Come in." The healer's voice was strained, and when Ian and Fiona stepped inside they both stopped in their tracks to find Gray caging her in against the wall.

The male had his hands on either side of Ophelia's head and was curving his body around hers in a very possessive way. He was staring down at her as if he wanted to kiss her senseless.

The female had a hand on the middle of his chest, her expression frustrated. "Get the hell back in bed," she snapped. "The only reason I'm not putting you on your ass right now is because you've been injured. Do you want me to embarrass you in front of Fiona?"

Gray simply growled instead of responding. Ophelia rolled her eyes and ducked out from under him. She was much smaller than him so she basically just stepped to the side. The male swiveled, tracking her actions as if he didn't notice, or, more probably, didn't care about Ian and Fiona.

"We need to talk about who attacked Fiona and you, and who took Ava." Ian wasn't going to waste time bullshitting. He wanted answers.

Now.

Ophelia held up a hand. "Finn's on his way down. Hold off on this conversation so you don't have it twice. He's the Alpha of this territory and you are in his house be-cause he's merciful." There was an edge to her voice as she looked at the three of them, clearly wanting to remind them who was in charge.

Ian just gritted his teeth. *Stupid shifter politics and hier-archies.*

"Of course we'll wait." Fiona shot both Gray and Ian a hard look as she went to sit down on a love seat against one of the walls.

Ian noticed that she seemed to be struggling, and he wanted to intervene and help her but wasn't sure if she would accept it. He didn't have any right to her. She wasn't his.

Not yet anyway, his dragon and demon side reminded him. But she would be very soon.

* * *

Fiona knew she shouldn't lean on anyone right now, but she kept her fingers linked through Ian's as they sat on the little sofa waiting for Finn to arrive.

Tension and adrenaline hummed through her, coun-terbalancing the strange weakness that had invaded her. It was as if part of her had died and no matter how much she called on her other half, her dragon remained unre-sponsive.

It was taking everything in her not to completely freak out. Because that would do no one any good and certainly wouldn't help get her friend back. She refused to believe that Ava was dead either. She was going to do everything in her power to save her.

She wanted to grab Gray and Ian and leave and figure everything out on their own. But the Stavros pack had taken her in and their healer had been very kind. She couldn't act rashly. Even if she hated waiting.

It was clear the others felt the same way. Ian was silent, a giant statue as usual, but his presence was soothing even if it was all-consuming. It had always been that way back when they'd been together. They'd hidden their relationship for as long as they could and when they'd been ready to leave together, to mate, her family had revealed they'd known everything—and that her mating with him wasn't an option. The fallout from that… She still couldn't think about that dark time. She'd had to kick him out of her life, to break his heart and hers in order to save him from her murdering psycho clan.

Which was why she couldn't believe he was sitting next to her and holding her hand as if decades hadn't passed.

Being so close to him again was wreaking havoc on her, and bringing up memories she didn't want to think about. She shoved them all back. Now wasn't the time to break down.

Just as she was about to jump up from her seat and go find the Alpha herself, Finn strode in, his expression dark. Earlier in the club she'd gotten a glimpse of him as the Alpha, but now she could see the true extent of his power. It rolled off him in waves.

"I've sent trackers to the area where you were shot. Now start talking." He glanced around at the three of them.

Fiona nodded once at Gray, even as she squeezed Ian's hand. She was so damn grateful for his presence right now. "I think you should probably start."

Gray stood and gave a respectful nod to Finn. "Long story short, a friend of mine found out some bad shit was going down in a Hell realm. We went there and my friend was killed. I barely escaped alive." He quickly launched into an explanation of what he believed was going on in the realm, relaying what he'd told Fiona earlier.

"And you don't know what this testing ground is for? Other than to see how well the drug kills humans?"

"No. But if they could weaponize this drug, turn it into an aerosol weapon…" Gray lifted a shoulder. "I can't say for sure, but it seems as if they want to kill a lot of humans. Not hard to figure out the end game is shitty for everyone."

The room went silent until Finn rubbed a hand over the back of his head. "Fuck."

Fiona could think of a lot of reasons half-demons or any number of supernatural beings would want to kill humans. Taking over the planet and ruling as gods was something she could easily see supernaturals wanting to do. She'd known plenty of arrogant supernaturals who didn't want to live in the shadows. Who wanted to rule the planet and make humans their slaves. And this realm was a lot more pleasant than most of the Hell realms she'd been in. Maybe they just wanted to take over the realm because they preferred it, or their own realm was dying. The "why" was important, but stopping whoever was behind this even more so.

"Do you think Ava is alive?" Fiona asked.

Gray looked her straight in the eye. "I don't know. She's not human so I don't think they can use her blood. They took her instead of killing her though, so I just don't know." He let out a frustrated sigh.

"But you have a good idea of who took her and where they went?" He'd been to the Hell realm. He'd know where the entrance was.

"Where they went, yes. And I made sketches of any face I remembered seeing in that realm. I don't know how much it will help though. And as far as who, meaning names? No, I have no idea."

"Is the entrance to the realm in my territory?" A hint of rage edged Finn's voice.

"It's on the border, but not quite in it."

Finn's jaw clenched once, and his pale blue eyes went wolf. "And you didn't think it necessary to tell me?"

There was a tense silence. "I should have. I apologize."

Finn blinked once in surprise, likely at the quick apology, before the anger was back. "I'll deal with you later," he growled at Gray, before turning to focus on Fiona and Ian. "I know you're going to go after your friend—"

"I'm going with her." Ian stood, but didn't let go of Fiona's hand.

She moved with him, wanting Finn to know that they stood together. Literally and figuratively.

Finn nodded, as if he'd expected it. "I'm going to set up a team and we'll all go together. Gray, I want those sketches immediately. And any information your friend had on whoever is behind...whatever this bullshit is."

"My friend had started a working list of missing humans. A lot of them are undocumented immigrants. Half-demons were taking people they knew wouldn't be missed. They don't want to draw attention to themselves. I'll get you that list as well."

"This sounds organized," Fiona murmured. Which wasn't good.

"If you have a laptop, I can pull up the sketches now. I've got the images saved in the Cloud," Gray said.

Finn pulled out his cell phone, made a quick call asking for a laptop. Then he turned to Fiona again. "How are you feeling?"

"Good enough." Not a total lie. "I'm ready to leave as soon as possible."

He watched her for a long moment, then turned to Ian. "Talk to you outside?"

Ian squeezed Fiona's fingers once, then dropped her hand before striding out with Finn. She wanted to go with him, to be near him, but stayed where she was. The faster she let Finn and Ian talk, the faster they'd get out of here and find her best friend. Ava had been the one constant in her life the last fifty years, more sister than friend. They *had* to find her.

CHAPTER EIGHT

"I'm going wherever she goes." Ian only spoke when he and Finn were in another room with complete privacy. He couldn't hear anyone else talking so he didn't think the others could hear them either.

"No shit. I just wanted to ask if you would be a team player for this op. You worked well with my pack before and I appreciate it. But I need to know what you're going to be like in the Hell realm. Because if you put my pack in danger…" There was a slight edge to his tone.

"I would never do that." He pushed back his impatience at the need to return to Fiona. He didn't like letting her out of his sight. Not even when she was in the security of the Stavros mansion.

Finn eyed him. "Will you be able to follow my orders? Because I can't have you disrespect me in front of my pack. And I don't give a shit if it's in another realm. I don't want to fight you, but I will."

Ian respected what Finn was saying. "As long as your orders don't put Fiona in danger or you don't try to separate me from her, we won't have an issue. I can follow orders." *Sort of. Maybe.* Damn it, he could. He'd do it for Fiona because her friend was in danger and Finn's pack would bring a lot of firepower. Right now it sounded like they needed that kind of backup to infiltrate…wherever they were going.

Finn sighed. "That's about what I expected. Also, I don't want Rory going with us. Is that going to be a problem with you?"

"No. Because Liberty would want to go with him." And there was no way that female needed to be back in any sort of Hell realm. She'd come a long way from the abused and frightened woman they'd found and he couldn't imagine her going back to one of those places.

Finn snorted in agreement.

Ian didn't actually think his brother would go if Liberty tried to insist on going with him. Ian couldn't see Rory doing that to her, not even on his Alpha's orders. Thankfully, Finn was a good Alpha and was going to circumvent the issue altogether by keeping Rory out of the op.

"What do you know about Gray?" Finn asked.

The question surprised him. He assumed the Alpha knew everything about the male since Gray lived in Finn's territory.

Ian shrugged. "I just know what Fiona has told me. She said she's known him since he was a pup. It sounds as if she saved him and his mom from a bad situation. But I don't know anything else." Not even the guy's last name. Not that he really cared.

Finn nodded, as if he knew that already. Or at least some of it. Because Ian didn't think he'd known Fiona had saved the male years ago. "I'm going to talk to Fiona alone. Are you going to lose your shit?"

Ian gritted his teeth. He understood that the Alpha needed to talk to her. Finn would want to ask her more about Gray in private, and even though Ian didn't like being separated from Fiona for even a moment, he knew he had to deal with it. Because he was going on this mission to rescue Ava and he didn't want to do anything to put his own brother at odds with the Alpha.

Somehow Ian grasped on to his civility. "I don't have a problem with that."

The only thing he would have a problem with was if Finn tried to separate them during the mission. Because nothing in this realm or any other would separate him from Fiona now that she was in his orbit again.

* * *

"You've been to Hell realms before, correct?" Finn asked.

"Yes. I've done various rescue missions with Ava. I didn't realize there was a gate along our borders." Fiona knew gates were everywhere but it bothered her one had been so close.

Finn nodded as if he believed her.

At this point she didn't really care what he believed. All she cared about was getting her friend back. "So when do we leave?"

"Within the hour. I know Ian will be a team player—sort of. At least I know he won't endanger my pack. I need to know how you handle yourself in battle situations."

It was a fair question since he didn't know her. "I'm not ancient, but I'm a freaking dragon," she said wryly. It didn't matter that she couldn't actually shift at the moment, she was still incredibly strong. "And you'll need either me or Ian to open the gate unless you have another way to do it." Because her dragon essence allowed her to open any Hell gate she wanted. Since she couldn't breathe fire she'd have to use her blood.

It was why, for so long, dragons had lived in ultimate secrecy. In the last few years they'd started to come out to other supernaturals a bit more. Predators like them could only stay in hiding for so long. And the strength of a clan was a powerful thing. It deterred others from attacking a dragon for the power of their blood. Taking on a single individual was one thing. Taking on a clan of dragons? Only someone suicidal did that.

"Okay. I know I don't have any jurisdiction over you. But I'm going to run this op." There was no give in the Alpha's voice. "Our number one objective is to save your friend. And we also plan to find out what the hell is going on. If there are other human captives, we're saving them too. Will you be able to take orders from me?"

"As long as they don't interfere with my saving Ava, or affect Ian negatively. And I won't be separated from him." *Nope. Not happening.* She didn't want to hurt Ian and she certainly wasn't a masochist, but she needed to stay with him. He was a dragon and she trusted him implicitly. It didn't matter how many years had passed. She would trust the male with her life in a way she couldn't trust anyone else but Ava.

Finn gave her a wry smile. "Fair enough. We have plenty of weapons and gear if you need. I know dragons don't favor carrying weapons for the most part, but you're free to use any of ours. Ian can show you to our weapons room."

Even though she wanted to ask how Finn knew that about dragons, she simply nodded. She'd just ask Ian later. "Thank you." For once she actually was going to stock up on weapons, considering she couldn't shift right now. The sick feeling in the pit of her stomach spread, making her flush hot then cold as she thought about what would happen if she could never shift again.

Never fly again. Never soar high above the clouds... She swallowed hard. Straightening, she shoved the thought away. She refused to believe that could ever happen. That this wasn't just temporary.

It had to be.

* * *

Ian was barely a foot from Fiona where they stood with a small team of wolves in front of the oversized whiteboard. Gray had drawn a very realistic diagram of the castle in that Hell realm where they thought Ava was being held. The male had serious talent.

Ian just hoped that was where she was and that she wasn't already dead.

"I don't know for sure, but I believe this is where the captives are, if there are any left at this point," Gray said, pointing to an area he'd marked *underground*. "There were two doors heavily guarded and I scented others past the doors. We weren't able to infiltrate it, however. But we were able to discover where their labs were." He pointed to another area of the castle. "And we were able to watch these beings long enough to figure out what they were up to."

Everything on the whiteboard had been labeled so they had a general idea of what they were looking for. But the castle grounds were heavily guarded as well. And after what had happened today, Ian figured the dragons and half-demons would increase their security. He just wished he knew *who* they were up against. He didn't like unknowns. So far Gray had told him he knew that dragons and half-demons were involved—an unlikely partnership.

Fiona shifted restlessly next to Ian, the energy humming through her wild. He wanted to ask her if she could sense her dragon yet, but didn't want to in front of the wolves. Like the other female in the team going on the op, Fiona had on leggings, boots and a heavy tunic since it was cold in this Hell realm. Once they crossed over he wasn't sure if that would trigger her ability to shift or what.

But he knew what would happen to him.

He'd be in his half-demon form. It always happened when he was in a Hell realm, whether he wanted it or not. He could turn dragon as well, but he shed his human side completely when he was there. The thought of Fiona seeing him that way had him on edge. She'd never seen him as anything other than a dragon or human. He'd never allowed it, even though she'd wanted to see it. He'd never wanted to disgust her. He forced himself not to think about her finally seeing him as a half-demon.

He'd just deal with it later.

As Gray continued going over the schematics of the castle and grounds, Ian watched Fiona out of the corner of his eye. Her long dark hair was pulled into a tight braid against her head and she had multiple blades strapped to her thighs. He was certain she had more where he couldn't see. Considering the amount of weapons she was bringing, he guessed she couldn't shift right now. It pained him that such an integral part of her was missing. At least she had training. That was one thing her clan had done right where she was concerned: made sure she could protect herself. They might have wanted their females to be seen and not heard, but they'd made sure they could defend themselves.

"When you're spit out into the other realm there's no telling where you'll end up," Gray said. "The time I went through I ended up roughly five miles north of the castle. My friend traveled over four times and ended up in four separate places. Each time it was roughly five miles from the castle, but in various directions, so it's possible the castle was built there because it's central to the entrance."

"What's the exit like?" Ian asked. Because exiting a Hell realm was always a bitch. In the last one he'd lived in, if someone wanted to exit, they had to dive down to the bottom of a very deep lagoon first. And the exit could only be used once a day so if someone had used it already, you had to wait another damn day to try again.

"At the top of a small mountain. About four miles up. The terrain isn't too rough but it's always foggy. Pea-soup foggy. And that fog is the only reason I escaped last time, because it camouflaged me."

"Any restrictions on exiting?"

The male shook his head. "Not that I know of. My friend said he'd used it more than once in a twelve-hour period. He'd seen others using it before him and he had no problem exiting directly after."

"Where does it lead to?" Finn asked.

"Same area as the entrance. Only about a hundred yards east of it."

That was fairly interesting. Most exits from Hell realms spit you out in a different place from the original entrance.

"You'll be staying here as my guarded guest until we return," Finn said to Gray.

For a moment the other male stilled, but then he nodded, his expression almost...pleased. Probably because the male wanted to spend more time with Ophelia. "Do you want me to lead you to the entrance?"

"Yes. My mate and Guardian will escort you back here once we're gone."

As if on cue, Lyra, Finn's mate, stepped into the huge training room. Her blond hair was pulled back into a ponytail, her grayish-violet eyes softening when they landed on Finn. The two of them moved toward each other like magnets.

Ian glanced away from them, a sharp sense of longing invading his veins. To see the two of them together, it was clear they were in love. He could have had that with Fiona. If things had been different. And they would be different as soon as possible.

"How long have you been in Biloxi?" Fiona's soft voice made him turn toward her. She was fiddling with the handle of one of her blades as she watched him, the nervous action out of character.

"Less than a year." If he'd known she'd been so close to him, he'd never have been able to keep his distance.

"Oh." She bit her bottom lip and it looked as if she wanted to say more, but at Finn's sharp voice they turned to him.

"Fiona and Ian will team up together. I'll be with Solon. And Chloe and Spiro will be a team." He started barking out commands of where they would infiltrate through and what the final game plan was for when they got there.

Ian listened, not saying anything when it was clear it was a solid tactical plan. For now, their plan was to save Ava, other captives if possible, and get samples of the drug. They also needed to find out who was behind this. But this was a rescue mission more than anything. With such a small but powerful team they had the element of surprise and strength on their side. Shit could always go sideways but that was to be expected.

He hated that Fiona was going when she couldn't shift. Hell, he hated that she was going to be in danger at all. But she was still a dragon, and even if he wanted to keep her protected and safe here, she'd never let him and the others go off to save her friend without her. He had to respect her strength, who she was. Her family hadn't, and he never wanted to be in the same category as them.

It didn't take long to pile into two SUVs. The drive was close to an hour and for the most part, it was silent, as everyone mentally prepared for the crossover and the potential battle they faced.

After turning off the main highway onto a gravel road, they traveled a couple miles through forest until they reached a dirt road. A decaying, wood sign was posted in front of what had been a gate but now was just two lone posts. The sign had once said KEEP OUT but the K, P, and U were missing.

"About twenty yards up there'll be a marked tree to the left of the road," Gray said from the far backseat where he sat next to one of the warriors. "We can go in on foot from there."

It was clear when they reached the tree. An X had been spray painted in red. *Subtle*, Ian thought.

"I didn't see any motion sensors, cameras or traps last time I was here, but things could have changed." Gray's voice was quiet as Finn turned off the engine.

They all filed out, including Lyra and Gabriel, who'd be escorting Gray back to the compound once everyone else had crossed over.

The trek through the sunlit woods was silent as they walked deeper into the thick trees and everyone scanned their surroundings for potential threats. Ian couldn't scent anything out of the ordinary, but that didn't mean threats weren't there. He hadn't forgotten how he'd seen a vehicle and a dragon carrying Ava vanish into thin air only hours before.

"This is it." Gray motioned to a small circular clearing in the middle of the trees.

Finn blinked at Ian questioningly. Without voicing anything he knew what the male meant. Ian nodded once. He could sense the invisible gates and all he had to do was breathe fire where Gray motioned to.

Ian waited as Finn said goodbye to his mate and Gray. Lyra and Gabriel stepped back far enough away from them that they shouldn't be pulled into the gate once it opened.

"Join hands," Finn said quietly.

"I'll have your back, Fiona," Ian said as he slipped his hand into hers, linking his fingers tight. As if there was ever a question of that.

"I know you will. You always did." Her expression was solemn, thoughtful, before she looked away from him and took one of the warriors' hands in her own.

"And you always had mine, didn't you? Even if you didn't want to tell me the truth about why you lied." He didn't care that he was saying this in front of others. He wanted her to know before they went through the gate. Because anything could happen, no matter the best-laid plans.

She turned back to look at him then. Her blue eyes widened slightly but the surprise that rolled off her was potent and raw.

Maybe she'd always thought that he'd believed her cruel words when she'd kicked him out of her life. At first he had, but it hadn't taken long for him to figure out that she'd lied about not loving him. That she'd pushed him away and mated with someone else in an attempt to keep him safe. By then it had been too late. He'd gone to her family's home and saw with his own eyes that she'd mated with someone else. *Now* he knew that to be a lie as well, but at the time... *Damn it.* The only reason he'd stayed away from her was because he truly thought she'd been mated. Once that had happened he'd assumed there was no chance for them. Ever. Because dragons mated for life in the most literal sense. If a mated dragon died, so did their mate.

Before she could respond, he turned, breathed fire where Gray had said the opening was. A swirling blue vortex opened up and sucked the six of them in. That protective instinct welled up inside him. He let go of the other wolf's hand and gripped Fiona to him, wrapping his body tight around hers as they fell into a maelstrom of raging wind and rain.

CHAPTER NINE

52 years ago

"You still haven't told me why you fight so much. You could do anything you wanted to, Ian." Fiona ran her long, elegant fingers through his hair as he laid his head on her lap.

A billion stars were splashed in the sky above them, a backdrop to a quiet Louisiana night. Not even the sound of crickets permeated the air. Probably because he and Fiona had the scent of predators. It didn't matter that they were in human form, their scent was still all dragon. And in his case, more.

He needed to tell her about his dual nature. He'd just been holding off because he didn't want to ruin their fledgling relationship. They'd been seeing each other in secret for two weeks and he looked forward to every time she was able to get away. She was the only reason he was still in New Orleans. Though tonight they'd flown far out of the city, north into quiet countryside.

"There's something I need to tell you. I'm not just a dragon." He blurted the words out. Now to figure out how to tell her the truth of what he was.

"I know. I mean, I don't know what you are. But you have the scent of something more to you. Something unique. And I don't recognize what it is." She continued

111

to stroke her fingers lazily through his hair. They'd finished flying twenty minutes ago and were now stretched out in the grass—unfortunately fully clothed again—and just enjoying the quiet, cold night.

Unfortunately he was afraid his words would ruin the peacefulness of the moment. And ruin everything between them. But he had to tell her. She deserved the truth. Deserved to know what kind of male he was before she linked herself to him.

"I'm a half-demon. My mother was injured in a hard battle. She'd managed to escape her attacker, but she was weak, healing from the long battle. My...sperm donor took her without her consent. He raped her." He remained preternaturally still under the stroking of Fiona's fingers. Which he realized hadn't stopped.

He'd assumed that she would shove him away in disgust once she knew what he was.

"I'm so sorry your mother had to go through that." Still she continued stroking through his hair as if what he'd said didn't matter. Or maybe not that, but she wasn't horrified by it at least.

"You don't care about my heritage?" he asked carefully.

"Of course I care. I care about where you come from. But if you mean do I think differently of you? No. Your father sounds like a monster. But you are clearly not. Is that why you fight so much? I don't know much about...half-demons." Her words were hesitant. She cupped his face then, her palm soft against his skin.

That vise around his chest loosened more than a fraction and he realized he'd been holding his breath as he let one out in a huge rush. Shifting slightly so he could look up at her, he nodded. "Yes. The urge to fight is always strong inside me. The fights allow me to take out my aggression." There were two ways for half-demons to let out their aggression. Fighting and sex. He'd always chosen fighting as his preferred method. As a half-dragon he had to be careful with his partners and fighting was simply easier.

Unless of course sex with Fiona was on the table. Then he'd choose that every time. But they hadn't crossed that line yet. He respected her too much and wanted to wait until he'd talked to her family. The truth of it was that what they said about his relationship with her wouldn't truly matter. He'd mate with her if *she* would have him. But it would be nice to have their blessing. Unfortunately, he wasn't sure that would happen once they found out his full nature.

"I love watching you fly," she murmured almost absently. "You're the most beautiful dragon I've ever seen."

He growled low in his throat at the unexpected compliment, at the surge of hunger her words sent through him. She always did that—told him how wonderful he was. He didn't feel that way. Never had. But she made him believe that just maybe he had a chance with a female like her.

Pushing up, he moved lightning fast until he had her pinned flat on her back against the soft grass. She wrapped her arms and legs around him, automatically arching into him. Her dark hair splayed around her face as she looked up at him, hunger and heat in her gaze.

"I'm not letting you go, Fiona," he murmured before brushing his lips over hers. She tasted like heaven. And his.

Only his.

"I'm not going anywhere." Truth was in every word.

He stroked his tongue against hers, needing more of her. Always more. He cupped the back of her head as he pinned her to the earth. He could feel the wild beat of her heart, the prick of her claws as she dug her fingers into his back. He wasn't sure how long they lay there kissing.

Time had no meaning when he was with her. Nothing else did.

Nipping at her bottom lip, he savored the groan she made when he slipped a hand under her flimsy top. She wasn't wearing a bra, something he was certain she did to make him crazy. Whatever the reason, he was glad for it. He'd been imagining what color her nipples were and tonight he planned to find out. She'd been shy about undressing in front of him before their flights and he'd respected her need for privacy. Something told him tonight was going to be different between them.

Her skin was smooth, perfect. When he cupped a full breast, she tightened the grip of her legs around his waist. He ran his thumb slowly over her hard nipple and groaned into her mouth when the wild scent of her desire permeated the air.

The past couple weeks he'd been holding back but tonight it was just the two of them in the vast spread of forest. He was going to taste more of her. As he nibbled his way along her jaw a gold and pale violet smoke surrounded them.

His mating manifestation. He was helpless to stop it. Which was why they had to be careful when they became intimate.

Right now in the middle of nowhere it didn't matter. No one was around to see. He'd sense any intruders.

He pushed up slightly and started to lift her shirt up, but she grasped the hem and tugged it over her head, moving faster than him. Her nipples were pale brown.

Growling softly, he leaned down and took one in his mouth.

She let out a gasp of surprise as he ran his tongue over the already hard bud, teasing and tasting her. As she slid her fingers through his hair, holding onto his head tightly, he palmed her other breast.

"Ian." The way she said his name was like a prayer.

It only urged him on and her scent was drowning him. It was a sweet, wild ocean scent that made him crazy, made it hard to breathe.

He moved to her other breast, circling her nipple with his tongue. He still couldn't believe he'd met this female, that she'd agreed to dinner with him weeks ago and that they'd been spending all their free time together. More than that, he couldn't believe she was here with him now.

She was out of his league, with an established clan that had immeasurable worth, yet she was here with him.

"Gotta taste all of you," he murmured against her breast before moving lower.

Her fingers tightened against his head, but he kept going until he reached the button of her jeans. They'd taken off their shoes before their last flight so all he had to do was unbutton them and tug them off.

He glanced up the length of her long, lithe body as he sat up between her spread legs. Her breathing was erratic, her eyes dilated. Keeping his gaze locked on hers, he slowly tugged the button out and pulled her zipper down.

Her breath hitched slightly, a pale blue fire dancing in her gaze and enfolding them just as his smoke did. It wasn't hot though, just a consuming presence. The smoke and fire were so thick he couldn't see beyond the two of them. Not even the stars above.

All he saw was her.

She was all that mattered anyway.

When he tugged her jeans down, she lifted her hips so he could get them off easier. Not bothering to pull off the little bit of lace she had covering her mound, he shredded the material at her hips so that it fell away.

She gave him a heavy-lidded look and lifted her hips to him as he bent between her open thighs, her fire growing brighter around them, consuming them.

He'd wanted to draw this out, to tease her more, but hell, he needed to see her climax. To taste it. To hear his name on her lips. To know he'd given her that pleasure. Him. Not some asshole her family wanted her to mate with.

"Ian…"

He froze at the hesitant way she said his name, and lifted his head. Heat was still there in her bright gaze, but she looked almost worried.

"I've never had anyone do this," she whispered. The normally confident female bit her bottom lip, her uncertainty clear.

"We can stop." His cock kicked against his pants once, but too damn bad. If she wanted to stop, they stopped.

"No!" She cleared her throat. "No. But...I just wanted you to know."

That was when it registered she meant... "You've never been with a male at all?"

She shook her head.

Fuck him. He'd guessed she was inexperienced but...a virgin. He nodded slowly, digesting that. The most primitive part of him was glad that he'd be her first. Not tonight, but soon. He knew he should walk away. He wasn't remotely good enough for this female, but he couldn't. Not when he knew she was his with a bone-deep certainty. Still, he wasn't sure about taking her like this in the middle of a forest. She should have silk beneath her body for her first time.

That didn't mean he couldn't bring her to climax, bring her toe-numbing pleasure. "We'll go slow and if you don't like something, tell me. We stop when you say we do."

She pushed out a sigh and nodded, relief mixing with the hunger in her gaze.

Moving down a little farther, he lifted her leg and kissed her inner ankle. If she'd never been with a male, he was going to give her everything she deserved.

He glided his lips over her soft skin, smiled against her ankle when her entire body jolted at the soft touch. Her fire and his smoke were out of control now. He wasn't sure how far they'd spread and didn't care.

Not when the scent of her hunger was driving him, urging him to mate her. His dragon rippled beneath the surface. Not with the need to shift, but his other side was telling him to claim this female.

Now.

He rolled his shoulders once as he lifted her other leg, dropped soft kisses up her ankle and calf. She shuddered each time his lips touched her skin. Taking his time, he kissed all of her until his face was directly between her legs.

"You're killing me," she rasped out, rolling her hips with clear intent.

The urgency in her voice eased the vise around his chest. He wanted everything to be perfect, but knew that was impossible. The only thing he could do was give her so much pleasure that she was exhausted with it. And keep giving it to her until she never wanted to leave him. Until she wanted to bond with him.

His demon half had no problem binding her to him with sex. Not at all.

He buried his face between her legs, growled against her slick folds when she gasped out his name. "Oh…Ian." She repeated his name over and over as he flicked his tongue up the length of her, teasing and learning her body.

She tasted like *his.* All sweet, honeyed perfection.

When he focused on her clit, she arched her back off the ground and dug her fingers into his head. "Right there!"

She was so damn reactive. He lifted his head for only a moment. "Cup your breasts. Stroke your nipples." He wished he had more hands, wished he could watch her as she touched herself, but all his concentration was on the tiny bundle of nerves guaranteed to bring her pleasure.

He increased pressure when she let out another moan, and kept stroking her clit, even when she tore her hands from his head. He heard a ripping sound even as she cried out in pleasure.

"Yes, yes, keep going, ah—" She broke off as her climax slammed into her.

Her scent rose, filling the air as she continued writhing against his face. He licked and stroked, savoring her taste, her cries of ecstasy, until finally she fell limp against the ground. He wanted to keep teasing her, to fill himself with her essence.

Though he was loath to move, she let out a small moan of distress. "Too much." Her voice was a whisper.

Pushing up, he stared down at her stretched out like a goddess. Her blue fire flickered all around her, calling to him like a siren's song.

"You're the most beautiful sight." His words were raspy, unsteady. And true.

"I don't know about that," she murmured, reaching for him. "You're incredibly—"

"Don't say beautiful," he growled before covering her mouth and body with his.

She stroked her tongue against his and he wondered if she liked her own taste, if this was too much for her.

When she slid her hand down over the front of his jeans, he stilled, lifted his head. Oh how he wanted her hands on him, stroking everywhere. He wanted to come in her hands, on her stomach, inside her. But... "I'm not taking you out here. You deserve better."

She frowned. "I want—"

"No." He just couldn't do that. "Let me give you something more. My bed, for your first time." Because he wanted to see her in his bed, stretched out, naked. Begging for his touch.

After a long pause, she nodded, but ripped the front of his pants open all the same and grasped his cock. Her grip was tentative at first until he groaned, rolling his hips into her hold. Maybe he didn't have as much control as he'd thought.

That was all the encouragement she needed. He covered her mouth again as she started stroking him, over and over, the feel of her hands on him about to push him over the edge.

It had been a long time for him, but stamina had never been an issue. Apparently until Fiona, because damn, she was actually touching him. *Fiona.* His female.

He savored the sensation of her gripping him, stroking him, until he couldn't take it any longer. He came in long, hard pulses, his come covering his stomach and hers until they collapsed against the soft ground.

He belatedly realized she'd torn out some of the grass and dirt earlier, which must have been that ripping sound. His smoke and her fire slowly abated, revealing the same night sky splashed with a billion stars. Everything was quiet around them, as it had been before.

Ian wrapped an arm around her as she snuggled against him. This had to be what heaven was like. Fiona in his arms, with his scent marking her.

"That was amazing," she murmured against his chest.

"You're amazing." He stroked a hand up and down her spine and cleared his throat. "I want to meet your family. I want to tell them about us. No more hiding in the dark." On this he would not bend.

She stiffened in his hold and moved slightly so she could look at him. "That's not a good idea. We should just leave."

Leave? What was she talking about? "Why? Because I beat your brother in a fight?" It would just show his family how strong he was. Sure, Colm might have issues with him, but that was something the male would get over.

"No. They want me to mate with a male from another clan."

At her words he growled low in his throat. No one would be mating with Fiona but him. His demon side was in agreement, ready to rip off the head of anyone who thought they could touch her. But she'd never even met the male. It wouldn't be happening. Once her family knew how serious they were, surely they'd get over it.

"They want to unite our clans. You don't understand what my family is like and that's my fault. I didn't want to tell you how awful they are because it's embarrassing. To them I am nothing. They only care about the heirs I can have and how strong I can help make the clan. I have no rights, no value. It's always about the males and the stupid clan."

Another growl tore from his throat. "You are worth everything."

She gave him a sad smile before she laid her head back on his chest. "Not to them."

He was silent for a long moment as he thought. She knew her family and how they would react. It went against his nature to run off into the night and escape as if they were common criminals. She deserved more than that. But if it was what she wanted, he would give her anything. All she had to do was ask. "Will you leave with me?"

She sat back up. "Yes. Just name the time." Her blue eyes were bright with an emotion he wasn't sure he quite comprehended.

"I need to set up a couple things and we'll leave within the week. Unless... No one hurts you, do they?" She'd never mentioned it, but the way she described her clan made him wonder—and shoved his dark nature right to the surface. If someone was hurting her, they'd die.

She snorted. "No. Not physically. I don't matter enough."

"Will they follow us?"

Fiona paused, then nodded. "It's likely. I'll leave a message letting them know I left voluntarily but they won't like it."

The wheels in his head were already turning. "I know a place we can live for a few years if we need to stay off the grid. They won't find us there." Once they were mated it wouldn't matter anyway. Because dragons were literally bound even in death. If one mated dragon died, so did the other. He doubted her family would bother with them then since she wouldn't be able to mate with someone of their choosing, but he would cover every option. Keep her safe.

"I'll go anywhere you are."

He brushed his lips over hers, immediately deepening the kiss. She was a drug, his addiction. He forced himself to pull back when he started getting hard again. She gave a slight protest, but laid her head back on his chest with a soft sigh.

"Why did you never search for your clan?" she asked after a few minutes.

"I had nowhere to start. And my mother never spoke of them so I didn't know if they'd rejected her, since it was too painful for her to speak of." There'd been no way to find them. No way he'd been able to figure it out anyway. "I wasn't even certain if others like me existed. I knew they must since I came from somewhere but…"

"Maybe we can search for them together." There was a note of hope in her voice.

"Do you need a clan to feel whole?" It wasn't something he'd considered. Because she was all he needed.

She shook her head quickly and met his gaze. "No. I've been alone most of my life anyway. It doesn't matter that I have a clan. Not when they treat me like an object to be used or discarded. They've given me everything and nothing at the same time."

He hated them for the way they'd treated her and vowed that he'd always keep her safe and treat her the way she deserved. "When I get back tonight I'll reach out to some of my contacts. Get everything in motion. We'll be gone by Friday."

Smiling contentedly, she laid her head back on his chest. For the first time in forever, everything inside him was settled. Calm.

CHAPTER TEN

"For a wolf who's housebound, you seem pretty damn smug." Ophelia eyed her only patient. Stretched out on the bed, shirtless, with his hands behind his head, Gray looked smug and sexy. Way too sexy.

"Of course I'm happy. I get to spend more time with you."

She narrowed her gaze at him. Everyone in the pack who'd met Gray in the past had described him as surly and a loner. But for some reason he seemed to have a permanent little grin whenever he was around her. The cheeky pup had even tried to cage her against the wall earlier and go all Alpha on her, as if he thought she'd what—like that display of dominance? And okay…her wolf had been very, very interested. It probably should have annoyed her more than it did, dang it.

"As soon as my Alpha and packmates are back, you're gone," she snapped harder than she'd intended. Ophelia was grateful he'd be gone too. Something about this Alpha rubbed her the wrong way. Okay everything about him rubbed her the wrong way—in all the *right* ways. He was all obnoxious and…sexy. *No, no, no.* He was maybe thirty and she was two hundred. Nope. Not gonna happen. He was a pup.

"Maybe I'll stick around. Ask him if I can join your pack." *Again with the smugness.*

"He'd never let you be part of the pack." And they both knew it. Gray was too Alpha. It surprised Ophelia that he was living in another wolf's territory but according to Finn the male had no desire to run his own pack or mix with theirs. So Alpha traits aside—meaning he was powerful enough to run his own pack and could never truly submit to another leader—he wasn't a threat to Finn or anyone else in the territory. Just because a shifter had the Alpha traits didn't mean they had the desire to run a pack. And according to pack gossip the male appeared to like living alone and hadn't made any power plays to take over territory. She'd never met him until today. Sure, she'd heard a couple of her packmates talk about how sexy he was, but she knew he'd never hooked up with anyone in her pack. And for some reason she was glad of that.

His eyes narrowed and he sat up in bed—his ridiculous eight-pack flexing with the motion. "And why is that?"

"Please. You're an Alpha." She stared at him for a long moment and waited for him to confirm it.

Instead he just stared at her, not bothering to hide his hunger for her. It took her off guard. She was over two hundred years old. Older than even Finn. She was one of the oldest members of the pack, and normally the males of her pack were intimidated by her. It didn't matter that she was small compared to almost everyone; she was the healer and everyone respected her.

Not this male. Gray looked at her like she was a female. A desirable woman he wanted to do bad, bad things to. And at that thought, she knew she needed to get the heck out of here. Because she liked the idea of that waaaay too much. She nearly snorted to herself. He'd probably be selfish in bed. At least that was what she was going to tell herself.

"If there's nothing else I can do for you, I'm leaving. If you need anything, call my cell or let your guard know."

He made a scoffing sound and rubbed a hand over his dark, unruly hair, his arm and chest muscles flexing. "You guys are guarding me? Seriously?"

She lifted a shoulder. She doubted it was necessary. He'd been fairly helpful to the pack and she didn't think he was going anywhere, but he was still a dangerous male. She could sense it. He was a predator just like her. Well, maybe not like her. He was more. They might both be apex predators but he was more physically dangerous than her. Her wolf sensed it. As the healer, she had a calmer nature and this male was wild and untamed under the surface. "It's not personal."

In a fluid—sexy!—motion, he swung his legs off the bed and stood. He stretched, looking more feline than lupine, and she had to force herself not to drink in every delicious inch of him. "Is it against the rules for you to give me a tour of the place?" he murmured, his gaze on her mouth.

"It's not against the rules. But I don't have time to waste on cheeky little pups." She turned around to leave, had taken one step toward the door when she felt his larger-than-life presence behind her. One of his big hands landed on the door to the side of her face, holding it shut and blocking her in.

He ran his nose along the side of her face, inhaling and not being subtle about it. "Cheeky pup?"

Heat flooded between her thighs. She wanted to turn around—and push him away or grab his face and bring his lips to hers. She wasn't sure which. So she didn't move. She couldn't trust herself around the male. Something about Gray brought out the most primitive side of her and she wasn't handling it well. She'd always been in control when it came to males and sex. But he made her feel the opposite right now. "You're young." Younger than her, anyway. Not that anyone could tell by their physical appearances. If anything, she looked younger than him.

Instead of responding he gently closed his teeth around her earlobe. The action was so damn bold. Her instinct should have been to shove him away, remind him that he had no right to touch her. She hadn't given him permission. None of her patients or packmates had ever been so bold with her. He wasn't touching her anywhere else. But that single contact had even more heat surging through her. She wanted to lean into him, to turn around and let him pin her up against the door while he devoured her.

Since that way lay insanity, she did the only thing she could. She elbowed him in the stomach hard and threw the door open. He didn't make a sound but thankfully stepped out of her way. She didn't look back as she hurried down the hall but she heard his muted laughter as she exited.

Frustrating male.

* * *

On the other side of the portal, Fiona found herself pinned under Ian on icy, uneven ground. The sky above was a pale green and everything was bitterly cold. When she inhaled it burned her lungs.

"You okay?" he murmured, moving off her so he could take in her appearance. He crouched over her, his expression worried as he looked her over from head to foot.

"I'm good," she whispered, unable to stop staring at him in his demon form. When they'd been together he'd refused to let her see him that way—much to her frustration. She couldn't believe he'd been ashamed of *this*.

Eyes wide, she drank in the now seven-foot-tall male with pale blue skin, unique swirling tattoos covering his arms and chest, and those familiar amber eyes she could easily get lost in. And he was completely naked, his clothes having shredded in the vortex when he'd shifted forms. He was definitely big all over. Something she was trying not to notice too hard. But she couldn't help but peek a little. Her self-control only went so far.

"Shit," he muttered, turning away and grabbing the bag of clothes he'd brought with him just for this occasion.

She still didn't tear her gaze away from his muscular ass until he tugged silky-looking black pants on. That was when she realized the others had formed a small perimeter around them and were making sure the area was secure.

Um, yeah, just like she should have been doing instead of ogling Ian. Inwardly cursing herself, she jumped to her feet and immediately took in her surroundings. She didn't scent any other beings nearby. She'd been in various Hell realms before; had seen some seriously creepy things. Now...there was no life that she could see, scent or hear. It was strange.

"We head east," Finn said, coming to stand a few feet away from her.

Ian moved lightning fast, putting himself in between her and the Alpha in a not-so-subtle defensive posture. She blinked once in surprise but knew she shouldn't be shocked. He'd always been possessive of her. And okay, she liked it. When the Alpha narrowed his pale gaze at Ian, Fiona stepped forward and linked her arm through Ian's.

He was stiff, but relaxed slightly at her touch.

She didn't bother asking Finn why they should go east. Gray's directives had been clear. There were small mountains surrounding them in every direction and one huge one to the west that went so high they couldn't see the top of it because it was covered in thick fog. The castle—their destination—would be to the east of the big mountain.

"Do you smell anything living?" she asked quietly as the three others moved to join them. She glanced around the surrounding forest. The tree trunks were a dark green, as well as the leaves. Gray had mentioned that the trees almost appeared to be alive. And not in the normal sense.

"No." Finn frowned, scanning the trees as well.

She shivered at the seeming lack of life. Even in her home in the country there were always the smells and sounds of the surrounding forest. She'd even gotten a couple foxes to trust her enough to let her hand-feed them. This utter silence was offensive to her senses.

"You guys know the deal," Finn continued. "We'll head there as a team then scope the entrance Gray told us about."

"Fiona and I will cover the back of the formation...if that's acceptable." Ian's voice was almost grudging but at least he'd tacked on the last bit of respect.

Finn nodded and motioned to his team. Without having to use any words they all fell into a formation, the male named Solon standing at the front with Finn and the other two lining up behind them. Fiona and Ian would follow and per their earlier plan they would all spread out in the forest, but not so far that they couldn't see each other. Except they didn't want to head off in a straight line.

Once they were in the thick of the green trees and fifty yards away from Chloe and Spiro, Ian spoke quietly. "How are you feeling?"

She didn't want to announce to everyone that something was seriously wrong with her. Because it was. She felt it in her bones. Whatever had been in that toxin wasn't working its way out of her system like it should have. It was making her feel tired and she still couldn't get in touch with her dragon. And that was terrifying. "Same. Maybe worse," she murmured, keeping her voice at a sub-vocal level even while continuously scanning her surroundings for any threats.

"We'll fix this," he murmured.

The way he said "we" ripped something open inside her. Swallowing hard, she broke his gaze. She was too terrified to think there could ever be a "we" with him. But now that he was back in her life again, a mere foot away from her... She blinked away the unexpected tears that stung her eyes. Being near him had her on edge and completely off-kilter.

"I'm sorry you have to see me in this form." Ian's words were stiff and unexpected.

Swiping at an errant tear, she snapped her gaze to his. "What are you talking about?"

"This." His expression was grim as he motioned to his now covered body. His clothes were loose, silky and all black.

"The only thing I'm sorry about is that you're not naked anymore." She didn't even think about them before she'd uttered the words. It just slipped out. She didn't want to send him mixed signals, but the male was magnificent and she wasn't sorry she'd told him—definitely wasn't sorry she'd finally gotten to see him like this. How could he think she wouldn't want to see him in this form?

Now he blinked in surprise before turning away from her. She wanted to ask him what he was thinking. And she really wanted to talk about what he'd said right before they'd been sucked into that vortex. But as they covered more ground she knew there was a bigger chance they'd stumble on guards or traps surrounding the castle, so she kept silent.

They needed to be vigilant. Because they were moving at almost human speed and watching for traps, it took about an hour and a half to cover five miles. When they reached the edge of the forest that led to the surrounding area of the castle, her breath caught in her throat.

The castle itself was up on a fairly large hill so that it appeared impenetrable and intimidating if someone wanted to storm it. But what they had in mind was a lot more subtle. She just hoped she was up to a battle if it became necessary.

She wasn't exactly exhausted but she felt almost tired. Which was unusual for her. Normally she never ran out of energy and always had some to spare. It was part of her dragon nature.

Instead of emerging from the forest and revealing themselves to any number of guards, many of which she could see up on the parapet walk and in the guardhouse, they remained hidden in the shadows of the trees.

After getting a visual of the castle, the six of them moved back into the trees quietly. Once they were about a hundred yards away, Finn spoke. "Considering the landmarks that Gray gave us, the entrance we'll be using is on the opposite side of the castle. Follow my lead."

Once again they fell into formation, this time moving at a quicker pace. She still struggled with not feeling like her normal self but keeping up wasn't a problem. Ten minutes later they were in the forest that merged with the back side of the castle.

There were another twelve half-demon guards on the parapet walkway and just as many on the ground. Ian could just call on his camouflage to protect him, but the rest of them couldn't. Including herself. Something she didn't want to think about.

Once they'd all gotten a good visual, they followed after Finn. She glanced at Ian for what felt like the hundredth time but he was in total warrior mode as he stalked through the trees.

When Finn made a hand motion for all of them to stop, they did. Ian was stiff, his posture making it clear he didn't like obeying another male. She understood because she felt the same. She'd been on her own for so long it was strange to be following another's orders. Though she'd do anything right now to save Ava. Including take orders from a wolf shifter. She was glad Ian was doing the same. Saving her friend was all that mattered. She just hoped they weren't too late.

If the topography was correct she knew they were close to another clearing where a small cabin would be. At least according to Gray. And she trusted that wolf with her life. He would never do something to put her in danger. Clearly Finn trusted the male as well, otherwise they wouldn't be here at all.

When they grew closer to the location of the cabin, Finn disappeared through the trees with a single order to "Stand guard."

Less than ten minutes later he returned with splatters of blood on his dark pants. It blended in with his clothes well, but her vision was exceptional and she could also scent it.

He made another motion that they should follow after him. Sure enough, a few minutes later they entered a clearing where the cabin was. The scent of blood and death grew stronger but Finn didn't slow down so they didn't either.

With sure strides, they hurried up the short set of stairs and into the cabin—where four half-demon males with pale green skin were dead. Body parts littered the kitchen and attached living room. And every one of them had their throats missing. She blinked. Finn was definitely an Alpha. She hadn't really doubted it, considering the territory he ruled and his reputation. Not to mention the actual power that rolled off him, but this was impressive. He clearly hadn't even shifted forms. He'd done this while mostly human so he'd probably just used his claws. *Wow.*

"We leave the bodies and enter through here." Finn shoved a table out of the way and lifted a hatch to a trapdoor.

Just as Gray had said it would be. Only Gray had entered without anyone knowing. He'd used a distraction to get the original guards out of the cabin, then snuck in with them none the wiser. Later, he and his friend had been discovered in the castle but as far as he knew no one was aware of how they'd gotten inside. If they had been, she knew there would have been more than these guards here.

"Since we don't know if they have backup or if there's a shift change soon, we need to hurry." Finn jumped down through the open hatch.

Okay then, they were heading in now.

"I'm going to camouflage myself." Ian started stripping as the other shifters followed after their Alpha. He tucked his clothes into his pack and handed it to her.

Fiona slipped it on her back and was able to easily reach her weapons—the crossbow tucked under the pack and the blades strapped to her thighs. It was foreign to rely on weapons other than herself but a dragon had to do what dragon had to do. Somehow she managed to avoid looking lower than Ian's face. Even if she wanted to get another peek, the timing was insanely inappropriate.

Ian surprised her by cupping her cheek gently with one big, callused palm. "If anything happens and shit goes haywire, I'm shifting to my dragon form and flying us out of here." He wasn't asking either. He was flat-out telling.

"Ian—"

He crushed his mouth to hers for a long, hard moment where all she could do was clutch onto his shoulders for support. The kiss was a harsh claiming and no matter how much she wanted to deny it, to remind herself that they had no chance together, after that one kiss she found herself hoping that just maybe they could find a way to make things work.

Not just maybe—definitely. She couldn't walk away from him again. Her heart couldn't take it and she didn't think his could either. When she'd left him, it had been like cutting off a limb, leaving part of herself behind. And she had, essentially. Because Ian was a part of her, embedded in her skin, her soul.

CHAPTER ELEVEN

The scents filling the underground of the castle were too many to sift through so Fiona stopped trying. She and Ian had split off from the others and were now on one of the lower levels. There had been a few close calls where they'd almost run into guards but she and Ian were quick.

Even if she couldn't camouflage herself now, when Ian blocked her with his concealed body she was hidden from others. Under normal circumstances she didn't like depending on anyone. While she hated that she couldn't reach her dragon half, having Ian to back her up was... Well, there was no word for it. But it felt right to have him at her side. And after that kiss she was still emotionally reeling even as she focused on their mission.

On instinct she reached out, felt Ian's hand even if she couldn't see him. He linked his fingers through hers as they slowed at the end of the hallway.

The hallways on this level were all stone, both the walls and floor. There weren't any paintings or decor, simply wall sconces with torches lighting the way every couple feet. Even with her hotter body temperature a continuous chill racked her the farther they walked. Apparently even that aspect of her nature had been affected by the poison.

This level was quieter than the other two they'd been on, and fear for Ava grew more with each second that passed.

Because the longer her friend was captive, the worse things would be for her. Fiona was going to make whoever had taken her pay.

Barely four feet in front of her, part of the stone wall suddenly snapped open—a hidden door. Fiona froze as a very familiar male stepped out of a darkened passageway with no lighting. There was no time for Ian to use his body to cover her, to hide her. She had nowhere to go. At least Ian was still hidden.

She stared and her brother stared right back. Colm blinked once at her, his blue eyes so much like her own. For a moment she froze, letting go of all her fear and panic. Why was her brother here? Was he in trouble? "Colm."

Fiona stared at her brother, whom she hadn't seen in decades. Of all of her brothers he'd been her favorite even if he'd been a bit of a hothead. They'd been the youngest, though he was still centuries older than her. He'd been so arrogant fifty years ago, the only other brother who'd wanted to buck their father's control. She hadn't been close to any of her brothers though—and none of them had attempted to help her escape when she'd been a prisoner.

"What are you doing here?" she whispered before glancing over her shoulder. She wasn't going to tell him about Ian yet. Maybe not at all.

"I should be asking you that. But I think I know." He motioned behind him when two armed half-demons appeared out of the hidden passageway Colm had come from. "Leave us. She is not an enemy. And no one is to touch her."

A sinking sensation filled her gut as she realized that if he was giving those males orders, then he was at least somewhat in charge here. He wasn't in trouble. *Oh, God. Oh, no.* A dragon had been at the site when she'd been poisoned and her friend taken. Had it been him?

Thinking fast, she decided to be as honest as possible. "Did you take my friend Ava?"

"We didn't realize who she was. We got a tip that a male we were hunting decided to talk to someone about my business. I did *not* know that someone was you. Are you alone?" he demanded.

Yes, she had to play this very carefully. "Do you see anyone with me?" The answer was vague enough and wouldn't give off the scent of a lie. "And just what the hell are you doing?" She kept her voice haughty, not letting any of her worry for Ian, Ava or Finn's people shine through.

"Don't worry about that now. I'll take you to your friend." He motioned that she should follow him down the stone hallway after he firmly shut the hidden doorway behind him. He gave her a slightly apologetic look that didn't reach his eyes. "I can't guarantee what shape she'll be in."

The sinking sensation grew worse. "What did you do to her?" She tried to call on her dragon out of years of instinct but felt absolutely *nothing*. The feeling of emptiness growing inside her was getting worse, making her want to all-out grieve for her loss. Somehow she forced herself to ignore it. All her focus had to be on getting to her friend.

Her brother didn't answer, just continued his hurried walk down the hallway. "Byrne is here as well. We broke away from Mother and Father a decade after you did."

That was certainly news to her. But then again, she hadn't kept in contact with her clan or brothers. "Why?"

He lifted a shoulder. The look he gave her was almost calculating. "Their vision was too small. They're happy living in the shadows like so many supernaturals. Happy to showcase their power among their own kind, not out in the open like it should be." He let out a snort of derision.

The sensation that she was walking a tightrope expanded inside her like a balloon. So she kept her expression as neutral as possible. "Vision?" Somehow her voice came out normal sounding.

"Yes. They're happy with the status quo. But we are *dragons*. We should rule the planet, not live in the shadows. To rule is our birthright."

Oh, sweet angels. He was completely mad.

Again, she kept her expression dispassionate and tried not to give away her feelings because unlike him, she wasn't crazy. And she planned to make sure all her friends and allies made it out of here. "We are dragons. The most powerful of all the supernaturals. But what else can we do? Humans would nuke the planet if they found out we existed."

That probably wasn't too far from the truth, considering how insane humans could be. When they realized they weren't at the top of the food chain it would probably start a ripple effect until country after country started nuking everything. That was a worst-case scenario, of course. But...maybe it wouldn't be so dire. She'd seen and met a lot of good humans over the decades. It just seemed that the ones in power were out of their minds with the need to control everything.

"Byrne and I are going to change things." he said, his expression gleeful, his blue eyes just a little too bright.

Before she could ask what he meant they reached a solid-looking door, this one not hidden to blend in with the wall. Colm pulled out an old-fashioned key and slid it in the lock. When they stepped inside what was clearly a prison, damp cold overwhelmed her senses. Holding her breath, she tried not to stare as the door slowly closed. She hoped Ian had made it inside with her. There were too many scents to sift through and she wasn't sure if he had. And it wasn't as if she'd heard the male. He was the ultimate predator, stealth personified.

Apparently they'd wasted no resources to heat this prison. There was just one big cage in the middle and it appeared to be reinforced with silver. A huge blue half-demon stood in front of Ava, trapped inside with her. He had no horns and wasn't over ten feet tall so he had to be a half-demon, not a full-blooded one.

Fiona's heart jumped in her throat until she realized the male appeared to be trying to protect her friend.

Ava stepped out from behind the male with a gasp as her gaze met Fiona's.

Fiona stared at her friend and realized that Ava looked to be in good shape. She'd expected... Well, she didn't even want to think about what she'd expected, but this was not it. Relief poured through her as she raced toward the door of the cage. "Are you okay?"

Ava hurried forward as well, but was careful not to touch the bars. Yes, they must be silver. Fiona was immune to silver, unlike vampires or wolves, so maybe the male inside was half wolf. "I'm okay. No one has hurt me. Not really."

"Get her out of this cage," she snapped at her brother.

At her words the male in the cage stepped forward and she realized he was bigger than she'd realized, about seven feet tall, just like Ian. And...he had the same pale blue skin and tattoos swirling over his body as Ian. Or at least the pattern looked similar. The half-demons she'd seen so far in this place were all pale green and none of them had been in a cage.

Her brother moved up next to her, his power rolling off him. "Don't give me orders, little sister. You," he said to the half-demon. "Stand back."

To Fiona's surprise the male did just that but not before snarling savagely at Colm. Once Ava was outside the cage she rushed into Fiona's arms. Colm slammed the door shut quickly as Fiona hugged her friend tight and held her close for a long moment before stepping back and turning to her brother.

Even though she wanted to scream at him for what he'd done, she somehow managed to keep her cool. She was still deep in enemy territory and not only that but Ian,

Finn and his people were here as well. And she was pretty certain that Colm or maybe Byrne had poisoned her.

Right about now it was instinct to reach for Ian but she had to act as if she was completely alone.

"Why don't you tell me how the hell you found out about this place?" Her brother's voice was deceptively quiet, his dragon in his eyes.

Thinking on her feet, she shrugged. The last thing she'd expected was to know who'd taken Ava, much less be related to them. She'd thought they'd have to fight their way out of the castle at the very least. "The male who came to me told me about the entrance to the Hell realm. Oh, your guards in that little cabin are dead as well." Might as well give him real facts. The guards were dead, even if she hadn't killed them.

"Fuck," he growled. Just as quickly he straightened, his eyes narrowing. "What happened to the male, Gray?"

She chose her words with care. "He was badly injured, a dagger of some sort to his chest."

He nodded. "Good. That's what he gets for sticking his nose where it doesn't belong. I'm going to escort you out of here and I never want to see you again. Not in this realm. If you come back I won't be so merciful."

She nodded, appearing to be the meek little sister that she definitely was not. "I don't care what you're doing here. I just want to leave with my friend. And you better stay out of my territory," she snapped, adding just a bit of heat. She couldn't be *too* meek. Not when he'd seen the carnage she'd left behind when she escaped the clan. She'd razed an entire compound to the ground.

A quick nod. "I'll stay out of your territory." Then he scented the air. "You smell like that half-breed. Have you taken up with that male?" Suddenly he was the angry brother she remembered, the one who'd been livid she'd been sleeping with Ian.

Shit. He must scent Ian in the room with them. Fiona certainly did by now, but Ian's scent was embedded into her. She blinked once, feigning confusion. "I have no lover." A truth. "What half-breed?"

Colm tilted his head slightly to the side. "That pathetic half-demon from New Orleans."

She let out a derisive snort even though it pained her to do so. What she'd shared with Ian had been precious, and her male was not pathetic. "That male was a way to escape." A sort of truth. He *had* been a way to escape. She'd also been deeply in love with him. "Turns out I didn't need him anyway." She rolled her eyes for good measure.

He started to respond when a half-demon of different coloring than the male in the cage appeared. "Sir, we have a situation."

Her heart rate increased. What if they'd discovered the others? She, Ava and Ian needed to get out of here right now.

Her brother nodded and then turned back to her. "Give me a few minutes. Do not leave this room."

She nodded even though she had no intention of following that order. When he left, she heard the lock click into place, but that shouldn't be a problem. She shoved out a breath of relief, knowing their respite was only temporary.

Just as it clicked into place, Ian's camouflage fell. Ava let out a gasp and the half-demon in the cage abruptly stepped forward.

"I don't smell blood, but did the male in the cage hurt you?" Ian demanded, looking like the fierce warrior that he was.

Ava shook her head. "No. He actually tried to protect me from the guard who kicked me in the stomach when they tossed me into the cage. And I wasn't hurt in any other way."

"Thank God," Fiona murmured.

Ian turned to the male. "What's your name? And why are you in here?"

"None of your fucking business."

Ian looked at the prison door and then back at the cage door. Then he let out a curse. "Are they using your blood for something?"

The male paused and then nodded. "Yes."

"I'm going to let you out but if you attempt to hurt these females I'll rip your head off then burn your body to ash. There will be nothing left of you."

Surprise flickered in the male's gaze, but he nodded. "I understand."

Using impressive speed and strength, Ian grasped his fingers around the bars and ripped the entire door free as if it took no effort. For him, it probably didn't.

The other male stepped outside the cage, lightning fast. "You're obviously not half wolf."

Ian shook his head.

"Thank you," the male continued. "I'll be leaving now. Stay away from the footbridge and moat. There are things in the water you don't want to deal with."

"Okay. There are others here with us. Wolves. If you hurt them, I'll hunt you down."

The male paused, then nodded before he hurried to the prison door and yanked hard, breaking the lock and pulling it open.

"There are more of us," Ian said quietly, pointing to himself. "You have other brothers."

Holy shit. Fiona didn't make a sound and the male didn't turn around. Just paused at the door, his back to them. Instead of responding, he eased the door open farther and rushed out into the hall where shouts of alarm were growing louder.

So Ian had another brother? They needed to talk about that later, but now they had to run. They'd gotten what they came for: Ava.

"We need to get out of here," Ian murmured as the three of them moved to the partially open door.

"Are we just going to let him go?" Fiona asked as they stepped out into the hallway. She handed Ava one of her blades, kept another firm in her grip.

"Fire in the battlement!" an angry male voice cried out from somewhere down the stone hallway. His voice echoed, making it difficult to pinpoint the actual location. A siren pierced the air, drowning out the man's cry of alarm.

"He's not our problem." Ian kept his voice neutral as he pointed toward the east. Now wasn't the time to discuss a new half-brother. The male had the same coloring that signified they shared a very distinct lineage. None of that shit mattered though if the male didn't want to come with them. They needed to get the hell out—he needed to get Fiona and her friend to safety. Clearly the people in the castle knew others had infiltrated it.

So no more being subtle. It was time to burn shit to the ground and make their escape. For Fiona's sake he hated that her brother was involved with this.

"Should we look for Finn and the rest of the team?" Fiona asked as she and Ava raced with him down the hall.

He paused at a door, leaned close to listen, then slammed it open to reveal a curving stone staircase. It was wide enough to fit his broad shoulders, clearly having been made for supernaturals. "No. We stick to the plan," he said as they started climbing the stairs. If anything happened or an alarm was set off, the plan was for them all to make their way separately to the escape route—the top of the biggest mountain. The exit from this realm.

And on the chance that not everyone made it to the mountaintop, they wouldn't leave anyone behind. But it made more sense if they all worked on their own, since they already had partners to aid in escape. His heart raced as they stepped out into another stone hallway floors higher. Getting Fiona and Ava to safety was his top priority and he hated not knowing the full layout of this castle.

The sound of boots stomping echoed way too close for comfort.

"In here," Fiona whispered as she tried the handle on a door. A draft of wind rolled over them as they ducked inside a big open bedroom and shut the door behind them.

"I have a plan. You might not like it," he said, his gaze on the thin, slitted windows set into the exterior stone wall.

"What is it?" Fiona's voice was cautious, her body language tense as the sound of booted footsteps grew louder.

"I'm going to burn a hole through this wall. My fire is hot enough to incinerate it. Then you two will ride on my back and we'll fly out of here."

Fiona and Ava both nodded.

Okay, maybe it was a good plan. "Stay behind me." He automatically held up his arms, shoving the two women behind him as he released a raging-hot stream of fire. Fiona should be immune to the heat, but all the same he gave both females a bit of his essence, protecting them from the inferno. When he was in dragon form, his fire was hotter but this would do the trick and it would give him enough room to shift forms so they could get the hell out.

The stone wall was stronger than he'd anticipated but under the heat of his fire it began to burn away. And burning stone was no easy feat, but he was a dragon. At the sound of the door slamming open behind them he stopped his fire and whirled.

Ava threw her blade at one of the armed half-demons, hit him through the eye.

Fiona did the same to another one, slamming right into his throat. Dark, thick blood spurted everywhere as the male fell to his knees.

Before he'd hit the ground, Fiona had her crossbow in her hands and was shooting rapid fire with the speed of a supernatural at the dozen or so males as they poured into the room like cockroaches. Their bodies started piling up on each other as Ian shoved Ava out of the way and released a stream of fire at them. His dragon side rejoiced at their short-lived screams. The darkest, most primitive part of him savored the sound and scent of their deaths. Both his dragon and demon relished the blood and violence. When he stopped, only ash remained scattered around the room.

"Well I think they're all dead." Ava's voice was as dry as Fiona's expression.

He didn't bother to respond, just turned and shot out another stream of fire. The stone blasted away, forming a giant hole.

Not bothering to take off his clothes, he let the shift roll over him. In a burst of light and magic, his dragon took over. Before he could scoop up the females, they were climbing onto his back.

A gust of icy wind whipped through the now destroyed room as he dove for the newly created entrance and broke through into the cold air outside.

Below them was utter chaos. He saw three massive holes clearly created by fire in various places around the castle. Finn and the others must have set up explosives. Good. It meant they were alive. If he saw any of them during the escape he would grab them up but for now, he was sticking to the plan. Those warriors were skilled and didn't need his help anyway. Right now, his concern was Fiona and her friend. He needed to get them to the realm's exit. Then he'd go back for Finn and the others.

CHAPTER TWELVE

The top of the mountain was colder than Fiona had imagined. Despite her higher body temperature and the fact that cold had never truly bothered her before, this place was different. And whatever she'd been poisoned with was affecting her more, especially after fighting with the half-demons. She was weaker. Not terribly, but this cold was actually affecting her like it would a human.

And she wasn't used to feeling weak. Ever.

They were the first ones here. No surprise, considering Ian had flown them straight to the top. It had been a rough ride and the three of them had ended up walking a good portion once he'd landed because of the terrain and fog—and Ian had killed five half-demons guarding the gate.

A blistering wind rolled over them as Ava crossed her arms over her chest. Fiona wasn't sure if it was from the cold or if her friend was being stubborn. Since vampires didn't get cold she figured it was the latter. "I'm staying with you guys. You rescued me and I won't leave the others." Ava's voice was heated.

"You need to leave. It will be easier for me to fly with just Fiona," said Ian. "The more people we get out of here, the better."

152 | KATIE REUS

"Please do this for me. I need to know you're safe."
Fiona put a bit of desperation in her voice and she meant
it. It didn't make sense for all of them to go back down the
mountain to the castle. "My brother already knows you
mean something to me since I came here to rescue you. I
don't believe he'd kill me. He'll be pissed that I brought in
other people." Who'd seriously messed up his castle. "So
you need to get out of this Hell realm while you can and
head straight to the Stavros estate. They'll give you shelter."

"I don't want to waste any more time," Ian snarled,
surprising heat in his voice. "You need to go."

Even though it was clear Ava wanted to argue, she
nodded. "Fine. But if you're not home in twenty-four
hours I'm coming back for you."

"Fair enough." Fiona turned and looked over the top
edge of the giant crater at the summit of the mountain.

According to Gray the gate would activate when
someone jumped into it. Fiona believed him, especially
since this place had been guarded. They were definitely
where they needed to be.

"Maybe you guys should give me a little more room,"
Ava said after giving Fiona a bear hug.

"We're going to be fine. I'll see you soon. Promise."
Fiona took a few steps back with Ian but could still easily
see across the gaping mouth of the gate.

Ian moved with her, his hand at the small of her back
in a protective gesture. One she liked way too much.
Thankfully he'd brought a couple extra pairs of clothing,
though he was down to his last set after shifting at the
castle and shredding everything again.

"I'll see you guys soon." At that, Ava jumped.

A sucking sound was followed by a burst of color spreading across the crater as a kaleidoscope of blues, greens and reds swirled into a vortex, taking Ava to the human realm.

Seconds later the gate closed. "She's safe now," Fiona murmured, relief sliding through her veins.

Ian immediately pulled her into his arms and she didn't fight him. Because she was freezing and because she wanted to feel his touch, she allowed the temporary hold. They needed to get out of there but for now she would be weak. Just for a moment.

"I didn't mean what I said to my brother in that prison. About you being a way to escape," she murmured against his chest.

He tightened his grip on her. "I know. I heard what you said and what you didn't say. And...at first when you told me you didn't love me, that you were mating with another male, that I wasn't good enough, I lost my shit. But after I managed to think clearly I knew you'd lied to me. About not loving me, anyway."

"Why didn't you come after me?" she asked, not looking up at him. She was glad he hadn't; her family would have made good on their promise and killed him before he'd ever gotten close to her.

His body tightened, but he didn't let go of her. "I...came to your estate the same night you kicked me out of your life."

Her head snapped up. "You did?" Her mother had told her he'd left town. And she hadn't scented a lie either. She'd been in chains, unable to see for herself. By the time she'd gotten free, she hadn't looked for him. She'd been too damn afraid to. Because she might have broken those chains, but she hadn't been free. She was pretty certain the only reason her family had left her alone all these years was because she hadn't chased after Ian. Well that, and she'd finally shown a spine and burned their home to the ground. She'd met Ava and they'd started working together. She'd given them no reason to bother her again.

"Yes. Your brothers told me you were in the process of mating. Your mating manifestation was visible from the house." His voice was raspy, unsteady, cutting through her as harshly as the icy wind whipping around them.

She pulled back to look at him, grief fracturing through her. No matter what, she could have never mated with anyone else. "I never mated with anyone." Obviously.

"I know that now. But I didn't then. I assumed it was too late for us. That you were stuck in a loveless mating. That you'd sacrificed yourself. Then...your mother dropped off a copy of your marriage announcement from the local paper. So I left town. I didn't want to risk seeing you with someone else."

She blinked, thinking back to that time. She'd been a captive, but... "My oldest brother, Flannery, mated around that time. That must have been what you saw. And my family must have created a fake announcement using their contacts. I married no one," she growled. Her heart twisted that Ian had thought she'd been with someone else, had actually mated *and* married another male. "I never could have been with anyone else." Her words were a whisper but he heard them. "I've never been with any-one since you." And she didn't want to know if he had been. Of course he must have though. He'd thought she'd been mated and it had been so many damn years.

Ian crushed his mouth to hers unexpectedly, his kiss all-consuming as his tongue delved into her mouth, his big hand cupping the back of her head in a dominating, possessive grip. She barely had a chance to return his kiss before he pulled back, his breathing harsh and erratic.

His amber eyes were glowing. "I haven't been with an-yone since you either."

She sucked in a breath as his words punched through her. That had been something she hadn't even thought to hope for. To know that he had been just as faithful to her made tears spring to her eyes.

"And I'm not walking away again, Fiona. After we de-stroy this place and return to our realm, I want the chance to court you again. You don't—"

"Okay. I want that too. More than anything." She would mate with him right now if their mating manifes-tation wouldn't give away their location. But that would be like a beacon to everyone in this realm. Not only that, mating was a huge step. They'd been apart for fifty years. Her dragon side might not care, but she wanted to get to know him again. "I need to be honest though. I don't know if my family will find a way to hurt you if we mate and—"

"When," Ian snarled.

She blinked. "What?"

"*When* we mate. Not if." His words were as savage as his expression.

Warmth filled her as she clutched his shoulders tighter. "When." The word stuck in her throat because she hadn't dared to hope that it was possible. That they'd ever have a second chance. That she could actually have happiness with this wonderful male. She cleared her throat. "Once we mate they won't come after you." Of that she had no doubt. Because once they mated, if her family killed Ian, it would automatically kill Fiona too. "But they might try to hurt you in other ways. To come after your brothers, your sister. Anyone you care about. My clan can be vindictive. Since you don't have the backing of a clan or a pack to strike back at my family... I have to tell you that. You need to think about this because—"

"There's nothing to think about." Again he was all snarls, something she found impossibly sexy. "My brothers are all strong. One's mated to a demigod with a crazy mother, and the other is part of one of the strongest wolf packs. As soon as we're out of here, we're getting mated. I'll court you after we've bonded. And I'll keep doing it for the rest of our damn lives."

She blinked.

"I decided I'm not waiting. We will mate as soon as we can." His eyes shifted from dragon, to demon and back to human as he watched her, almost daring her to challenge him.

A rush of heat and want flooded her at his possessive tone. This was her male. Fiona went up on tiptoe, pressed her lips to his, savoring his taste and raw, masculine scent, unable to get enough. Somehow she pulled back, even as another rush of heat invaded her. The brief taste wasn't enough, would never be enough. "As soon as we're out of here, you're mine forever."

"Damn straight," he growled.

If he understood the potential threat and was okay with it, she would be too. Because the truth was, she couldn't walk away from him again. There was simply no way.

"You ready to go look for the others?" Because they'd been up here long enough as it was. The most selfish part of her wished they could simply jump into the vortex and return to the human realm so she could claim Ian forever.

But she could never, ever do that to the people who had risked their lives to help a female they didn't even know. She owed them. And Fiona would make damn sure every single one of them got out of here alive.

"Wear this," Ian murmured, handing her a thick black cloak that was more like a hoodie from the human realm. But the material was different.

She held it up to her nose and inhaled before putting it on over her battered clothing. She wondered if he knew how cold she was right now or if he just wanted her to wear it to put his scent on her. Either way she was grateful for it. As soon as she tugged it over her head the warmth of the material helped get rid of some of the chill.

Now it was time to find the rest of their team and get home.

* * *

After stripping off the rest of his clothes and tucking them into his pack, Ian let the shift take over him until his dragon was in control. The only thing he could truly think about right now was the fact that Fiona had just agreed to become his mate.

He hadn't expected that at all. If anything, he'd expected a lot more resistance. He'd been up to the challenge of convincing her that the risk from her family was worth it. Because he sure as fuck wasn't afraid of them.

He hadn't been afraid of them fifty years ago either. But she had been. They'd controlled her, kept her a virtual prisoner. If not literally, then mentally. And now that time had passed he understood her fear better. Unlike him, she'd been sheltered, controlled, *manipulated.* Her clan was all she'd ever known. To her they were terrifying and all powerful. And he had been alone. She'd been afraid for him.

Before Fiona could climb on him, he gently scooped her up with one of his paws and tucked her close to his chest. By holding her this way she wouldn't get the brunt of the wind on his back as he flew down the mountain and into enemy territory. She'd seemed unnaturally chilled as he'd held her moments before. He wondered if it was because her dragon was sleeping, and it worried him.

As she curled into his paw, he lifted off the ground. A sense of rejuvenation and power invigorated him as he flapped his wings, climbing higher and higher. The fog surrounding them was thicker than he'd even imagined. He'd never been in a Hell realm like this before. One so damn cold.

Despite the name "Hell realm," the realms weren't hot. Not all of them anyway. The one he'd lived in for the last few decades before settling in Biloxi had been relatively mild as far as the weather. But it had been a brutal place to live in all other ways. Some days he missed it but now that he'd found Fiona again, he would live in the Arctic as long as she was with him.

As he breached above the fog, he immediately scanned for any potential aerial threats. From what Fiona's brother had said, one of her other brothers was in this realm as well. Which made for two big threats. He had no doubt he could take them on, but he didn't want Fiona to get caught in the crossfire. Literally or figuratively.

No, he wanted to find the others and get everyone out of here. Then they could come back and take this place down. They would need more shifters—probably the whole pack—to end what was going on here. And Ian wanted to find his new half-brother as well. But he wouldn't risk Fiona in an effort to do that.

The pale green sky was a bit darker than it had been even an hour ago. It was always hard to judge time in a place like this. The various realms had similarities but many things were different, including the passage of time. The growing darkness could indicate that it was close to nighttime here or it could indicate something else.

He dipped down the mountain, careful to stay above the fog. He might have exceptional sight but no one could see through that soup or more than ten feet in front of them.

He was aware of the cold as he flew faster and faster but because of his dragon nature it barely affected him.

His camouflage was firmly in place as he flew back toward the castle and the fog dissipated. Plumes of thick, dark smoke filled the air. More than when they'd left. So Finn and his crew had clearly done some damage. And maybe Ian's new half-brother. Who knew? And who really cared. The only thing that mattered was that this place was destroyed. They also needed to check if there were more captives, but for now they needed to find Finn and the others.

As he began to circle the castle and surrounding area, he automatically searched for any familiar faces. When a blast of dragon fire shot in his direction, a sharp burst of orange and red flames meant to kill, he automatically flew upward, keeping Fiona protected against his body. She might not be able to reach her dragon right now, but she should still be able to withstand dragon fire.

But if she couldn't, just in case he gave her more of his essence to protect her.

Heat licked at his tail as he tried to avoid the onslaught of fire, but because of his natural ability to withstand another's fire for a limited time, he was unharmed. Unfortunately he couldn't see his attacker. And when another blast from above shot right at his face, something told him that his attackers—and there had to be more than one—could see him clearly despite his camouflage.

Which meant they had something in their possession made from dragon fire. It would likely be a blade or a piece of jewelry. *Damn it.* If someone possessed anything made from the rare fire, it gave them the ability to see any and all dragons, no matter if they were camouflaged.

A rage like he'd never known overtook him. Just because he couldn't see his attackers didn't mean he wouldn't fight back. Hell, he was going to destroy them.

He embraced the darkness welling up inside him as he released a stream of blinding blue fire. A screech tore from his chest as he flew in a big circle, releasing the fire in every direction he turned.

An answering cry filled the air as he glimpsed a pale silver dragon under the darkening sky. It had to be one of her brothers. He'd seen Fiona in her dragon form before and she was a pale silver that glistened like the finest jewels.

A dragon plummeted toward the castle grounds below, one of his wings limp as he slammed against a wall. Stone rained down in all directions.

Another blast of fire shot at Ian. He rolled his body midair, diving in the same direction the dragon had fallen. He shot another stream of blistering hot blue fire at the fallen dragon. The fire engulfed the beast and the air was filled with horrifying screeches that raked over his senses. He hadn't expected the rare blue fire, but he wasn't going to question it.

He soared back toward the sky as stream after stream of orangey-red fire licked all around him. But none of it touched him.

He blasted out fire again in every direction but as far as he could tell he didn't hit anything else. When the sky suddenly plunged into darkness, he made a split-second decision. He wanted to stay and fight, to find Finn and the others—but he needed to get Fiona to safety.

He'd lived in another Hell realm for a long time and the time changed from day to night there quickly, just like here. And at night terrifying things tended to come out.

While he didn't doubt his ability to take on any threat, right now wasn't just about him.

It was about the woman he loved.

He'd already destroyed one big threat. Now it was time to find shelter for the two of them. Finn was a strong Alpha. He should be able to take care of himself and his wolves for a few hours.

CHAPTER THIRTEEN

"We should be safe here." Ian glanced around the small cave, looking for any crevices someone might be hiding in. But he doubted there was anyone inside.

He couldn't scent anyone and the cave was only accessible from the air. He'd seen it at the top of one of the mountains as he and Fiona had been flying farther and farther away from the castle. He'd wanted to put as much mileage as possible between them and the threat before touching down.

"Did you see any creatures or animals on the mountain before we landed?" Fiona sat against a boulder, using it to prop herself up. She shivered, making him frown. She wasn't injured so the poison must still be affecting her.

"No. I didn't see anything while flying." And that wasn't normal in these realms. In the one he'd lived in so long, the creatures that had come out at night were something from a nightmare. Even for him. Things that looked like a cross between a hellhound and scorpion and walked around on sharp talons had been one of the tamer creatures in that realm.

Moving quickly he pulled his pants out of the bag and tugged them on. Fiona was still wearing his hoodie, and from the way she'd been shivering earlier he knew she needed it more than him. He sat next to her and wrapped

163

his arm around her shoulders, pulling her close. "I don't know how long nightfall lasts here but we'll rest for a bit." At least there was only one way in and out of this cave. And even if someone was scouting from the sky, they wouldn't be able to see him and Fiona.

"How are you feeling?" She snuggled tighter against him.

"I should be asking you that. What's going on with you? Are you getting weaker?" Dammit, he should have sent her back with Ava.

"Not weaker. But I still can't feel my dragon. Maybe this is what it feels like not to be a shifter. So I don't know if I'm getting weaker or if this is just a side effect of whatever was done to me."

Rage against whoever had hurt her filled his veins but he shoved that emotion back. Right now was about her. "I'll get you to the exit as soon as we leave this cave, and then return to the castle for Finn and the others. I can find out more about what poisons they've been making."

"I'm not leaving without you. So don't ask it of me. I spent decades without you, Ian." Her hand had been resting on his chest gently. Now she clenched her fingers into a ball against his heart as she met his gaze. "I can't be separated from you again."

There was a desperation in her eyes that he understood well. His heart opened up at her words. He didn't want to leave her either. But he wanted her safe more than anything. More than he even wanted to mate with her. Because she was his to *protect*.

"We'll talk about it in the morning."

Her jaw tightened once, but she laid her head on his shoulder, which told him just how tired she must be. "I feel bad that we're separated from the others. I'm worried about them."

"Finn is a powerful Alpha. You had to feel it." It was undeniable. Humans probably even sensed it, though they wouldn't know why it was they were on edge around the male. Finn would be fine.

She nodded. "I did. There's only one other wolf I've ever met who had that kind of power rolling off him."

"See? They'll be fine. They'll probably just go wolf and hunker down in a den for the night." It wasn't in Ian to worry for others. Well, anyone else other than his family or Fiona. And Finn wasn't the type of male someone worried about. But Ian wasn't surprised that Fiona was concerned. That was just her nature.

"Tell me about your family," she murmured.

He stroked a hand down her spine as he held her close. He didn't want to talk about his family because it would open up the conversation about her own family—and he was pretty damn sure he'd killed her brother earlier. "We'll talk about that later." He wanted her to get some sleep. Which made him think... "Are you hungry?"

She shrugged slightly against his chest. "I ate one of those energy bars. I'll be fine. I don't want to go hunting for anything."

Yeah, that wouldn't be necessary. Concentrating hard, he focused on the one place he always transported food from when in a Hell realm.

"What the—" Fiona jerked back slightly, stared as a plate with a gyro and sautéed vegetables appeared in his hands.

He handed it to her as he concentrated again. A second later a plate of grilled lamb appeared in his hands. "Which one do you want?"

"How the heck did you do that?" she demanded.

A wicked grin spread across his face. "Discovered that trick a decade ago. I can transport some things directly from the human realm—small things. Like furniture, food, stuff like that. There's a jackass chef I screw with on occasion." Though it had been close to a year since he'd done it, since he hadn't been back to a Hell realm in that long.

She blinked and looked down at her gyro. "Wait… So you just transport food from some guy's restaurant?"

Ian laughed, his grin growing wider. It felt good to mess with that asshole. "Yep."

"He probably thinks he's losing his mind."

Ian shrugged. "He deserves it."

"What did he do to piss you off?" She apparently decided she didn't care where he'd gotten it and took a bite.

"I was at a restaurant once with Rory, and the chef—who's also partial owner—came out into the main restaurant and made one of his waitresses cry. Just berated her for nothing in front of everyone." It had taken all his restraint not to beat the shit out of the guy or burn him just a bit—Rory had made him see reason. Instead he'd messed with the dude on an epic level for about a year straight. Now he just did it occasionally.

"That's super mean but also pretty funny." Shaking her head, she took another bite.

They were silent as they devoured their food. He needed more energy than this but he'd wait until Fiona was asleep and conjure more food from the asshole's kitchen. The wind outside the cave was the only noise he could hear. No wings flapping overhead, no would-be attackers or predatory creatures trekking up the mountainside.

Once she was done, she set her plate to the side and he did the same with his before pulling her into his arms again. He set his chin on the top of her head, enjoying this quiet with her even at the most inopportune time. "You need rest."

"I'm not ready to sleep and I want to know what you've been up to the past fifty years. I thought about you far too often." Pain he understood well faintly laced her words.

"I thought about you too. All the time," he murmured. "Especially when I stroked myself off."

She jolted at his words and looked up to meet his gaze. Her cheeks were flushed pink and a pale blue fire had started to lick along her arms. "I thought about you when I touched myself too."

Ah, hell. Yeah, now wasn't the time to do *this*. He swallowed hard and realized that his mating manifestation had started to reveal itself. The smoky substance should be hidden enough in the cave, but there was no guarantee it wouldn't spill out of the opening. Not to mention if hers started full force, he didn't think they'd be able to hide it. Her brilliant blue fire was too bright and would light up the entire mountain. They might as well put up a big neon sign telling their hunters where they were.

"Okay, let's talk about family."

She gave him a small grin as her own fire dimmed. "I think that's probably the smartest idea. Even if it's not what I want to be doing right now."

He wanted to ask her what she'd rather be doing, but knew the answer would push him over the edge. "So...family. I met Rory not long after you and I parted ways." Such a civil way to describe what had happened between them. Not wanting to dwell on the past or to see sadness in her eyes, he continued. "We fought together in supernatural fighting rings for a while, moving from place to place and making as much money as we could. In some instances, we would actually fight each other in the ring so no matter what happened we both came out on top. Then we started making investments with our winnings. Rory is really good with numbers and he taught me." Ian was still nowhere as good as Rory when it came to investments, but he held his own and they'd both grown damn wealthy over the last fifty years.

Her expression softened as she laid her head back on his chest. "I know I've said it, but I'm so happy you found family. Rory seems so protective of Liberty."

"Yeah. They're a perfect fit." Just like he and Fiona were. And he wasn't letting her go.

"Tell me about your other brother. You said he's mated to a demigod?" There was a touch of surprise in her voice.

So he told her about his brothers and sister and how having a sister was a little strange. He wanted to go all overprotective on her but she'd made it clear she was strong enough to take care of herself. Didn't stop him, Rory and Bo from trying.

"You guys threatened to go beat up one of her exes because he stole from her?" Fiona asked after he'd told her a story about Cynara.

"Yep." Because brothers looked out for their siblings. He knew their threat to hunt down the bastard who'd hurt Cynara was a little psycho from a human standpoint. But not from a supernatural one.

"Do you plan to look for your other brother? The male from the prison cell?" she asked sometime later, her voice soft.

"I don't know. Probably." He wanted to know if the male was like him and his brothers. If the guy was more like their father then Ian wanted nothing to do with him. "What about you? I have the information from Finn's file but it's bare. And I want to hear it from you anyway." He didn't want to read about her life, he wanted to hear what she'd been doing since they'd been apart.

He still couldn't believe she hadn't taken another lover but maybe he shouldn't be surprised since he hadn't either. And he didn't care if it was primitive of him—he was glad she hadn't been with anyone else. That no one had ever touched what was his. Their dragons had chosen even before they'd gotten to know each other. Their dragons were damn smart.

"I don't want to lie to you." She was silent for a long moment and he wasn't sure she would continue so he remained silent, waiting. "My family put me in chains so I wouldn't chase after you. I was kept in prison. For a year."

He stilled at the shock of her words. She'd been in chains? Imprisoned? Fire burned the back of his throat and he fought the urge to let his dragon free. Someone would pay for that very, very soon. He and his brothers would see to it.

"They told me you left almost immediately. And once I was free I didn't look for you. But I did look at the records of your home and they'd been telling the truth. At least I thought they were. You left days after they'd imprisoned me." There was so much raw agony in her voice that it shredded him.

All he wanted to do was hunt down her entire clan and destroy them all for the pain they'd caused her—and for what they'd done today. If he'd thought for an instant she'd been kept prisoner, he'd have razed their home to the ground and rescued her all those years ago. But he thought she'd been mated. With another male. Even if it had been what he'd assumed was a loveless mating, she'd been off-limits to him. "If I'd known—"

"I know. I didn't want to tell you because I knew it would hurt you but I don't want any secrets between us. *Never* between us."

He nodded before gently brushing his lips over hers. "I want to kill every single one of them." And he just might, once they got out of here.

Her lips pulled into a thin line. "I think you killed one of my brothers."

Yeah, he thought the same and he didn't feel any guilt over it. He'd just been avoiding talking about it. "I do too. But I didn't expect that blue fire." He'd heard of it, but the way he'd been consumed with the need to protect Fiona had been different than anything he'd felt before. Even decades ago she'd never been in danger—not that he knew of—so that protectiveness had never manifested itself.

"What was that?" Her breath was warm against his chest as she cuddled against him.

"I've heard some members of the Stavros pack talk about it. There was a dragon who lived with them for a while and one of their packmates mated with him." He smiled thinking about Victoria. "She's a research nerd and discovered something to do with a blue mating fire. I believe it only exhibits itself when someone's mate or future mate is in dire straits. It can break through another dragon's natural ability to shield." He didn't want to apologize for killing her brother because it would be a lie, but wondered if he should. "He was attacking us, Fiona."

She lifted her head to look at him. "I know." Anger glinted in her blue eyes. "And I hope you don't think I would ever be angry at *you*. Those people are not my family. They haven't been my family for a long damn time. I don't actually care which brother you killed. They might not have put me in chains but they didn't stop my parents from doing it. And the more I think about it, I realized that whatever dragon was at the ocean with me and Gray had to have either been behind the attack that poisoned me, or at least sanctioned it. My brothers had to have known about it. And when we saw Colm he didn't mention anything about that poison. Makes me wonder if…"

"If what?"

She shook her head and swallowed hard. "I'm getting worse. I didn't want to say anything but I almost feel as if my body is weakening, and it makes me wonder if

I'm...dying. What if they injected me with what they've been injecting in those humans and it has an adverse effect with my chemistry as well? It could be the only reason my brother let me go. Because he assumed I'd die. Technically I guess he didn't let me go. We escaped. But he let Ava out of the cage and I assume he'd planned to let us free—until things went crazy and he saw you."

Ian had thought that her brother had let her off fairly easily. She'd invaded this realm and killed his guards and the male had seemed as if he'd let both Fiona and Ava go. It had all seemed too easy. Ian had been so damn desperate to get her out of that castle, he hadn't cared that Colm hadn't attacked her on sight. But if her brother thought Fiona would die maybe that was why. Or...maybe he was tracking her? Ian immediately dismissed that thought. If he'd been tracking her, they'd have been located by now.

He clenched his jaw once as his dragon rippled beneath the surface. The remaining brother would pay. "We'll find out what he did to you. You're not leaving me. You're not dying." He refused to allow it to happen. And if she did, he was going into the afterlife with her. There was simply no question about it. "Let's get some rest."

Because they had no idea what tomorrow would bring and they had to be ready.

CHAPTER FOURTEEN

52 years ago

"Are you nervous?" Fiona watched Ian, unable to hide her surprise at how tense he was. She'd arrived at his place less than ten minutes ago—after sneaking out of a party one of her clan members had thrown—and he'd offered her a glass of wine. Which he'd nearly spilled. Twice.

Now they were sitting in his living room. Unfortunately. She wanted to get straight to his bedroom and get to the good stuff, but he'd wanted to sit and "talk." She couldn't imagine about what though. Tonight was *the night*, and as far as she knew there wouldn't be much talking.

"No. Yes." He rubbed a hand over the back of his head in an out-of-character nervous gesture.

The male was always so damn confident about everything. He walked into a room and simply dominated it. It was just who he was. Hungrily, she watched the way his forearm flexed before he dropped his hand back to his lap. That hand should be on her body.

She'd never seen him like this. She was the virgin, but he seemed more nervous than her. Way more nervous. Maybe he was worried for her? "I'm not going to break."

"I know," he rasped out. His gaze dipped to her mouth and she felt the heat in his look all the way to her toes.

And just like that her mating manifestation kicked into high gear, the pale blue fire the same color as her eyes spreading out over her body. It was strange—she'd heard about it from her family but had never witnessed it before.

And there was no controlling it. Not technically. Staying away from Ian would surely control it but not when they were alone together in his house and he was looking at her like he could eat her up. "And why are you sitting all the way over there?" She picked up her glass of red wine and tucked her legs under her on the long couch.

All the furniture in his living room was oversized, just like him.

He didn't move from the big leather chair. "If I move any closer you're going to be naked in a few seconds." His amber eyes glowed brightly and the smoke of his own mating manifestation was already spreading out across the floor.

"How is that a bad thing?" Putting her glass back down, she stood. Enough was enough.

She'd been waiting for this for what felt like forever—since she'd met Ian at least. She'd never imagined a male like Ian could even exist but now that he was in her life, she wasn't letting him go. She was going to take what was hers and she wanted him to do the same. They belonged together. Soon, just a couple days from now, they would be leaving her clan behind forever. They would never accept him as her mate and she would *not* live without him.

"What are you doing?" His voice was raspy, unsteady, as he stared at her. His knuckles had turned white as he clutched the sides of his chair.

Slowly, she lifted her peasant blouse over her head, keeping her gaze on him the entire time. Once the shirt was over her head, she tossed it to the floor. Like usual around him, she hadn't bothered wearing a bra. It made him crazy so she made sure to never wear one. She liked affecting him because he did the same thing to her.

Next, her fingers moved to the button of her jeans.

Ian's gaze tracked her movements, his breathing harsh as he watched. His erection pushed against his jeans, his reaction to her undeniable.

Seeing how she affected him made her feel powerful, a little more in control. She'd tasted him all over but tonight she was going to feel him inside her. He'd been the one putting the brakes on, wanting her to make sure she was ready to mate. Well damn it, she was ready.

As she shoved her jeans down her legs, revealing that she'd forgone all undergarments, he growled low in his throat.

Oh yeah, that was the reaction she'd been looking for. She stepped out of her jeans then kicked them away. Cool air rushed over her skin but she barely felt it.

Moving slowly, she strode toward Ian until she was standing directly in front of him. His growl reverberated around the room, his bright amber eyes scorching. When he didn't make a move to touch her, just sat there like a statue, she cupped her mound.

Aaaand...that snapped him out of it. "Mine," he growled, yanking her wrist until she fell on top of him, straddling him.

Moaning, she bent to kiss him as he surged up to meet her mouth. He wrapped his arms around her, his callused hands stroking over her arms, back, legs, breasts, anywhere he could touch. Shivers rolled through her as he couldn't keep his hands off her.

She could feel how much he trembled beneath her as they ate at each other's mouths. Energy swelled through her and she was vaguely aware of the light show she was making. His place was on the outskirts of the city but he had neighbors a few miles away. If they saw it, they saw it.

She wasn't stopping.

After trying to release one of the buttons on his shirt—and failing—she ripped all of them free. Moaning, she pressed her breasts to his chest, shuddering as she rubbed her already tight nipples against his rock-hard chest.

He growled something she couldn't make out against her mouth then stood, carrying her as if she weighed nothing. Seconds later he had her stretched out on the thick, soft bundle of blankets in front of the fireplace.

There was no fire going but they didn't need the heat.

"I love you, Ian," she whispered right as his mouth latched onto one breast.

He froze, going impossibly still for a long moment. They'd basically admitted their feelings to each other. At the end of this week they were leaving together and were mating, but they'd never actually used the L word.

But she needed to say it. Heck, she needed him to hear it. He'd opened up to her about all of his past, and while he'd had a mother who had loved him, he'd never had anyone else in his life. Until her. And she didn't want him to doubt for one second how she felt about him. "I'll always love you," she continued. "No matter what."

In response, he cupped her mound, slid a finger into her already wet sheath and growled softly against her breast.

"Ian." She arched into his hold as he slid another finger inside her.

He flicked his tongue over her aroused nipple as he began sliding his fingers in and out of her.

Okay, maybe he couldn't say the words back just yet. She knew how he felt though. He showed her every time they were together. Right now she didn't want to think. She just wanted to feel every delicious thing he was doing to her.

She dug her fingers into his shoulders as he began moving lower, lower. "Not this time." He seemed to be obsessed with going down on her—not that she was complaining. But she desperately wanted to feel him pushing deep into her.

Her blue fire was wild around the room, the pale flames dancing over every surface. Even Ian's dark, smoky manifestation couldn't hide her fire. She didn't think anything could at this point. She felt as if her fire could take over the whole city.

He looked up the length of her body and gave her a wicked grin. "I'm tasting what's mine first." A soft, demanding growl.

Her cheeks warmed up at his words and when he withdrew his fingers, only to replace them with his mouth, she let her head fall back as he started teasing her into near delirium.

He was incredibly talented with that mouth, something she was very grateful for. She slid her fingers through his dark hair as she neared climax. He'd brought her to countless climaxes over the last few days and she was ready for it, her body automatically tensing for that release. He'd learned what she liked so quickly it scared her a little.

She had no secrets from him, this wonderful, strong male who would soon be her mate. Maybe not tonight, but she couldn't wait much longer. Her dragon half was going mindless with the need to be claimed and claim him right back, clawing at her, demanding she mark him.

Right before she would have come, he tore his mouth from her. "Ian..." Her stomach muscles tightened in protest, all the muscles in her body pulling taut as her orgasm was withheld from her.

Moving quickly he stood and stripped his jeans off with incredible speed. Standing above her with nothing on, the male looked like a god, as if he'd been carved from marble and made just for her. His long legs were cut, muscular lines of perfection, and his cock... Another rush of heat flooded between her legs.

She'd seen and tasted it before but the male was huge and all hers. "Get your ass down here," she murmured, putting bite into her words.

His dragon flickered once in his eyes before he was back on top of her, this time crawling up her body like he was a predator and she his prey. She welcomed being completely claimed by him.

He cupped one of her cheeks, his hold shockingly gentle as his cock pressed against her entrance. "I love you."

To hear him say the actual words set something free inside her. She hadn't realized how badly she'd needed to hear them. Her throat was too tight to respond, but she wrapped her arms and legs around him, urging him on.

He kept his gaze pinned to hers as he slowly pushed inside her. She gasped as her inner walls stretched to accommodate every inch of him.

His jaw was clenched tight, his expression as fierce as she'd ever seen it as he stared down at her. "Never letting you go," he whispered before pushing all the way to the hilt.

"Ian." She'd never felt so incredible in her life. Shifters were built different than humans so unlike the pain that human females could sometimes feel, she only experienced...heaven.

There was no other word for it.

"Love when you say my name," he growled. When he reached between their bodies and tweaked her clit, she jerked against him.

Then he started moving inside her, oh so slowly at first, definitely teasing her. She dug her fingers into his back, scraping her nails against him. "More." She needed faster, harder or...something. Her body was on a razor's edge and she needed—

He crushed his mouth to hers and began thrusting inside her.

Too many sensations overwhelmed her—the feel of his thick cock pulsing inside her, his lips against hers and the perfectly wicked way he was teasing her clit.

He had the right amount of pressure to drive her absolutely wild. Her heart beat out of control as he teased, stroked and pushed her right to the edge of sanity. She just needed a little more but it was as if he was restraining himself.

She moaned against his mouth, wanting to tell him she needed more again, but she wasn't sure what she needed.

He tore his mouth from hers, nibbled little kisses along her jaw and neck. The sweet sensation sent shivers scattering through her entire body. Her inner walls tightened around him with each thrust.

"Want to feel you come around my cock," he whispered darkly. "Want to hear you say you're mine." There was that bite of darkness to his words again.

"I'm yours." She could never be anyone else's. That was a fact she knew without a doubt.

"Say it again." He thrust harder.

"I'm yours, Ian."

He growled again, the sound as untamed as the male himself as he bit down on her earlobe. The bite set her off and her inner walls clenched tighter and tighter the harder he thrust into her until her climax slammed through her, a tidal wave of pleasure she felt as if she couldn't contain. Nothing could contain her right now.

A blast of pale blue fire shot from her, rippling out across the room and up the ceiling as her orgasm slammed into her.

"Fiona." Ian growled as he let himself go, joining her with his own climax. His canines descended as he stared at her, as she met him stroke for stroke.

For a moment she thought he'd bite her, complete the mating, but he buried his face against her neck instead, shuddering as he came inside her.

She wrapped herself tightly around him as her climax crested higher and higher. When she could finally see straight, she loosened her grip on him and opened her eyes. She was vaguely surprised to see flickers of blue still dotting the ceiling but dismissed it.

She stroked her fingers down his back, filled with so much love for the male she felt as if she couldn't contain it all.

When he lifted his head to meet her gaze, his eyes were pure dragon. "Did I hurt you?" A trace of fear threaded through his raspy voice.

She shook her head and cupped his cheek. "Not possible... You could have bitten me," she whispered, not trusting her voice not to crack otherwise. She'd thought he would mark her, claim her for good. It was what she wanted and she was pretty certain he did too. So she didn't understand why he'd held off.

"I want to wait until we're away from here. Until you've had time to fully embrace leaving everything behind. I want to mate with you more than my next breath, but I need you to be sure." His eyes were human again as he continued. "Dragon matings are for life. I...don't ever want you to regret mating with me. Even if every second that you're not mine is torture."

She cupped his cheeks with her hands as tears stung her eyes. He brushed his lips over hers, his kiss immediately deepening as she arched into him again. His thick cock was already hardening again, making her moan into his mouth.

How could she not love this male? He wanted to wait for her—even if she knew without a doubt he was *it* for her. Fine, they'd wait until they'd left her clan far behind.

Then he'd see just how damn serious this was for her. There would be no looking back. No regrets when it came to the two of them.

CHAPTER FIFTEEN

Colm stared at the pile of his brother's ashes he'd had moved to the banquet hall hours ago. No one was in here to disturb him as he tried to get his mind wrapped around what had happened—and to reformulate his plans. He couldn't understand how his brother, Byrne, had been taken from him so quickly. They'd had that half-breed dragon in their sights. They'd even prepared for a situation like this in case any other dragons decided to screw with them.

It had been risky but when they'd relocated here, Colm had created a dagger using his dragon fire. It gave him or his brother—or anyone—the ability to see other dragons, even in camouflage, as long as it was in his or whoever's possession. Most dragons never made anything out of dragon fire for that very reason. And he usually kept the dagger locked up because he wouldn't risk it falling into the wrong hands and allowing himself to become vulnerable. But he'd needed the extra security in case something like today happened. Now he was glad he'd been smart enough to be prepared.

He might be working with half-demons, but he sure as hell didn't trust any of them. He trusted no one but himself and his brother. He swallowed hard, still not processing that his brother was truly gone. He would grieve later, once their mission was finally complete.

Now he knew for a fact that his stupid sister had lied to him. She'd said she'd come alone but she'd brought way more intruders than he'd imagined. Including that dragon from fifty years ago. She wasn't mated to him though, because he would have scented it on her. So that was a strange development, but maybe the male had mated to someone else and was simply helping her. No matter why the other dragon was here, Colm would destroy him. He should have done it fifty years ago but his family had promised Fiona not to if she stayed away from the male. Now they'd both die.

He'd worked way too hard to see this operation brought to fruition to have it ruined by that stupid bitch. The only reason he'd even planned to let her go was because she'd been hit with one of his poison darts. She wasn't going to live much longer. Maybe a week maximum, since she was a dragon after all. But he didn't think it would be longer than that.

Unfortunately he had more problems than just her now—like those other shifters who'd infiltrated this realm. He had to stop them as well as Fiona and her half-breed before they escaped.

One of his lieutenants stepped into the banquet hall, letting the heavy door shut behind him with a thud. The male nodded respectfully at Colm. "I've sent twenty men to guard the exit of the Hell realm."

"Are you stupid? That's not enough. My sister is a dragon and the male with her is a dragon as well." A half-dragon with a unique kind of fire he'd never seen before. It had incinerated his brother, causing him to burn and die so quickly. He never even heard of something like that blue type of fire, much less seen it. But he wasn't going to tell this half-demon that. He might be working with them but he was still the superior race and he only told them things on a need-to-know basis. "Send thirty more," he snapped before the male could speak. "And make sure they are all armed with crossbows and poison darts."

"Respectfully, sir, are you sure? We've lost that half-demon and our supply is small."

Colm inwardly cursed because the male was right. They'd been mixing that half-demon prisoner's blood with human blood—as well as another secret ingredient—and while they had a large supply of humans, they didn't have another half-demon. Not one like that male anyway. His DNA was unique. "How big is the party out hunting him?" He didn't micromanage because he trusted his lieutenants to do their jobs, but he'd also been out hunting the wolves and his sister before returning to the castle. Now it was time to get his shit together. He needed to be on top of *everything*.

"I still have three hunting parties out right now. But darkness has fallen and we'd just be running around in circles even with our trackers. This land is too vast."

Even though the male was right, Colm still didn't like it. But he'd learned to adapt over the years. That was why he was such a strong leader. Unlike his arrogant father. That male would see how strong Colm was when he finally took his rightful place in the world. "Fine. Get three more hunting parties together and be ready to go at daybreak. I don't think he'll try to exit right away. That male is too shifty and he'll try to wait us out." Waiting would be the half-demon shifter's mistake. They'd hunt him down before that. No way would Colm let him escape. Not when he needed him so desperately. "I'll lead one of the teams. We leave as soon as it's light."

The male simply nodded and stepped out of the room, leaving Colm with his brother's ashes. Sighing, he stared at the pile. He needed to get rid of it.

Thousands of years ago dragons had been hunted and sacrificed for any number of things: their blood, bones, ability to open gates of Hell. Even though Colm didn't think his brother's ashes could be used against him, he decided to scatter them in one of the few bodies of water in this realm. It should render the ashes useless. He was going to make that half-breed pay for killing his brother. Make him bleed and suffer until he begged for death.

CHAPTER SIXTEEN

Ian focused his senses as they quietly walked down the mountain in the early daylight, concentrating on scents and sounds. If anyone tried to attack them, they were getting ashed.

Earlier he'd flown halfway down the side of the steep incline with Fiona riding on him, but since he knew her brother had the ability to see him when he was camouflaged, he didn't want to make them bigger targets. Now they were on foot and using the trees as cover from any aerial threat.

"How are you feeling?" he asked quietly as wind whipped over them. He barely felt the cut of it, but Fiona shivered slightly as their boots crunched over the snowy ground. The tunic she wore was thick, but he'd given her his own, telling her that he wanted to spare it from getting shredded in case he had to shift at a moment's notice. It revealed more of his blue skin, his lineage markings, but she truly didn't seem to care. It erased his fear of her rejection or disgust.

"I'm good." She gave him a small smile and while it definitely reached her eyes, she still seemed a little winded.

"I'd like to carry you."

She shook her head. "No. But thank you."

He started to argue, but stilled at a new scent trickling in on the air. He held up a hand.

Immediately she stopped next to him, withdrawing one of her blades as she glanced around. The wind was the only sound and though the scent was subtle, he recognized it.

His half-brother dropped down from the trees about twenty yards in front of them wearing dark pants and a tunic. He moved like a feline, with a liquid grace Ian had never seen in the wolves. Ian tensed, ready to go into battle if the male had brought others with him, but the half-demon held up his hands, palms out in a peaceful gesture.

"I'm alone. And I'm here to tell you that the fucker in charge of this operation has added guards to the exit gate. At least thirty half-demons. But by now maybe more. I was up there a few hours ago before daybreak and there was no way I could have fought through all of them. They've created a sort of net over the actual gate and I'm not sure what it's made of. It looked metal. Maybe silver. I didn't want to risk getting tangled in it."

"Why are you telling us?" Ian kept his voice neutral. He might be related to this male via blood but that didn't mean anything. Because this guy still had their father's blood running through his veins. Ian did too but he'd also been raised by a loving mother and he knew that made a difference, especially since he had to fight his dual nature all the time. He was just lucky that his dragon side was a hell of a lot stronger than his demon side.

"You saved my life. And…I want to get out of here, but I also want to meet the rest of my family if you're telling the truth."

"I think we would all like to get to know you better. Once we're sure we can trust you." There was a bite to his words he couldn't contain. If this male ever became a threat to his family, to the people he loved—to *Fiona*—Ian would end him with no problem.

"Okay, that's fair enough." He cleared his throat and ran a hand over the back of his neck, making the sleeve of his tunic slide back. It was weird to see another male who wasn't Rory or Bo with the same lineage tattoos marking his skin. "I spotted the wolves you said were with you a few miles to the west of here. They hunkered down for the night and blended into the shadows so well I wouldn't have seen them if I hadn't known where they were before. That was hours ago so I have no idea if they're still there but if you're looking for them—"

Ian nodded. "Lead the way. But what I said before stands. If you fuck with me or try to hurt anybody with me I will destroy you."

The male didn't seem offended at all as he nodded. "I wouldn't expect anything less. By the way, a dragon? Our asshole sperm donor sure got around." There was serious disgust in his voice, which made Ian smile. Maybe he'd end up liking this male after all.

"He did." And if Ian ever saw him again, he'd kill him. Or die trying. "What's your name?"

"Javier. And I'm a hybrid wolf/jaguar. My mother's a mixed breed and I received her genes. I only shift to wolf, but the jaguar gene is still there."

Interesting. Though Ian wanted to link his fingers through Fiona's, pull her close, he just remained at her side as they walked, alert for any danger. "My name's Ian.

And this is Fiona. She's mine." He thought it was already pretty damn clear, but he was making sure this male had no doubt she was taken.

Fiona just gave a slight smile as her cheeks flushed pink, but didn't respond otherwise.

Javier nodded. "I figured you guys were together. How old are you anyway, if you don't mind me asking? I'm thirty."

Christ, that made him feel ancient. "I'm a little over a hundred."

"And I'm eighty-two." Fiona's voice was soft as she scanned upward, taking in the all-green trees, looking for any would-be attackers.

The matching green bark and leaves were strange, just as Gray had said they would be. Ian hadn't seen anything to indicate the trees were alive enough to harm them, but he still wanted to be aware. In the realm he'd lived in before, most of the tree trunks had been a bright red and the sky lavender.

"Jeez," Javier muttered.

Ian smiled to himself at his half-brother's tone.

They walked in silence for the better part of an hour, using the trees and shadows as cover. Ian saw that Javier was just as vigilant as he was and, points to him, he didn't stare or give Fiona any lingering looks. Ian wasn't sure how the male could keep his eyes off her when she was perfect, but he was glad for it. He was already worried enough for her; wanted to get her the hell out of this place so Ophelia could examine her again.

"I'm pretty sure your friends are currently watching us. Are they going to attack me and ask questions later?"

Javier said quietly as they stepped into a clearing of sorts. The green-on-green trees had grown slightly more spaced out, but they were still able to use the shadows as cover.

Not that it would matter if the wolves were close enough to hear. And Ian was certain they were. He'd scented them roughly five minutes ago as they'd been walking.

He figured Finn was trying to ascertain if this male was a hostage or a threat to them and how he should respond, so he'd given the Alpha the chance to make his own opinion. "You can come out if you like," Ian said quietly. "The male is with us." Though if he could be trusted remained to be seen.

As if it had been choreographed, the four wolves in human form dropped from the trees, as silent as ghosts. Finn looked every inch the warrior he was as he eyed Ian's half-brother. He looked over Fiona with just a hint of concern and Ian wondered if the male saw how pale she appeared. But Finn didn't say anything. He looked at Ian next with a question in his eyes.

"For now, I'm trusting him. But that leash does *not* go far," he said, even though he knew it would likely insult his half-brother. At this point he didn't care. His only concern was keeping his mate safe and getting her out of this realm so they could find help for her.

"And no offense taken," Javier muttered under his breath.

Fiona let out a small chuckle, making Ian smile a little bit too. This female owned him.

"Who are you?" Finn's question was asked quietly, but the power in his words was unmistakable. Before he'd even finished speaking, the other three wolves in human form fanned out and took up guard around them in a spread-out triangle.

It was strange, but the longer Ian was around the male the more he realized how much raw power the wolf actually had. And he was a good leader, had trained his wolves well.

"My name's Javier. I was taken from my farm in Alabama—it's a cattle and agriculture farm. Some people who worked for me started going missing and the police were as stumped as anyone else. It's a rural area though, so I didn't expect much. A lot of the people were seasonal workers so it wasn't uncommon for me to lose workers without notice. But this was getting to be too much. So I went to this bar that some of the men frequented on their nights off and I saw these females who were definitely shifters luring my workers outside. I followed. And I ended up in this shithole because I was stupid enough to try to take on a bunch of half-demons by myself. I'm strong in this form but there were twenty of them and I wasn't prepared," he muttered, disgust in his voice.

"Once we got here, they started using my blood and mixing it with humans' and something else. From what I can gather they were trying to create a certain cocktail and apparently perfected it with my blood. All I know is that it kills the victim within days."

Finn nodded once, taking time to digest his words. It lined up with what Gray had told them. "Whose territory do you live in?" the Alpha finally asked.

Javier blinked. "Um...my own. I own my ranch. No mortgage. Everything's paid off."

Finn just frowned but didn't respond. Maybe Javier didn't know that there were various territories around the world and that if you were supernatural and lived in one, you were under the jurisdiction of the Alpha—whoever he or she might be. Now certainly wasn't the time to tell him.

"He's also my half-brother," Ian added when it was clear that Javier wasn't going to tell Finn.

Finn didn't look surprised, but the male rarely did. "What are you? I can smell wolf on you but there's something else. Something other than the demon."

"Obviously I'm a half-demon. But...my mother was a mixed breed, half Jaguar, half wolf. That's likely what you smell. My dominant gene is wolf and I only shift to wolf and demon, but the other nature is still in my DNA, still in my blood."

"According to Javier there are guards around the gate exit," Fiona murmured, her tone grim. "But we did get Ava out."

Finn nodded. "How many guards? And what are their skill levels?"

"Last I was there was a few hours ago and it was dark as well as foggy. Using mostly my sense of smell I would say a couple dozen. But by morning I guarantee there will be more. They know there's only one way to escape. Or I assume there's only one way to get out of this hellhole. As far as skill level...they're all fighters, as far as I know."

Finn looked at Ian. "Are there often more than one exit in these realms?"

"No. But this one is different than any I've ever been in. I expected creatures to come out at night but it was just silent and cold."

Javier nodded again. "I know they have creatures native to this realm—according to one of the dragons—but they remain in the few water sources including the moat around the castle. I heard some half-demons talking about the viciousness of them. But from what I've gathered just by eavesdropping that's one of the reasons they picked this place. They wanted the freedom to do whatever sick thing it is they're doing without dealing with extra threats. It was a specific tactical decision."

"We're going to talk more about this operation later," Finn said, authority in his voice. "But for now I want to get out of here and bring back the rest of my pack so we can clean this place out."

"Did you find any humans?" Fiona asked him. Even though she was pale, her voice was strong.

"Not directly. I scented a lot of death on one of the lower levels, but..." Finn cleared his throat once. "We were discovered and had to set off a few distractions to escape."

Fiona just snorted.

Finn turned to Javier, his gaze speculative. "Not all those explosions were from us."

Javier lifted a shoulder. "I did what I could. And I'll help you bring this place down. These beings are monsters. I didn't... I didn't know there were so many different supernatural beings until I got dragged into here. I've been to Afghanistan and Iraq—I was in the Corps for eight years. I thought I'd seen it all," he muttered, scanning the area again, clearly on alert.

"I'm sure there's a lot you don't know." Finn's tone was even. "If you fight with my pack—and you don't betray us—I'll give you sanctuary in my territory and I'll speak to the Alpha of the territory you're living in and let him know you don't know all the supernatural laws."

"Ah…okay." Javier looked at Ian questioningly.

"I'll explain it to you later. This is a good thing."

"Thank you, then. And I'll fight regardless of what you offer," Javier said. "These guys need to be stopped."

Finn gave him one of the first real smiles Ian had ever seen from the Alpha. "All right, then. Let's go do some damage."

CHAPTER SEVENTEEN

"This won't take long," Ophelia said.

"I'm really okay." Ava perched on the edge of one of the beds in the healing ward, her foot tapping nervously against the floor.

Ophelia simply nodded as she ran her hands over Ava's head, arms and chest—though not actually touching her. Using her healing gift, she checked for any internal trauma. "Is there anything else you need to tell me? What we talk about here is private. I don't even tell my Alpha. This relationship," she motioned between the two of them, "is sacred." Thankfully she hadn't felt any physical issues going on with Ava, but vampires healed as quickly as any other supernatural being.

"No. I swear it. I was thrown into a cage with a half-demon but he didn't hurt me. He actually protected me," she murmured. "I didn't expect it."

"Lyra, Finn's mate, and our Guardian, Gabriel, will want to speak to you when we're done." Ophelia had insisted she check out Ava first. The female had been kidnapped and taken to a Hell realm; anything else they wanted to know would wait.

The vampire nodded. "Of course. I'll tell them everything I know."

"I'm going to get you more blood and I've already got one of my packmates setting up a room for you. I have no

197

authority over you but I believe it would be smarter for you to stay with my pack right now. Until the others get back at least."

"I don't mind staying here. Fiona sort of ordered me to anyway." Ava snorted, a grin pulling at her lips. "She's like an overprotective mother bear."

"That's not a bad thing."

"No, it's not." The pretty vampire smiled and lay back against the bed. "Would it be okay if I rested here for a bit until they want to talk to me? I feel like all my energy has been sucked out of me and I just need to lie still."

"Of course. This place is insulated so you'll have ultimate privacy. There's a phone if you need to contact me for anything and I've got a few packmates out in the hall if you need something immediately. Do you need to wait to talk to Lyra and Gabriel?"

"No, but I don't feel like moving to another room."

Ophelia nodded. "Okay. I'll let them know you're good for questioning. You can get this over with as soon as possible. By the time they're done I'll be back down here with your blood."

Ava gave her a grateful smile. "Thanks."

As Ophelia left the room, she nodded once at her packmate Taylor, who was leaning against the door outside Gray's room. Her vibrant red hair was pulled back into a tight braid and she looked bored.

Taylor brightened and pushed up from the wall when she saw Ophelia. "Hey, mama."

She smiled at the nickname. Many of her packmates, especially the younger generation, called her mama or some form of the motherly endearment. "Hey. How's our guest?" *Too sexy for his own good Alpha wolf Gray.*

Taylor snorted. "Fine, I guess. Man, that male is hot but he's freaking grumpy and snarly."

Ophelia hadn't even realized she'd started to bare her canines in an aggressive manner until Taylor blinked in surprise. Ophelia had never done that to anyone before, and it was pretty clear that she was getting all possessive because of Taylor's "hot" comment.

Taylor grinned and opened her mouth to speak but Ophelia held a finger to her friend's mouth. "Say anything and I shred you."

Taylor just snorted again and batted her finger away. "You want to take over my shift?"

"Bite me," she muttered, heading down the hallway. The last thing she needed was to be anywhere near that obnoxious wolf. First she had to bring Ava that blood. Then she had to check on three packmates—all of whom were pregnant. They hadn't had any pups in the pack in a while and now it was like something was in the water.

Once she was done with the checkups, she was going to relax and watch a movie for the next couple hours. With Finn and a small team of warriors in a Hell realm right now it was very possible that she'd have injured packmates to deal with soon. She knew she needed to rest and be ready for whatever came their way.

After the pregnancy checkups, she found Jason in one of the game/movie rooms. She didn't have the energy to talk and be friendly. Yeah, she could have gone back to her actual room but she didn't feel like being quite so separated from the rest of the pack. Her wolf was in a weird mood right now. And she blamed it on a certain wolf currently under the same roof.

"I just put in a movie," Jason said, the younger wolf stretching out on the well-worn couch.

"I don't even care what it is. You just getting off your patrol shift?" She collapsed next to him and let out a sigh to finally kick her feet up. She felt as if she'd been going nonstop the past week, and Gray's mere presence in the mansion was making her edgy and out of sorts.

"Yeah. Want to relax a little in case shit goes down. You talked to Lyra about anything interesting?"

She nearly snorted. Wolves were so damn nosy. "Uh, no." And even if Ophelia had, she likely wouldn't share any information with Jason. Sometimes she could but there was a hierarchy in the pack. Jason was a warrior but he was young and if he needed to know something, one of the senior warriors would let him know—not her. As healer and one of the oldest members of the pack, she was privy to almost everything. "You're smart to be prepared though." And she hated that her packmates might be headed into battle soon.

The mission Finn was on now with the others was part recon and part rescue but Ophelia knew deep down that it would end in bloodshed. If not now, then once they went back. Because with what Gray had said was going on—Finn wouldn't stand for that. He would put an end to people being kidnapped and killed, no matter what. It was part of his Alpha nature to protect those who needed it.

As the movie came on the gigantic television screen on the wall, she relaxed, letting her head fall back against the couch and kicking her sock-clad feet up on the equally well-worn coffee table. The pack had quality furniture but since they were wolves and generally rough all around they tended to buy industrial-type stuff that could withstand the roughhousing of shifters.

"So what's up with the 'guest' downstairs?" Jason asked sometime later during one of the many car chase scenes.

The movie they were watching was over-the-top ridiculous but there was a lot of eye candy of the male variety so she wasn't complaining, since it temporarily distracted her from Gray. "What about him?"

"Just wondering why Finn's keeping another Alpha here."

Ophelia shrugged. "You're super nosy today."

Jason gave her one of those adorable smiles she was sure had made plenty of shifter females his own age drop their panties, and wrapped an arm around her shoulders. "Come on. I've been working shifts nonstop and have no gossip."

She laughed and leaned her head on his shoulder. Shifters were the worst when it came to gossip. Like middle schoolers. Worse, even.

A soft growling sound had all the hairs on the back of her neck standing up. Before she'd turned around, she scented him.

Gray.

Sitting up, she looked over to the open doorway to find Gray and Taylor standing there—Taylor with a big freaking smile on her face. *What the hell?*

"And this is one of our game rooms where the pack likes to unwind," Taylor said, motioning with her hand. "You know Ophelia, and this is Jason."

Next to her Jason pressed pause and stood. "Hey man, nice to—"

Gray just stared at him in the way Alphas could do when they were pissed, trying to force the other individual to submit.

Oh, no. This was not good. Jason already had an Alpha and for another to stare him down would mess with his wolf. She was already pushing to her feet even as Jason started to growl low in his throat.

"Taylor, you need to get the heck out of here, and Jason, you're going with her."

Jason didn't tear his gaze from the threat. "I'm not leaving you—"

"Now!" she snapped, using her healer voice. "That's an order." Hierarchy was a funny thing in packs and even though she wasn't a warrior, as healer she was revered by all.

Jason paused only once, giving Gray a hard look before averting his gaze. Because he had no choice. Gray was more dominant through and through.

Once they were alone Gray kicked the door shut behind the others, his expression dark as he stalked toward her.

Oh, hell no. "What's the matter with you, you freaking caveman? You can't come in here and—"

His mouth was on hers in a savage claiming before she realized he'd managed to cover the distance between them. Everything around them faded away as his tongue danced against hers. With one big hand, he cupped her cheek and jaw and his other he wrapped securely around her, pinning her tightly to him.

And there was absolutely no hiding his very clear reaction to her.

She should push him away. Punch him right in the face. Instead, she moaned into his mouth, arching against him even as she knew she shouldn't be doing this. By letting him go all caveman and kiss her, she was telling him this behavior was acceptable. Damn it, she shouldn't be giving in to this ridiculous display of his. But...she loved the way he tasted, loved the way he'd just completely taken over and gone all crazy Alpha. She dug her fingers into his shoulders, holding him tight. She'd been thinking about this male nonstop and here he was, devouring her mouth with his.

Just as suddenly as he'd started, he pulled back, stared down at her. His normally bright green eyes had gone a shade darker as he simply watched her, his breathing harsh and erratic. Leaning down, he rubbed his cheek against hers in a surprisingly sweet gesture.

"I don't like his scent on you," he murmured, continuing to rub against her.

Damn it, she needed to stop this, but... "He's just a pup. Just one of my packmates," she whispered, needing to somehow assuage the rage she could feel underneath Gray's surface.

"Still don't like it. Don't want anyone else's scent on you but mine." The way he rasped it out and wouldn't look her in the face told her how hard this was for him to say aloud. He was making himself completely vulnerable.

She shouldn't like that either. They didn't even know each other. "I like your scent on me." *Crap. Did I just say that?*

He pulled back to look at her and there was unmistakable triumph in his gaze when he met her own.

Ah, hell. Things had definitely just shifted between them. And she was pretty sure that she was not ready for what this sexy-as-sin male wanted from her.

* * *

Ian landed quietly about thirty yards from where he knew Fiona and the others were blending into the shadows of the forest. Finn had asked him to do an aerial recon of the top of the mountain. It was a hell of a lot easier for him to fly and check things out than for everyone to trek up the mountain into a potential trap.

Once he was certain that there weren't any threats nearby, he shifted to his half-demon form and hurried to the thick cluster of trees. Finn stepped out of the shadows first with Ian's bundle of clothes in his hand.

"Well?" the Alpha asked.

Ian shook his head as he tugged his pants on. "It's too hard to see anything. The fog is too thick, even with my acute eyesight. But I could smell at least fifty separate individuals. There's a small army up there."

Not completely impossible odds, but fifty half-demons with an unknown level of skill against the seven of them. He was certain that they would prevail in the end, but there might be casualties. He wouldn't risk going into a battle like that with Fiona. No way in hell. Not to mention that one of Fiona's brothers was a dragon and could be up there as well, so half-demons plus a dragon. While her brother might not be up there, they had to work on the assumption that he was—to expect the worst.

Finn was quiet for long moments as Ian finished getting dressed. Finally he said, "We'll head back to the castle. Look for survivors and raid the lab. I've been talking to Javier since you've been gone and he says the lab is one of the most fortified areas. But if they've sent out hunting parties, and I have no doubt they have, the castle will be weakened. Now is the time to strike them even though we're smaller in numbers."

Ian had promised to follow the Alpha's orders unless he thought those orders would put Fiona in direct risk. Since he thought that trying to escape the Hell realm right now with all those guards would put her at more risk, he had no problem following the Alpha's lead. "I can do an aerial recon and then we can all head in on foot. Unless you think we should split up?"

Finn shook his head. "No. We need to stick together this time. They know we're here. I don't want to push our luck with the aerial recon. Those dragons saw you before, even when you were camouflaged."

True enough. Ian fell in line with Finn as they moved deeper into the woods. Immediately he scanned for Fiona, and found her standing next to Chloe. It soothed his primitive nature to know that she was safe with others—and that she was with another female. He knew it was archaic but his animal and human side didn't give a shit. They embraced who he was. As he scanned her in one sweep, concern filled him. Maybe he was being paranoid, but she looked paler.

Getting to those labs was of utmost importance. He wanted a few moments alone with his half-brother to see if the male knew anything about the poison Fiona had been hit with but that wasn't possible right now. Instead he moved to her side and brushed his lips over hers, just for a brief touch. It was amazing how her simple touch or taste grounded him in a way he'd never thought possible. In a way he hadn't experienced in fifty years. "You okay?" he murmured.

She simply nodded, her face slightly drawn.

"When we go in, you and I are a team." And he'd have her back no matter what.

A smile ghosted her luscious mouth. "I've got your back."

As they moved through the woods this time, everyone was silent and on high alert. It was disturbing how quiet the strange forest was. No sounds from any animals was wrong on every level. And there was something in the air. Something that made him feel as if they were being watched. But he couldn't scent anyone, and going on what Gray had told them he assumed it was the trees. Which was creepy as fuck.

When they neared the bottom of the mountain, Finn held up a hand but Ian had already scented the threat.

Twenty individuals, give or take, if he smelled correctly.

Fiona already had one blade in her free hand, but she dropped his hand and pulled out another dagger as they all moved into a circle, spanning out in preparation for an imminent attack. Ian remained within ten feet of her as the pale green half-demons moved out of the trees like cockroaches.

Yep, twenty in all. Silently they started to move in a circle, trying to trap the seven of them inside.

Since Ian didn't fully trust his half-brother, he made sure that he could see the male out of the corner of his eye. To his surprise, Javier was the first to move into action, racing straight at a group of half-demons, a blade clutched tightly in hand. Ian wasn't sure where he got it from and he didn't care.

Someone from the other group let out a loud battle cry and the silence was shattered in an instant as the half-demons screamed and the wolves howled. It didn't matter that they were in human form. Their howls filled the air, a clear call to action.

"Stay close to me." It was a subtle demand and Ian didn't care if it pissed Fiona off. He would keep her safe at all costs.

Adrenaline punched through him but unlike the others he didn't shout or cry out, he simply raced at the nearest group of half-demons and unleashed a stream of blistering fire. Two males screamed, but the sound was cut short as their skin and bones burned away at an accelerated speed. Two neat ash piles replaced what had once been their bodies, with little bits floating away.

Out of the corner of his eye, he saw Fiona slice off the head of one of the warriors. Then another, and another. She could take care of herself, something he needed to remind himself of. Even if she was weaker than normal, she was still clearly skilled. And she was a dragon, whether she could feel her animal or not. He had to respect it. Still, he hated that she was draining herself, now of all times.

"Traitor to your own kind!" one of the half-demons screamed at him as he raced toward Ian.

Traitor? All right. Instead of using his fire, he let his claws unleash and sprinted forward in a burst of energy. The warrior raised a blade and slashed down, aiming for Ian's heart. He dodged to the side and kicked out as he did. His foot slammed into the male's stomach.

With a grunt, the warrior flew through the air but landed nimbly on his feet. The male danced to the side and drew back his blade before hurtling it at Ian.

His instinct was to duck away from it, but Fiona wasn't in his line of vision and he wasn't sure of her exact location. As it flew at him he shifted slightly to the side and raised his arm as a shield. The blade pierced through his forearm, followed by ripping agony. Better than slicing through his palm.

He ignored the pain and tore it out. Then he hauled it behind his head and, putting all of his force behind the throw, hurled it back at the male. *Swish, swish.* It flew end over end through the air. The male's eyes widened as he tried to dodge the deadly blade, but the point slammed into the warrior's head, right between his eyes.

Swiveling before the body had hit the ground, Ian saw that Fiona had taken out two more males. Javier had his back to her and was fighting like a trained warrior.

The clash of blades sang out in the forest, a familiar song to him. He released a stream of fire, mowing down two males who were attempting to gang up on his half-brother.

Screams filled the air but quickly died as the threats turned to more piles of ash. His fire was that same blue as the day before. He felt jacked up on adrenaline and emotions, as if nothing could contain him. Though his dragon rippled beneath the surface, he shoved the beast back down and sliced off the head of another attacker with his claws.

A dozen more warriors spilled out of the forest and Ian let his dragon free. In a burst of light and magic, his other nature took over. It was time to end this. They needed to get the hell away from here and he needed Fiona safe.

Blue fire tore through the air as he obliterated the new threat. He let out all the rage he was feeling, built up for decades upon decades. Rage that they were in this realm at all. That he'd lost so many years with Fiona. That she'd been poisoned and there wasn't a damn thing he could do about it right now. That she was in danger, and not safe at home, mated to him.

Fuck every single one of these monsters.

"Ian. Stop." Fiona's soft voice stilled everything inside him immediately, made him calm his fire.

Silence descended for a long moment as he stared at pile upon pile of ash, some scattering in the wind.

Unfortunately he'd set a few trees on fire in his attack as well. And that was when he heard the rumbling.

The earth shook violently as nearby trees began to uproot themselves.

What. The. Fuck.

Without thought he plucked Fiona up in his paw and dropped her onto his back. Then he did the same with

Javier. Before he had a chance to grab the others, the four wolves had already started climbing on him. They were heavy but he would be able to lift off.

Using all of his strength he soared upward, his wings slicing through the icy air with precision.

Starbursts of pain erupted throughout one of his wings as he cleared the top of the trees. One of the trees had attacked him, scraping along his wing with... Branches, claws? Could trees even have claws? He shook the thought off.

They were getting out of here. Ice burned his lungs as he soared higher and higher. Though he wanted to head straight to the castle, he decided to fly far away in the opposite direction. They needed to put some distance between the half-demons they'd just killed and come in from another angle completely. That meant lot of flying for him.

His injured wing burned as he flew but it hadn't done any actual damage so at least he could still fly.

He wasn't sure how much time passed as he continued his flight, and if he had to guess he covered at least sixty miles in a huge circle before he rounded back to the south side of the castle grounds. He flew as long as his body could take it before landing in what he thought was a safe position.

He wondered if the trees somehow communicated with each other and whether the nearby trees would know that he'd killed some of their own but it was a risk he had to take. If he didn't land soon he risked falling from the sky and injuring the woman he loved more than anything. His landing was harder than he'd intended, his entire body jolting as he made contact with the ground.

After the others had disembarked from his body and he'd shifted forms, he didn't have to concentrate very hard for his half-demon side to take over. A rush of much needed energy shot through him as he underwent the change. He was weak but not as weak as he would have been if he hadn't been in this form. Something about being a half-demon in a Hell realm gave him more strength. He wasn't quite sure how it worked and didn't much care.

"Are you okay?" Fiona's hands cupped his cheek before he'd fully stood.

Breathing hard, he nodded and gathered her into his arms, not caring that he was completely naked.

Finn strode up next to him and held out a change of clothes. "This is all I have. I don't know if it will fit but it's better than you walking around with your junk hanging out."

A smile twitched at his lips but all he did was nod his thanks and take the bundle of cargo pants and pullover sweater.

"How weak are you?" Finn continued. "Don't bullshit me."

Ian understood why Finn was asking. He was part of this team and the Alpha would need to know Ian's capabilities for any upcoming battle. "I'm okay to fight but I need food." And he couldn't draw on enough energy to transport food from the human realm. Screwing with that chef right now would be perfect, but after a quick try, he couldn't muster the concentration or energy to do it.

Finn nodded again. "We'll get you some. Thank you for what you did."

Fiona murmured her thanks as well, her expression concerned as she watched him. She never had to thank him for taking care of her.

"Is anyone else going to talk about how creepy those freaking trees were?" Chloe asked, staring at all of them with wide eyes. "Those trees uprooted themselves. *Up-rooted.*"

Javier let out a short laugh. "Those things are terrifying. But from what I understand they only attack if they are attacked."

The female wolf just shook her head, muttering something under her breath about getting back to her own realm.

"Okay," Finn said, his voice all Alpha. "We're going to head in through the south side and make our way to one of the lower levels. Everyone is an enemy. Kill on sight. If there are humans captive we'll save them."

"Priority should be getting to the lab," Ian said quietly. Because while he wanted to save humans, he wanted to find out more about the poison because it didn't appear as if Fiona's body was counteracting it—and she was a dragon. She should have already staved off any weakness. As of right now even her scent was weaker. It was strange and he wasn't sure what to make of it. He hadn't noticed it until a few minutes ago but now that he had, it was as if her scent was fading.

Finn paused to look at Fiona, then back at Ian. An emotion Ian couldn't define crossed the Alpha's face before he nodded. "Agreed. We get to the lab first. You," he said to Javier. "You're going to take point with me."

Javier nodded and hurried to fall in line with Finn. But Ian noticed that his half-brother shot Fiona a worried look.

Which told Ian that he wasn't being paranoid—she was definitely paler and they had to notice the difference in her scent as well. He moved to her side and wrapped his arm around her shoulders. She leaned into him with no compunction—which spoke volumes. "We're going to figure out what they poisoned you with and we'll fix this. I promise." Because there was no other option. He wouldn't allow it.

Her mouth pulled down. "If there's no cure—"

"There will be." He cut her off with a savage snarl and hugged her close. He refused to let anything else happen to her. He refused to let her… He couldn't even think the word.

CHAPTER EIGHTEEN

52 years ago

"Why are you acting so awkward?" Fiona whispered to Ian even though they were the only supernaturals in this establishment. It was a little hole-in-the-wall jazz club that had only been open for a few years according to the man who'd let them in. She'd overheard some humans talking about it and wanted to see it for herself.

Ian stood stiffly, with his back to a wall as the quartet of men began to set up their instruments. About fifty other men and women were crammed into the small, bare room, drinking from flasks and smoking while waiting to hear the music. The women had on sparkly cocktail dresses and the men all wore suits. Fiona loved this era and loved the change in clothing, adored being able to dress with more freedom. Everything around her was changing and soon she was going to make the biggest change of all in her life.

"Relax. You're with humans who have no idea what you are." A tall black man moved into their line of vision with a smoothness that bordered on supernatural. But he was human. He held out a hand to a wary Ian, a big smile on his face.

Ian took his hand, shook once. "Who are you?"

"Name's Thurman. Senior." His Cajun accent seemed to get thicker as he spoke.

"What do you mean by humans?" Confusion tinged his voice.

The man's smile remained in place. "I know what you are. What both of you are. Never thought I'd get to meet one of your kind, and now you're all over the city. Surprised to see you folks in a place like this though."

Fiona stilled momentarily, but shook his outstretched hand as a waft of smoke washed over her from a nearby patron. "What are you?"

"A seer. Some call me the Magic Man of New Orleans. I'm training my boy to take over for me soon enough, but he's out of town for a protest right now. He'll be sad he didn't get to see you." He shook his head, his expression disappointed for his son.

Fiona glanced at Ian once, lifted a shoulder. It was a little strange that the human was just telling them what he was, but this was New Orleans after all. The humans who lived here seemed to be different than humans she'd met elsewhere.

"You've seen others like us?" Ian asked, seeming slightly more guarded.

The man gave another genuine smile. "I ain't never seen anyone like you. But," he nodded once at Fiona, "I've seen plenty of your people along St. Peter's and Chartres tonight, *chère*."

Fiona stilled at his words. She'd left her family's compound discreetly a few hours ago. She hadn't snuck out exactly, but she also hadn't told anyone where she was going. Lately she'd started to exert her independence, and so far there hadn't been much pushback. It had been little things—going on shopping trips by herself without telling anyone. Running errands alone. Which shouldn't be a big deal in the first place, but her clan could act insane about such things where females were concerned. When she'd gone to that party with her brother weeks ago it had been a win as far as she was concerned.

Her family had only allowed her to go because they wanted her on display to other supernaturals, basically. To show others how beautiful members of the O'Riley clan were. *Ugh. So stupid and gross.* But she didn't care about the reasoning, because she'd gotten to meet Ian—and her entire world had changed. Soon she'd be leaving with him and never looking back.

Fiona wasn't sure if the man sensed her distress, but his next words soothed her. "The owner just put out the 'at capacity' sign. No one else is getting in the joint for the show, *chère.*"

Next to her she felt Ian relax just as she did. They could enjoy the show without the worry of running into her family. Tonight had been a risk, she knew that. And Ian hadn't even wanted to come. So they'd arrived independently and at different times. They shouldn't have to hide their relationship, and okay, she'd liked pushing the envelope a little tonight. Because she was proud of Ian, proud that they were together. She hated that they had to hide what they meant to each other. She couldn't wait until the day they could walk down the street holding each other's hands without having to hide.

Soon. She kept telling herself that over and over.

"Thank you," she murmured.

"There's also an exit out back if you want to use it when the show's over." Before they could respond, he'd turned and blended into the crowd. Though he couldn't blend too much considering how tall he was.

"That was a little weird." She looked up at Ian, who was still scanning the place. When she saw how tense he was, she realized how selfish she was being. "Let's just get out of here and go somewhere outside the city. I'll go out the front, you go out the back and we'll meet up somewhere."

He opened his mouth to respond and the first note of music filled the air. A saxophone. She turned, as did everyone else in the cramped place. A murmured hush fell over the crowd until the only other noises were the rustling of clothing.

As the men started to play, that changed, with people swaying side to side, some shouting out their approval with others starting to basically dance in place.

Jazz was like a language unto itself, and to her it represented America. There were a lot of things she didn't like about the country, but more that she did—and it was why she didn't plan to leave anytime soon. There had been so many changes in the last few years; the humans were finally having their civil rights revolutions all over the world. It was damn time she did the same—that *all* supernaturals followed suit.

The emotion coming from the musicians as they played the saxophone, trumpet, piano and bass was…indescribable. But she felt it all the way to her soul. As if they were speaking to her, to everyone, telling a story of sorrow but triumph. Which felt a little silly to think, but her body vibrated with energy and excitement.

Ian moved in behind her, wrapped his big arms around her and swayed in time with the beat of the music with her. She could feel his energy pulsing through him as if it were her own.

"I love you, Fiona," he murmured against her neck, sending a shiver spiraling through her. She barely heard his words over the music but they rushed over her just the same.

"I love you too." *More than anything.*

"I'm glad we came tonight." He tightened his hold around her and for a moment she felt as if they were the only two people in the world. As if nothing and no one could touch them—as soon as Ian's contact came through for them.

They needed to make a clean escape so there was no way to track them. She hoped that one day they got to return to New Orleans because it was where she'd met Ian for the first time.

Where she'd felt alive for the first time.

CHAPTER NINETEEN

Colm walked around the piles of ash, his rage growing heavier, thicker by the second. Anger consumed him as he calculated how many men he'd lost. This was not acceptable.

"Two trees have moved." One of his warriors decided he was too stupid to see the obvious.

Colm didn't respond, just reined in his fire. Barely. Scanning the disturbed area of the forest, it was clear that two trees had uprooted and replanted themselves elsewhere. The trees were quick when disturbed but Colm had no doubt the beings responsible for this were faster. They were long gone by now.

Given the ash, that disgusting half-breed had killed his men. And even though there were dozens of footprints mashed together where his men had been massacred, he could see a clear pattern of footprints leading down from the mountain.

Continuing to ignore the small group of men with him, he stalked north, following the footprints in reverse. There were seven sets. He'd had reports of four wolf shifters. Not to mention his sister and that half-breed. There was her vampire friend as well. He couldn't imagine the half-breed captive working with them so that male must still be on his own somewhere.

221

"What do you want us to do?" one of the more skilled half-demons asked, moving up next to him so silently Colm hadn't even heard him approach.

He'd have to pay more attention to this one. "Keep the exit guarded but we're headed back to the castle." From the pattern of footprints he could only guess that the group of seven were headed there. But that still left Javier, the other half-breed. Colm needed that male. His blood was incredibly valuable.

He could always find humans. They were nothing. But Javier...his blood was unique. Colm never would have known about him either if not for his other partner. A partner he planned to destroy once he'd taken over the human realm. That would be tricky, but he had no problem double-crossing that monster. Especially when that male would slice off Colm's own head in an instant. They were simply using each other to take over the human realm, something Colm understood.

"We lost a lot of men," the male hedged.

No shit. He sighed, running the calculations in his head. "Send a runner to the exit. Pull down another fifteen men to bring to the castle."

The soldier nodded and stalked over to his small group of men. Once the order was given, one of the half-demons took off. That was taken care of and now it was time to head back to the castle.

He hadn't planned to call on his partner so soon, but it looked as if he might have to. Especially since this new threat to their plan had arrived unexpectedly. He wouldn't let his pride get in the way. Not when his brother had already been killed. No, he'd call in backup.

The kind of backup that would annihilate everyone who didn't belong.

Everyone except Javier. He was keeping that male around. Then it would be back to business as normal. He'd start killing humans on a massive level. Once they managed to make their drug in aerosol form, it would just take planning and patience. This little stumbling block would be a distant memory soon.

* * *

52 years ago

Even in his drunken state, Ian scented others entering his property. In his current mood, he was ready for a fight. A really brutal one. Maybe he'd even die.

At this point he didn't fucking care. Didn't care about anything. He'd gone to Fiona's estate last night to kidnap her, to just take her away from her family. Because her bullshit story about not loving him was just that: bullshit. He knew what they had was real. That she loved him as much as he loved her. Her family must have forced her to leave him, scared her or something.

But when he'd seen her mating manifestation at her family's estate, bright and clear for anyone in the Garden District to see, he'd wanted to die right then. She might love him, but she'd still mated with another male. Now there was no chance for them. Ever.

So he'd come back to his place and had drunk the equivalent of a liquor store in the last week. Not that it changed anything. Knowing she was with someone else, letting someone else touch her—

He unleashed a stream of fire that incinerated the couch across from him. The leather went up in flames, then quickly turned to ash, scattering across the wood floor.

Shoving up from his seat, uncaring about the destruction, he stalked to the front door at the sound of light footsteps on his porch. God, if someone was here to attack, they weren't being subtle.

He yanked open his front door and came face to face with Fiona's mother. The female was the spitting image of her; looked more like a slightly older sister than her mother. Seeing her made his gut clench.

The tall female held out a newspaper for him. It had been folded over, open to the marriage announcements. *What the hell...*

His gut tightened even more as words blurred before him. There was no picture because supernaturals went out of their way to avoid cameras, but words like *Fiona O'Riley...married on...* He crumpled the paper before burning it. As the flaming pieces fluttered to the front porch, he glared at the female who was still standing in front of him.

"Why are you still here?" he rasped out. She'd clearly just come over to pour salt in his wound. *Well, job done.*

Her lips pulled into a thin line, her blue eyes cold. "As you can see, my daughter is officially off-limits to you now. You should leave the region. My sons want you dead and you'll only be hurting yourself further if you stay." She sniffed once haughtily, cringing a little. "And you stink. You want her to see you like this, a pathetic drunk? Go find a female on your level and leave our clan alone." Without waiting for a response, she swiveled, her high heels clicking loudly as she descended the short set of stairs to the front walkway.

He scented others from her clan nearby. It was disgusting that they'd let a female deliver a message to *him*. A renowned fighter nicknamed "Beast." But they must have known he wouldn't hurt a female unless provoked, no matter how much he loathed her.

When she reached his driveway she started stripping, getting ready for her flight, no doubt. So he slammed his door shut and stalked back inside.

Glancing around a place that had never felt like a home until Fiona had entered it, the dagger in his chest sank even deeper.

What the hell was he thinking? He couldn't stay here now. Her mother was right; he needed to leave. The thought of seeing Fiona in town with another male—he'd want to kill the male but he couldn't. Not without killing Fiona because of the way dragons mated. That was something he could never, ever do.

Throwing his head back, he screamed out his rage in fire and pain. All around him the home burned, destroying her scent, erasing every single memory he had of her. He wanted this place completely eradicated, the one place he'd felt truly happy. He didn't want to remember how she'd felt beneath him, how she'd told him she'd always love him. He had to destroy everything that reminded him of her.

Almost.

He still had one picture tucked away in his pocket and he wasn't getting rid of it. Apparently he truly was a masochist.

His throat ached by the time he was done, the amount of fire he'd released completely draining his reserves. He hadn't even thought it was possible to run out of fire, but he hadn't been able to stop himself. As his fire died he surveyed his surroundings. There was nothing left of the house. Not even the foundation was standing. He wondered if any of his miles-away neighbors had seen the light show. Didn't really care. There were no sirens in the distance so maybe not.

Eerie silence descended around him, so loud it hurt his ears. Numb with grief, he stripped off his clothes and curled them into a bundle so he could carry his only remaining belongings. He didn't care about the clothes, but he wasn't leaving Fiona's picture behind.

"I wish I could," he muttered to himself, his throat raw and for some reason not healing. It was as if his fire had burned too hot for his body to fully repair. Whatever. He didn't care if it never fully healed. His heart would not.

Letting go of his beast, he allowed his dragon to take over, to soar high into the clouds away from his past, from Fiona, from everything. Needing to escape the vicious pain clawing at his chest.

CHAPTER TWENTY

Fiona tried not to inhale too deeply as they hurried along the cold, stone hallway far beneath the castle. They'd killed about twenty guards over the course of the last half hour as they cleared the floors. And they'd found cells upon cells of dead humans. Mostly males, but a few human females. It appeared as if some had taken their own lives and others had died of poor treatment. She shoved her rage back down. It wouldn't do them any good now. She'd save it for when they destroyed every single being involved in this.

They were on the last floor, the one Javier had said he'd been taken to on multiple occasions so a human doctor could draw his blood. Fiona couldn't believe a human was in this place voluntarily but maybe Javier was wrong and the doctor had been forced through blackmail or just brute force. Either one seemed like a strong possibility.

Now all she smelled was blood and death. The offensive scents rolled over her and she doubted they'd find anyone alive down here—but they had to try. So far they'd passed four cells, all splattered with blood. But there was no one inside and there were only two doors left.

At a scraping sound, they all stilled. Ian was camouflaged but he held her hand securely in his. Finn was taking point with Javier, no surprise.

Up ahead, Javier murmured something so quietly it must have been subvocal because she couldn't hear him.

Finn nodded then turned to the nearest steel door and slammed a booted foot against it. It flew open, and moving in a cohesive unit, his three wolves still in human form spilled into the room, weapons up.

There were a few shouts but they died quickly. By the time she and Ian strode through the doorway there were two dead half-demons on the floor of a surprisingly pristine lab and a...human man wearing a lab coat. The human stared at all of them, the fear rolling off the older white male potent. The acidic scent was stronger than even the blood and death. Tables had been set up on the stone floors. Beakers, test tubes with glass stirring rods, racks for the tubes, multiple burners and a whole lot of other equipment she didn't recognize covered most of the flat surfaces.

Her heart beat a little faster, a staccato rhythm in her chest. She was getting weaker by the second and while she'd tried to hide how run-down she felt, she didn't think she was doing a very good job of it. It had been impossible to miss the concerned looks from Ian and even Finn and Javier.

"Be right back," Ian murmured, squeezing her hand before dropping it.

She frowned for all of a second before the human doctor was lifted off the ground by a seemingly invisible force.

The male with graying hair clutched at his throat, his eyes growing wide as Finn strode up to him with the swagger of an Alpha.

Finn crossed his arms over his chest, his eyes flecks of blue ice as he stared at the human. "You saw what we did to those half-demons. We've taken out a hundred of them so far and we're not done. The hand you feel wrapped around your throat? That's my buddy Ian. He's a mother-fucking dragon and his mate was poisoned by some shit I'm guessing you created. He's restraining himself. If he wasn't, you'd be missing your throat. Now, he's going to let you down and you're going to talk. If you don't...we'll keep you alive for months. Maybe years. The pain will be never-ending and you'll wish you were dead. But the sweet release of it will never come. Not until you're a husk." He leaned in close, looked up at the male hovering in the air, frantically clawing at his throat as he stared in horror at Finn. It appeared as if Finn said something else but Fiona couldn't hear him.

Whatever it was, the man in the lab coat urinated on himself. She scrunched her nose as the sharp scent filled the air. But she kept guard at the door, peering out into the hallway for a visual even though she couldn't hear anything.

Chloe stepped out with her. "I'll keep watch," the she-wolf murmured.

Fiona nodded but stayed close to the door anyway. If they were attacked she'd back the female up. She might be feeling weaker than normal but she could still fight. Blade in hand, she turned to see the doctor fall to the ground and Ian suddenly drop his camouflage.

Coughing and gasping for breath, the doctor stared up at Ian—and urinated again.

"Come on dude, that's just nasty," the male named Solon muttered.

The human might not have even heard him. All he did was stare between Finn and Ian, two terrifying forces of nature.

Finn crouched down, and if he was trying to make himself less scary, he failed. "We're going to start small. I'm going to ask you some questions. You will tell the truth—and we'll scent if you don't. If you lie..." He jerked a thumb to Ian, who stood staring like a...well, a pissed-off seven-foot-tall half-demon.

The male nodded once, the action jerky.

Fiona might have felt a little bad for the man under different circumstances but he was behind her poisoning and countless others'. She was all out of sympathy.

"Tell me your name." Finn's voice was low, a sharp edge to it, which was probably scarier to this human than if he'd yelled.

"Dr. Bianchi."

"How long have you been here?"

"On and off maybe a year."

"Are you here voluntarily?"

"No." *Lie.*

The room went eerily quiet.

Ian's head tilted slightly to the side, the movement so small she might have missed it if she hadn't been watching so intently. Wordlessly he grasped the male's wrist and a snap filled the air—followed by a scream of pain. Ian did it so brutally and efficiently.

For a moment he looked back at her. Not at the Alpha. Her. As if... What, for her permission? She wasn't sure.

"We need the truth from him," she said quietly. Not just for her but for any others he might have poisoned. She knew the only reason Ian was holding off from demanding to know about the poison right now was because they needed to get a gauge for how truthful this male was, to see what they could do to him before he broke.

She didn't care what Ian did to this male. She wanted to live. To have the life with Ian that had been stolen from them. She refused to believe they had this second chance only to have it ripped apart. Life was such a fickle bitch she knew that she could very well die but... Hope sprung eternal, apparently. Because she hoped with every desperate fiber of her being that she and Ian got that second chance. Got to have a life together, children, a family.

So whatever he needed to do to get the doctor to talk was fine with her.

Ian nodded once, turned back to the human who was groaning, his eyes glassy with pain as he held his wrist to his stomach.

Finn made a clucking sound which under other circumstances might have been funny. Still crouching down, the Alpha shook his head. "I warned you, doctor. Now, are you here voluntarily?"

"Ye...yes," he rasped out.

"Better. Let me guess. You did it for money."

The male nodded.

"I'm going to need an audible answer."

"Yes. For money. And...he promised me a place in the new world. Homes, wealth, anything I want." His voice shook and his eyes were still glassy but he seemed to be focusing well enough.

Fiona hoped he held out through the questioning. She wanted to shout at them to get on to the questions about the poisoning.

"We already know about your boss's stupid plan to take over the human realm."

"Not ssss...stupid." He shook his head once.

To Fiona's surprise, one of the wolves walked over with a glass of water and held it to the doctor's mouth. After he took a sip, he continued. "They have a plan and...a partner." He whispered the last part, the terror in his voice no match for the stink of it rolling off him.

"We'll get back to the partner bit. For now, tell me about this poison. We know you've been mixing human blood with my friend Javier's blood." Finn looked over at Javier.

The doctor's gaze trailed after him, as if seeing the half-demon for the first time. He blinked then started shaking when Javier gave him a cold smile.

"Yes. I have." The doctor's voice shook but at least he wasn't slurring. "It's more than just the two mixed bloods. I've added...other ingredients and had to process it. And none of it's written down. You need me if you want to replicate it!"

"Is there a cure for the poison?" Finn asked, ignoring the small outburst.

Fiona held her breath as she waited for the male to answer. There had to be one. All the muscles in her body tightened as time passed in slow motion.

The doctor cleared his throat, rasped out, "Yes."

A lie. The scent was overwhelming.

No cure.

On instinct she called on her dragon. Felt nothing. Not even a hint of her dual nature, her other half. The vast nothingness clawed at her, made her want to scream at the unfairness of it all.

Ian growled low in his throat as numbness spread through Fiona like slow-moving lava, scorching yet holding her immobile.

"What did I say?" Finn's voice was that familiar icy calm.

"There's no cure," the doctor said but didn't look at Finn. All his attention was on Ian—a seven-foot pale blue warrior who was completely naked and clearly ready to rip this guy's head off. "There's a hint of magic and...another blood in the mixture."

"What type of blood?"

The male paled and he shook his head. "It'll kill me."

It? Fiona frowned.

Ian leaned down, got in his face then cursed as the doctor started convulsing. "What the—I didn't touch him!"

The scent of blood filled the air.

Cursing under his breath, Finn stretched the human out on his back as the man gasped out his last breaths.

When Ian and Finn stood up she realized what had happened. Blood gushed out on the floor, covered his pants as it pooled everywhere. The doctor had sliced his femoral artery. Crimson pooled out around his body and his pants were completely soaked with blood.

"What the ever loving hell," Solon snarled.

Clearly the dead human had been hiding a scalpel in his pocket. They hadn't even checked him because why would they? Even though fear laced her veins she stepped into the room and started scanning the shelves. There were books and notebooks they might be able to use. She sure as hell wasn't giving up. "We need to take the samples," she murmured, moving to a makeshift refrigerator. It wasn't like one in the human realm but the doctor had created an icebox of sorts to store vials of blood. They were all labeled.

"Found a carrier." Ian was next to her in seconds, a cushioned case in hand. Clearly what they'd been using to transport the product to the human realm. She wondered how it managed to survive the exit, but the case appeared sturdy and padded. And they knew for a fact that someone had been selling this shit in the human realm per Gray, so it must survive the trip just fine.

Fear bubbled up, wanted to take over, wanted to drown her with the knowledge that she was dying. But she ruthlessly shoved it back down. What the hell was she going to do? Panic? Freak out? No. That was for weaker beings. She'd deal with this head-on and if she discovered that there truly was no cure, that no one could help her, well... She'd spend every last second she could in Ian's arms. For now, they had work to do.

Once they'd packed up everything they might be able to use later, utilizing all their packs and any bags in the lab, they headed out. It was time to go.

Ian had dressed again and wasn't bothering with camouflage at this point. The castle was eerily silent as they moved up a flight of interior stone steps. Finn wanted to go out a different way than they'd come, to eliminate as many threats as they could.

But there were none, not even in the great hall. All the hairs on Fiona's arms stood on end as they reached the main exit to the castle courtyard. Beyond that would be the moat but they still had to make it through the courtyard first. Unfortunately she could scent many, many others outside.

Damn it. Maybe they should have left another way.

The main door, at least thirty feet high and just as wide, was open, revealing a drawbridge. She couldn't see anyone but she could scent them.

"I'm going to call Colm out for a death match," Ian said, looking at her. Not Finn but her.

She sucked in a breath. Death matches between supernatural beings had a long history. After a fight to the death, the victor walked away free and clear without interference from the loser's comrades. It was an ancient practice and she wasn't sure of the original language it came from, but death match was pretty much understood by all supernaturals. "Ian—"

"I have to. It's the only way we'll all make it out of here without losing anyone. I can scent at least a hundred half-demons out there and I'll still have to take on Colm. I won't be able to protect you while I'm fighting. I won't risk losing you again. Never again." There was no give in his voice before he turned and shouted out "Death match! You and me, Colm! Now!" Ian's naturally raspy voice echoed out loud and clear for anyone in the castle courtyard to hear.

Ian was strong, capable, but…she couldn't stand the thought of losing him again. Of him being in pain. *No, no, no.* She wanted to scream at him to stay with her, for them to escape through another exit, but she knew her male. Knew he wouldn't back down from this challenge now that he'd extended it. He was too honorable.

Silence descended for a long moment before another shout filled the air. "Agreed. Victor walks away. No interference during the battle."

Ian turned to Fiona, cupped her cheek gently. She turned into his callused palm, her throat tight as she stared into his amber eyes. "Come back to me." It was all she could force out.

He looked as if he wanted to say something, but simply nodded and turned from her. Immediately she felt the loss of his touch, but everything else came back into focus as he strode away, a warrior going into battle.

She watched as he stopped next to Finn. "It's the only way," he said to the Alpha. "I kill Colm and the others will be honor bound to let us go."

"They're half-demons," Finn said.

"I'm a half-demon." His voice was wry.

Jaw tight, Finn nodded. "If they don't hold to the bargain, we'll destroy them."

Ian nodded once, shot Fiona a look of undeniable love that broke her heart before he strode out through the main doors. The light from outside bathed him, highlighting every inch of raw strength and power in his huge body.

Finn gave his wolves a sharp look and they fell in line with him, following after Ian, but Fiona was already moving past them. The Alpha didn't give her orders and she was going wherever Ian did. She'd follow the male into any battle, into Hell itself.

Never again would she be separated from him. Not until she took her last breath.

The truth was, she wasn't even sure she could abide by the laws of the fight. Because if her brother was close to killing Ian, she was going to intercede. She wouldn't be able to stop herself.

CHAPTER TWENTY-ONE

Ian kept his expression neutral as he strode out into the courtyard of the castle. Only now did he realize why Colm had agreed to fight him.

Finn's wolves—and Ian's brothers and sister!—armed to the teeth, some covered in blood, were in the courtyard as well, facing off with a bunch of half-demons. And they were evenly matched.

Ian wondered if the Alpha had known his people were coming or if they'd just shown up. He'd find out soon enough.

Now he was in warrior mode. He was going to kill Colm. Then they were getting the hell out of here.

Ian kept all his focus on Colm. The male looked cocky, just as he remembered him the first time he kicked his ass.

This fight might be to the death, but it was just another fight to Ian. Just another ring. Just another bully to put down. Because that was all Colm was. A bully. He was on a larger scale than most but he wanted to take over the human realm because he thought he was better than everyone else.

Ian couldn't dredge up any guilt that this was Fiona's brother either. Hell no. Especially not since this bastard had known she'd been poisoned, had maybe done it himself. Had been fine letting her leave because he thought she was going off to die.

That wasn't happening. But this male was about to die.

Ian looked between Colm and the half-demon next to him. He didn't recognize the male, but that meant nothing. He didn't know anybody from this realm. "I want your word that the victor leaves unscathed. You know the rules. Will you abide by them?"

"It doesn't matter. I'm going to kill you and then I'm going to kill all of your people." Colm's voice was cocky, his expression smug.

Ian looked at the half-demon instead of Fiona's brother. "When I kill your leader will there be bloodshed or will my people and I walk away?" Ian was certain that Finn would end up destroying everyone here eventually, but Ian's priority was getting Fiona out of here and to the healer.

"Everyone leaves except that half-demon, Javier, if you win." He shot a sideways glance to Colm and then straightened. "It's a moot point since you will lose." But there was a hesitancy in his voice.

If Colm heard it he didn't acknowledge it. But the half-demon's words were good enough for Ian. At least for now. Because he wouldn't trust this male or any of his comrades—and no one was keeping Javier from leaving either. At this point Ian was fairly certain that with Finn's wolves and his own brothers and sister—he was still pissed that Cynara had shown up—they would be able to take on this army.

But he'd already called for a fight to the death. The truth was he wanted to kill the bastard, wanted to rip Colm's head from his body. "Rules?" Because there would always be rules. Unless this fool wanted to go fully dragon. In that case Ian would destroy him in seconds.

Colm must have known that because he shifted once on his feet, clearly losing some of his cockiness. "We stay in our two-legged form. No flying and no fire."

"Fine. What about claws and canines?"

"All fine. Just no fire. Same rules as fifty years ago."

A grin spread across Ian's face. He'd never been one to talk trash in the fighting ring but he couldn't help himself right now. "I remember how fifty years ago turned out. This time I'm not letting you walk away so easily."

Colm simply glared at him and ripped his tunic over his head, tossing it to the side.

Ian did the same, stripped off his tunic and weapons. He didn't need them. He'd seen Colm's moves and they weren't impressive. Though many years had passed so Ian knew he couldn't get cocky. That was a mistake he'd never made. He didn't underestimate his opponents.

He had a feeling Colm was going to underestimate him, however. Ian was in his half-demon form now. Bigger and stronger than the first time they'd clashed. But Colm had this ridiculous notion that the blood in his veins made him superior.

As they both stripped down to just loose pants, everyone moved back, creating a huge circle around them. It was shockingly quiet, or maybe he'd just tuned everything out. The only thing he could hear was the wind whistling. But he could barely feel the cold; he was too jacked up on adrenaline.

Staring at Fiona's brother, he only saw a slight familial resemblance in his espresso hair and blue eyes. This male exhibited none of her warmth, her goodness, the very essence that made her who she was. No, this male was everything that was wrong with the world. And Ian was going to end this now.

In a fight, he worked second by second. The ultimate goal was obviously to put his opponent down. But everyone fought differently and he had to adapt to his opponents' fighting styles and use both their strengths and weaknesses against them.

Out of the corner of his eye, he saw his siblings—Rory, Bo, Cynara and even Javier—move in so that they surrounded Fiona. Yeah, he trusted and respected Finn, but he knew his family would protect her in a way no one else would.

Just like that, everything else fell away. He could truly concentrate on this fight knowing that she was protected. As protected as anyone in this realm could be.

He lasered in on Colm, watching the way the male moved, the agile way he stepped, how he'd already released his claws.

Ian needed to make the first strike. It would be a psychological blow to the obnoxious dragon. The male who thought he was better simply because of the blood that ran through his veins.

His own dragon rippled beneath the surface, the need to release his fire and annihilate this threat overwhelming. But he shoved it back down. He wouldn't dishonor the fight. Though the truth was if it came down to it and Fiona was in danger, he would break every rule there was.

"I'm going to kill her when I'm done with you. The only smart thing she ever did was not mate with you. But she's still a whore," Colm snarled, taking a step closer.

Ian let the male's words roll off him. Soon he'd mate with Fiona. This piece of shit was simply an obstacle.

"She cried out for you a few times when my parents locked her up—"

Ian moved lightning fast, slamming his fist into the center of Colm's face, crushing his nose even as he slashed out with his other hand, raking his claws across Colm's chest. He dug deep, ripping away flesh before the male flew back in the air under the impact of Ian's punch.

Colm slammed onto his back ten feet away. Gurgling, he jumped to his feet. His nose was clearly broken and even though they healed at a rapid speed, it would hurt like a bitch.

Not only that, it would hurt Colm's ego. Which was what Ian wanted.

Colm rushed at him, claws out and body tense. Ian dodged to the side, and the male swiveled, following his movements. Then he lunged at Ian and they fell on each other like savage beasts.

Pain fractured up his side as Colm dug his claws into Ian's ribs but he ignored it, ignored everything but the driving need to put this male down.

He slammed his fist against the other male's kidney, then his ribs, then stomach. He felt his own body being pummeled but it was easy to ignore as he continued beating the shit out of Colm.

He brought his fist up, slamming it against Colm's already broken nose. The other male cried out in pain even as he drove his fist against Ian's chest. Digging in with his claws Colm tried to break through Ian's chest cavity, no doubt to rip Ian's heart out.

Ian slashed out with his own claws, going straight for Colm's neck even as he slammed a fist down against Colm's clawed hand.

He broke the contact from his chest, and Colm sliced at Ian's forearm, trying to make Ian stop choking him. He still didn't release his grasp—until the other male kicked out at Ian's knee.

He heard the snap before he felt the break and tumbled back into the dirt. Even though he was already starting to heal, his body was exhausted from the long flight and no food.

Growling low in his throat, he took pleasure in the fact that Colm's throat was shredded and bloody. He balanced on his good leg, tracking Colm's movements as he started to slowly circle him.

He could feel his bones and ligaments knitting back together but his knee wouldn't be healed by the time Colm attacked.

The other male lunged suddenly, moving in low as if to tackle Ian. But Ian had learned not to allow his weaknesses to slow him down in a fight.

Calling on every single reserve in his strength he had, he crouched low and sprung high into the air. He put most of his pressure on his good leg but there was no choice but to use both. Agony ripped through him, but it was a small price to pay as he came back down and landed on Colm's back.

He wrapped his arm around Colm's neck and squeezed tight, even as he wrapped his legs around the male. His knee might be broken but he had a lot of strength in his thighs.

Colm bucked at him, trying to dislodge him. Ian rolled onto his back but didn't let go. Using his claws, he punched his fist through Colm's back. Another surge of adrenaline pummeled through him as he wrapped his fingers around the male's beating heart.

Growling, Ian yanked his hand back, and loosened his hold around the dragon shifter as he shoved to his feet. Blood pooled in the grass and dirt of the courtyard, spilling out in a rush around the fallen male's body.

Ian tossed the heart to the ground, and moving quickly, snagged one of Colm's daggers—the one crafted from dragon fire. No one else would be getting their hands on it. As he sheathed it, he started scanning for Fiona. She stood in the middle of his siblings, but shoved them out of the way as she ran to him.

She didn't even pause, didn't care that he was covered in blood and had just killed her brother. He didn't let his guard down, was completely aware of the half-demons watching as she jumped into his arms.

He held her tight, never wanted to let her go. If she didn't care about the blood, he would let it go as well. They were free to leave. If the half-demons kept their word.

As he scanned everyone he realized he didn't see Javier anywhere.

"He's gone," Fiona murmured, as if she'd read his mind. "Finn sent him away with some of the samples, told him to try to escape out the gate." Her voice was so low he barely heard her.

He shifted slightly as the half-demon who appeared to be Colm's partner stepped forward. On instinct, Ian shoved Fiona behind him even as his siblings, Finn and a handful of wolves came to stand next to him. To his annoyance Fiona elbowed him so that she could move next to him as well.

"Do you agree to the rules of the fight?" Ian tensed, ready for another battle.

"We do." The male's expression was grim. "You have free passage to leave. If you return, any agreement is null. This is only in accordance with the rules of the fight."

"We could just end this right now," Finn said quietly. His blue eyes blazed his wolf nature, his rage clear. "Kill every single one of you for all the humans you killed."

"It wasn't by choice." He gritted his teeth even as truth rolled off him. "The dragons had a partner and they overtook our realm. We've harmed nobody here until recently. And we've had no choice but to follow orders."

"Partner?"

The half-demon nodded, looked around. "Where's Javier?"

"Don't know, don't care." Ian wanted to get the hell out of here now. "You want him, you better find him. We're leaving now."

The male's jaw tightened, but he nodded even as he called out an order to "Find Javier."

"If you truly had no choice, why do you want the half-demon now?" Finn asked.

The male's pale-green face went ashen. "We still don't have a choice. If we let him escape, we all die."

Ian wasn't particularly concerned if these half-demons died, but the fear on the male's face was real. Even so, he dismissed it. If Finn wanted to worry about what was going on here, then he could. He wrapped an arm around Fiona's shoulders and shot Finn a hard look. "I'm leaving."

The Alpha nodded, and for that, Ian was grateful. He had no doubt the Alpha would return and likely kill every living being here involved with kidnapping and killing humans, but for now they could get Fiona to Ophelia.

"And you all better back the fuck off right now. If I see one of you draw a weapon or make a move I don't like toward one of my wolves, you're all dead." There was no give in Finn's voice as he stared down the half-demon.

The male nodded and stepped back, giving them a wide berth. Finn turned to his pack as Ian turned to his brothers. He wanted to ask them what the hell they were doing there, especially since Bo was supposed to be on his honeymoon. He actually couldn't believe that Nyx wasn't here. Which likely meant his brother was going to get his ass chewed out when they returned home. And Ian would make damn sure his brothers and sister made it home.

"Where's Nyx?" he murmured to his brother.

Bo just bared his teeth at Ian.

Surprised by his brother's show of anger, Ian blinked. "What the hell is that for?"

"You go off to some Hell realm and your female is poisoned and you don't let me know?" His brother's amber eyes had gone nuclear.

"You were on your honeymoon—"

"I don't want to hear it! We're family." His voice was a savage snarl.

Before Ian could respond, the earth rumbled, similar to when the trees decided to say "fuck you" to science, before the earth rose up around them in a wall of terror, rocks, and deafening noise. Ian threw himself over Fiona, shielding her body with his as the sun of this realm was blocked out and—

"What the fuckety fuck is this?" Cynara's shocked voice made Ian raise his head to see that they were in a...dome?

A dome made of what appeared to be glass or something similar encapsulated them. His heart raced out of control as he glanced around, saw all of his siblings except Javier. It was him, Bo, Rory, Cynara, and of course Fiona who looked as shocked as he felt.

"What the fuckety fuck indeed," Fiona murmured, pushing to her feet.

He could see the wolves and half-demons past the glass of the dome but from the way the others were looking around in confusion—he didn't think they could see inside.

As another rumble started, the ground about fifty yards in front of them split open and blue, sparking electricity poured out in waves of energy.

Oh, no. This wasn't good at all.

CHAPTER TWENTY-TWO

Fiona stared in horror as a huge demon climbed out of a hole that shouldn't be there. It closed with an ominous rumble after he'd stepped onto the hard surface of the ground, as if it had never been there at all.

Demons weren't supposed to have access to Hell realms or earth. Not without a crap ton of blood sacrifice. Yet this... *Holy shit.*

At least twelve feet tall with horns, the male was the same pale blue as Ian and his brothers and sisters, but the difference between half-demons and a full-blooded one were crystal clear as she stared at his massive body and horns. And as far as she knew, demons didn't have human forms. They could glamour themselves but they never actually changed forms. Not like half-demons.

"Ian," Fiona whispered, drawing two blades out of their sheaths. "Is that your father?"

"Yes." The word was a savage growl, more animal than anything else. He made a move to step in front of her, but froze.

Looking around, she realized that the others seemed stuck in place as well. Their faces were set in tense lines but no one was moving. "Can you move?"

His foot slid forward a fraction, but it was very clearly forced. "No."

249

Frowning, she shifted her own body and realized she could move just fine.

The huge demon stretched to his full height and rolled his shoulders, looking around at everyone in the dome. He frowned once as his gaze passed over Fiona but he barely acknowledged her as he looked at the others.

"My children." His voice echoed in the dome, deep and as creepy as his bright red eyes.

A shiver of terror twined through her.

"What did you do to us?" Ian snarled. All his muscles were tense as he fought the invisible hold that his father clearly had on him.

"I'm just holding you in place for the time being. Where is my other son?" He let out an angry snarl as he scanned the dome again, as if he thought Javier would appear from nowhere.

"He escaped!" This time Bo shouted it.

The demon king bent down and shoved his hands into the dirt and grass. A ripple went out along the ground, circling out from where he was crouched. After a moment, he stood and gave the most terrifying smile she'd ever seen. His teeth were like blades, and pain and suffering echoed in his eyes. If they ever made it out of here, she'd be having nightmares for sure. This...thing was Ian's *father*? It was hard to believe such a vicious-looking creature could have sired someone as sweet and protective as Ian.

"Javier is still here." His voice echoed, that same low octave sending another shiver through her. It was like multiple voices echoing instead of just one.

"*You* were the silent partner of the dragons?" Ian demanded, his voice only a fraction calmer than before.

Stepping forward, the demon headed to Rory first, nodded as he spoke. "Yes. They were stupid enough to think I'd keep my word once I had what I wanted."

"And what is that?" Ian asked.

The male didn't respond as he moved on from Rory and continued his long strides, walking up to Bo this time. Bo spat on the male. Instead of retaliating, the demon just laughed, the sound echoing all around before he continued to Cynara. Though in her half-demon form, her hair was still the same shocking purple. The way he looked at her made Fiona want to vomit. He didn't remain long, but continued on to Ian, who had sweat rolling down his face, arms and chest now, mixing in with the drying blood. It was clear he was struggling to fight the invisible hold, because Ian sure as hell wasn't afraid.

On instinct, Fiona stepped in front of him, wanting to spare him if his father attacked. It appeared as if she was the only one who could move. While she was weakened and might not be able to shift into a dragon, she would still fight.

The demon tilted his head to the side a fraction. "Aren't you a sweet little treat," he practically crooned at her.

"And you're disgusting." She clutched her weapons tightly, fantasizing about sinking a blade between the creature's red eyes.

"Fiona," Ian snarled. "Get away from him!"

No, she wanted to keep him talking. At least long enough to find out what the hell he was up to. "Why were you working with my brothers?"

His eyes flashed a neon red, and the scent of sulfur rolling off him made her fight back bile. "Some of that should already be obvious."

She swallowed hard, staring up at him. "I know that my brothers wanted to take over the human realm."

He snorted, and a puff of smoke escaped from his nose, the sight of it bizarre. "They wanted the human realm and I was more than happy to give it to them. While they go to war with the humans, I plan to take over every single Hell realm—with the help of my children." His red eyes flashed bright again as he looked past her at Ian. "You weren't supposed to kill that arrogant dragon just yet."

"Sorry to have screwed up your plans." Ian's voice was icy calm.

"No matter. You moved up my schedule for involving all of you, but now that we have the right formula I'll find someone else to start killing humans. Someone else can take up that war while we focus on what's important."

"We're never going to help you." Rory spoke for the first time, his wolf in his gaze instead of his demon as he glared across the dome at his father. "You know we all hate you."

"Oh, I think you will. You all share my blood, my…appetites." His voice dropped a few octaves. "You can only fight your nature for so long before it eats you up inside. You think your mates will stay with you? That they've changed you? That they love you?" His maniacal laughter echoed off the glass as he swiveled back to face Fiona. "This one would betray you in a heartbeat if I gave her back her dragon. Because she *is* going to die. I can smell it. Within two days, maybe three, given her bloodline."

Fiona felt herself pale, even though deep down she'd known the truth. There was no other way to describe how it felt inside, as if she could feel herself shutting down. She wasn't even in pain, just so damn tired. As if she could sleep for a thousand years. Just fall into a Protective Hibernation and rest. But it wouldn't be a hibernation; she wouldn't be waking up from this.

She wanted to know how the demon knew she'd been poisoned in the first place, but couldn't find her voice as she stared into his red eyes.

"He's a liar! Don't believe him," Ian snarled.

His father looked past her at Ian then with an emotion that might be called pity if it wasn't so mocking. "If you don't believe me, just ask her. She's dying. But I will cure her if you align yourself with me. All you have to do is say yes and your female will be whole again."

"Lies," Ian snarled.

A jolt of power surged through Fiona. She stumbled back into Ian's chest as she felt the first inkling of her dragon blossoming inside her. *Oh God.* She'd missed her.

"Fiona?" Ian whispered, his breath warm against her. She felt his fingers skate against her arms, but his touch was faint, as if he was using all his strength for that one action.

"I'm okay." She wouldn't look at him, kept her focus on the demon a few feet away.

"Tell him," the demon murmured. "Tell him you have the first hint of power back. That you can feel your dragon again. Here's a little more," he murmured, injecting her with even more power.

Her dragon pulsed inside her, growing in strength as it spread through her like kudzu looking for purchase.

"I would rather follow her into the afterlife than ever align myself with you," Ian snarled.

"But would *she* rather I cure her? That is the question." The demon focused on Fiona again, his gaze a bright crimson as another jolt of power swelled through her. "As long as I'm alive and my son works with me, you have your dragon back."

Her fire tickled the back of her throat. Oh God, he hadn't been lying. She could feel her dragon again, feel it taking over her in a rush of raw, wild power that was so familiar she wanted to weep. Her beast wanted to be free, to soar, to burn. Which meant she'd only get one chance at this.

She wasn't sure how he was holding his children immobile or how much power he was extending, but if she could attack him maybe it would weaken him or break his hold on them. There was no way for her to know unless she tried. And she was damn sure going to try. Even if she died in the process. Saving Ian and his family would be worth it. Saving Ian was worth everything.

"If I can't convince you to work with me by curing your sweet little dragon, maybe..." He swiveled his head to look at Cynara, who was still glaring daggers at him. "Maybe if I hurt your little sister enough you'll realize there is no other option than to work with me." His head snapped back to face Ian. "I've spent over a century building an army of children and you ungrateful shits will do what I say. You'll be gods in these realms!"

Slaves, he meant.

"Never," Bo snarled again.

The demon simply shook his head. "You'll all give in eventually. It took enough planning simply to get Javier here. Another ungrateful child."

"*You* got Javier here?" Ian asked.

"I orchestrated it. Why do you think the dragons had their people kidnapping humans from areas where my children live? I knew eventually one of you would nose around and manage to end up here. Javier is the only one not aligned with anyone powerful and he didn't know about you all. He was the easiest target. I wasn't sure his blood would work, but I should have known. His mother was such a delicious treat." He absently rubbed a hand over his growing erection.

Revolting.

Fiona curled her lip up in disgust but froze as another thought occurred to her. "Your blood has other capabilities, doesn't it?" It was almost impossible for his kind to make it to the human realm, but demon blood was incredibly powerful. "Was that how my brother and the others were able to disappear into thin air in the human realm? They used your blood somehow?"

The demon simply smiled, showing razor-sharp teeth. "It's likely they did, yes. Now enough questions! I'm going to let this dome down and we're going to destroy everyone out there who opposes us. This will be our main base of operations and I'm no longer waiting in the shadows."

A low rumble filled the dome, the ground shaking beneath them. "If you make this hard for me, I'll rape your sister and make all of you watch. Then I'll toss her to—"

Fiona's dragon shoved to the surface in a sharp burst of power. This was it. Her only chance. Though still in human form, fire exploded from her in a rush of rage and heat. She screamed out her anger and fire, directing it all at the huge demon only a few feet away.

His own scream ripped through the air as she coated him in blue flames. As he stumbled back she dove at him, blades in hand. She slammed them into his stomach as she continued burning him, her flames licking along her skin without harming her, but destroying him.

He lashed out, his claws slashing against her chest as he writhed in agony. She stumbled back under the impact but breathed out another stream of fire—a bright wintery blue. It began to eat away at his face, but he wasn't going down without a fight. She vaguely heard Ian screaming at her, but all her focus was on taking this monster down and freeing Ian and the others.

The demon's claws extended but suddenly Ian and the others seemed to snap free from their invisible chains.

They rushed at him like a pack of wild animals, falling on him, tearing him limb from limb as he screamed and tried to fight back. Fiona had never seen anything so brutal, but she couldn't tear her gaze away from the carnage.

The four of them ripped into him, savaging him with a righteous fury. They seemed immune to any of his blows, immune to everything he tried to throw their way.

Body parts were tossed to the side as they continued ripping, ripping, ripping. With each killing blow they delivered Fiona weakened, her body losing all of her dragon strength, her beautiful inner beast pulling away from her.

When Cynara lifted his head high like a trophy a moment later, Fiona felt the last of her dragon's power fade from her. He hadn't been lying when he'd said that her power only lasted as long as he was alive.

"This is for my mother!" Cynara screamed, throwing the severed head against the nearest dome wall.

The horns pierced the glass and Fiona shuddered as cracks started to form into a spiral, circling out from the head in an unnatural coil.

Craaaaccckkkkk.

This place was coming down around them! Before she'd taken two steps toward Ian he sprang at her, shifting midair into his dragon form.

House-sized, Ian's wings snapped out, glittering like precious jewels as the glass shattered all around them into…ash. It dusted her skin, cascading all around them and the others in the near vicinity, but all she could focus on was the beautiful dragon of gold, violet and lavender who moved over her, his body appearing to be liquid or smoke.

He snarled loudly, keeping her trapped under him as he surveyed their surroundings. The Stavros pack and the half-demons watched Ian carefully. She didn't blame them. His body was coiled tight, the aggression rolling off him palpable.

"The demon is dead," Bo announced to everyone, coming to stand next to Ian, his other siblings right with him. Cynara looked as if she was in shock, but Rory had his arm around her shoulders. "And we're all leaving right now. I miss my mate," he muttered more to himself before he started to climb up Ian.

Fiona just blinked in surprise, then sagged against Ian's leg. He was still in his sentry position, not budging as the wolves moved into action.

The enemy half-demons who'd been working with her brother set their weapons down in unison, as if it had been choreographed.

"You want to carry me in your paw or do you want me to ride with your siblings?" she asked quietly, knowing he'd hear her regardless. Her energy was fading, her chest was still bleeding, and she needed to sit, to sleep. She'd just used up the last of her energy and knew they only had a couple days left.

At the most. Only two days with the male she would die for. Her heart cracked much like the dome had, but she held her tears at bay. If she broke down now, she'd never stop crying.

Now that the dome was down all the scents and sounds rolled over her, a little overwhelming. But she was able to tune out everything and everyone except Ian.

Her wonderful male who'd just had to kill his own father. The male had more than deserved it, but she knew it had to hurt Ian that he'd come from such a monster. Fiona understood because of her own family. She hated who she'd come from as well, hated that their blood ran in her veins. He would be suffering now and she wanted to do everything she could to soothe him.

Ian scooped her up in a paw, held her protectively close to his chest and launched into the air.

She curled into his hold, allowing herself to close her eyes as he flew them high into the air. Maybe she should be more concerned about the Stavros pack but she knew they'd have no problem leaving. The half-demons had surrendered their weapons and no one could stand against a pack that strong anyway.

Right now she wanted to get home and to spend her last couple days with Ian. She didn't think his father had been lying about her being close to death. Inside it was as if her dragon had already died. The tears she'd shoved back started to leak out, rolling down her cheeks even as she tried to hold them off.

She didn't want to die! She wouldn't even get to mate with Ian, not bond with him. Not truly. They could make love before she died, but they couldn't link themselves to each other. He wouldn't be able to bite her, to solidify the final act of mating. If he did, he'd die with her. At that thought a sob rose up but she squashed it. Her chest shook as she silently cried, not wanting Ian to hear her.

She wanted to slash out at the world if it was true, if there truly was no hope left for her. But if there wasn't, she was going to enjoy every last second of her time on this plane with Ian. Feeling sorry for herself wouldn't do anyone any good.

CHAPTER TWENTY-THREE

Fiona pushed up from the chair, her legs a little wobbly. She hadn't wanted to lie down even though she was tired. She'd been afraid she wouldn't be able to get up.

The news Ophelia had just given her drove home the final punch of truth. After leaving the Hell realm they'd come straight to the Stavros mansion to see the healer. Ophelia had made quick work of her chest wound, but Fiona had known from Ophelia's sorrowful expression that the final news wouldn't be good. There was no cure.

"It can't be fatal," Ian snapped.

The petite, dark-haired healer leaned against the edge of the bed, her arms crossed over her chest. "I'm so sorry, Fiona. I've done a battery of tests and I haven't been able to find anything to counteract this. I've been in contact with various healers from across the species, all over the globe. Vampires and shifters of every kind, including dragons."

"Did you contact Arya?" Ian asked.

Fiona wasn't sure if she should know the name but it didn't sound familiar.

Ophelia shook her head. "Not her specifically. But I talked to the healer of her clan. And I sent samples of Fiona's blood."

"Why can't you just use your magic and heal her?" Ian shoved up the sleeves of his long-sleeved black T-shirt.

He was trembling with rage, so Fiona placed her hand on his forearm.

Ophelia had already explained all of this to them but Ian simply wasn't listening to what she'd been saying. And Fiona didn't want to waste another second here. She was heartbroken and yes, afraid, but she wanted to spend the rest of her precious time with Ian and only him. "Ian, she can't heal it because of the chemistry, probably because of the demon blood used. She's not God."

His eyes were pure dragon as he looked at her. "I'm not losing you," he snarled.

Tears stung her eyes as she cupped his face, even that much movement a struggle. Fiona heard Ophelia murmur something about leaving them alone before she shut the door behind her, closing the two of them inside.

Fiona didn't bother blinking her tears away now because damn it, this hurt. "I'm not going to waste our time. Let's go. Either your place or mine, I don't care. Let's take what we've got and make every moment count."

"We can find someone—"

"You know I only have a couple days at most. Let's spend them together. Please. At least tonight." Because she didn't want to squander her last few hours or couple days hunting down a cure that might or might not exist. She certainly didn't want to die, but she and Ian had so little time.

His jaw was clenched tight, his huge body trembling so much she saw his dragon rippling beneath the surface.

If he was dying it would shred her inside so she understood his pain. Hell, she was shredded inside right now, knowing she wouldn't get to spend eternity with the male she loved. Life was such a bitch.

"Give me one second." Ian pulled his phone out and texted someone before shoving his phone back in his pocket and pulling her into his arms. She was surprised he'd taken the time to text someone, and vaguely curious as to who he'd contacted, but at this point just wanted to get back to his place or hers and get naked before she was unable to even move.

"I'm not dying without feeling you inside me again. Your place or mine?" she whispered.

Instead of answering, he simply growled and lifted her off the ground. Guess she'd find out soon enough where he planned to take them.

Fiona closed her eyes, resting to conserve what strength she had left. As long as she was with him, it didn't matter where they went.

* * *

Ophelia shoved open Gray's door without knocking. She knew it was rude but he'd just have to deal with it. She was an old wolf and sometimes she had a lot of attitude.

He jolted up from the bed, and the look on his face when he saw her, as always, was full of heat and hunger. "To what do I owe this pleasure?" he practically purred.

"You can take me out on a date. Sometime next week so you've got time to plan. And it better be something awesome."

His face split into a wide grin. "Not that I'm not happy, but why the sudden change?"

Seeing Fiona and Ian, two people who wanted nothing more than to spend just a couple days together, knowing that was all they had, broke her heart. And here she was, being a coward for absolutely no reason. At least not a real one.

Yes, Gray was a pup, but he was all man. Which meant they would definitely butt heads because she had a strong personality. Something told her it would be completely and utterly worth it. "I just decided to see if you can handle all this." He started to respond but she held up a hand. "There's something else I need to tell you..." She shoved a hand through her hair, searching for the words. Then just blurted, "I can't find a cure for Fiona."

"What?" His smile melted from his face even as he turned ashen.

"I've been running nonstop tests the past forty-eight hours and I've been in contact with every healer I know. So come on, you can help me in my lab."

He didn't argue, just hurried toward her and fell in step. "Where is she?" Guilt rolled off him in waves and she knew it had to be because he was the one who'd pulled Fiona into this.

"She and Ian left not too long ago." Ophelia might have told Fiona and Ian that there was no hope, but that didn't mean she was going to stop looking for someone who could help her. She'd already exhausted all of her resources but there were supernaturals all over the world. Maybe she could get in touch with the right person, someone who knew how to counteract demon blood. Because as far as she could tell, that was what was blocking her healing magic. "You know any healers? Any magic men?"

Gray lifted a shoulder as she shoved open the door to her lab. "I'll call everyone I can think of."

Ophelia simply nodded and flipped on the lights. It was time to get back to work.

* * *

Cell phone up to his ear, Bo paced his small office as his mate, Nyx, watched him along with Rory, Liberty, Cynara and Javier. "Yeah, no, I understand. Thanks for trying." He resisted the urge to shatter his phone into a thousand pieces. He could put it back together with his magic, but that would take time he didn't have.

He'd called a friend of a friend—of a friend—about trying to find someone who might be able to heal the female his brother loved. Every single person in the room except for Javier, who didn't know any other supernaturals, had called everyone they thought might be able to help.

Nothing had come of it.

"I hate this," Liberty rasped out, distress in her voice as she shoved up from Rory's lap. "There's got to be something we can do for them!"

Bo wanted to scream in frustration. The only thing that stopped him was when Nyx placed her hand in his, pulled him close. "I've tried calling on my mother," she murmured quietly. "She's not answering me."

He cupped his mate's cheek, not surprised Nyx had contacted her bitch of a mother. "Don't contact her again. The price will be too high." And he was determined to help his brother without her goddess mother interfering.

"Arya's on her way," Liberty said quietly, her voice watery. "Maybe she'll be able to help."

Bo simply nodded as Rory pulled Liberty into his arms. Arya was a powerful, ancient dragon who'd given Liberty the gift of immortality. But Fiona had been poisoned with something that contained demon blood. It wasn't of this realm and it was deadly. He didn't know of anything that could counteract it and searching Google sure as fuck wasn't going to help.

Cynara jumped up suddenly, her purple hair pulled back into a tight braid against her head. They hadn't even had time to talk about what had happened back in the dome. He was sure they were all equally glad that their asshole of a sperm donor was dead, but all that mattered at the moment was Fiona and Ian. "I'm going to New Orleans. Want to get there before sunrise."

"Why?" Bo asked.

"There's a magic man there who might be able to help us."

Holy hell. Of course. "Thurman."

"Well get back over here," Nyx said to Cynara. "No sense in driving."

"Oh, right." Cynara moved next to Nyx, took her hand as Bo took her other one.

As Liberty and Rory each touched one of Nyx's shoulders, Bo realized that Javier was staring at them.

"Uh…what are you guys doing?" His half-brother—it was going to take some getting used to the fact that he had another one, and likely many more yet unfound—lifted an eyebrow, eyeing them as if they'd lost their minds.

"As a demigod I can travel pretty much anywhere in seconds," Nyx said. "As long as I've been there before or—Whatever. I'll explain the rules later. Just make sure you're touching me when I make the transport, and we'll all go together."

"Be careful where you touch," Bo growled low in his throat.

Javier simply rolled his eyes and stepped forward. "I'm going to need some serious therapy soon."

Bo tensed, readying himself for the transport. He'd go anywhere, do almost any damn thing if it would save that female's life. Because something told him that if Fiona died, Ian wasn't long for this world.

CHAPTER TWENTY-FOUR

Ian followed Fiona's scent to his living room. He'd flown her to one of his homes, in the mountains of Tennessee, wanting her all to himself. Though he'd thought about taking her to his beach house in Biloxi since it was closer, he'd known that their mating manifestation would be too bright there and anyone might see.

Here they had ultimate privacy.

Curled up in front of the fire on a pile of quilts and with a fuzzy blanket pulled over her naked body, she was sleeping. She'd been exhausted when they'd arrived so he'd fed her and insisted she get some rest. Her half-empty glass of red wine was on a nearby table along with a half-eaten platter of snacks.

He checked the clock on the mantel. It was a little after two in the morning. She'd been asleep for hours and had made him promise to wake her up…a couple hours ago. But she'd looked so peaceful he hadn't wanted to. Okay, he had, but he'd managed to hold off. After rechecking the house, even though he had security and they were in the middle of nowhere on the side of a mountain—and he'd scent anyone who tried to breach his place—he decided that it was time.

Now…he was going to do something she'd probably hate him for, but she'd get over it. She'd *have* to.

269

He'd promised her that he wouldn't mate with her, that he wouldn't link himself to her irrevocably. He'd lied. This had always been his end plan if there wasn't a cure. He wasn't waiting a moment longer.

Fiona was his and if she was going to die, he was going into the afterlife with her. He wouldn't risk anything less. He was half demon, half dragon. Theoretically it could take him centuries upon centuries to die naturally and meet up with her again. And that was assuming there *was* an afterlife.

No. If she was leaving this plane, he was too. He knew himself well enough that once she was gone he wouldn't last regardless. His heart would simply stop beating without her. Or he'd go into a battle he knew he couldn't win.

And he didn't want her to die alone. Couldn't stand the thought of it. Mind more than made up, he crouched down in front of her. He was already naked, so not bothering to pull the blanket off, he simply lifted it up and brushed his lips over one of her ankles.

She stirred slightly, then let out a raspy, sleep-heavy laugh. "This is the best way to wake up," she murmured, rolling over onto her back and shoving the blanket off.

He looked up to find her watching him with those bright blue eyes that reminded him so much of the vast ocean. He could easily drown in that gaze. "I'm going to kiss every inch of you." He lifted one of her legs, but kept his gaze pinned on hers as he raked his teeth over her inner ankle.

She shuddered and slightly moaned as she watched him intently. "I love that wicked mouth."

"I love you." He nipped at her calf now, slowly making his way up her leg.

In all the years they'd been separated, she hadn't changed. She was just as sweet as she'd always been. The way she'd stood up to his father yesterday, hadn't judged Ian or his siblings for the way they'd torn into the male like savages, or him for killing her brother. And she was heartbroken to be leaving him. She'd even tried to make him promise that he'd be happy, that he'd be open to finding someone else in the future. He nearly snorted at that bullshit.

There would *never* be anyone else. Not if he lived a thousand lifetimes.

He was just grateful he had her back now. No one ever said life would be fair. It sure as fuck wasn't. But at least now he got to have his Fiona for another day. Maybe two if they were lucky.

Everything bad in his past fell away at that thought. There was only the here and now.

Him and Fiona.

"You're amazing." Fiona's sweet voice was drowsy as she stretched out her arms over her head.

He scraped his teeth along her inner thigh, causing her to jerk from the contact. She slid her fingers through his hair as he ran his tongue along her slick folds.

He'd planned to tease her a little longer, but his patience was over. He was barely keeping it together, barely containing the need to mate with her, to *mark* her—and he had this fear that she'd realize what he was up to, would somehow read his mind and stop him.

That wasn't happening.

"Ian." She moaned out his name as he flicked his tongue around her pulsing clit. The little bundle of nerves peeked out from her folds, simply begging for him to pleasure her.

He was more than happy to oblige and planned to spend every last moment on this earth pleasuring this female.

He placed his hands on her inner thighs, held them open. "I fantasized about your taste over the years," he murmured, not looking up at her, but keeping his attention right where it should be. He teased her clit again, then paused to continue. "Thought I'd imagined how sweet you were."

She simply moaned, dug her fingers into his scalp. "Less talking." Her words were tinged with desperation.

He smiled against her mound, remembering how impatient she'd been once upon a time. Still was, apparently. "I couldn't have imagined this," he said before burying his face between her legs again.

She arched up off the blankets as he ate at her like a desperate man. When he tasted her, kissed her, teased her, he felt starved. As if he'd never get filled up, never get enough. She was his last meal and he was going to enjoy every inch of her delicious body.

When he slid a finger inside her tight sheath, her inner walls clenched around him. She was so damn tight and ready for him.

His cock pulsed between his legs, thick and heavy, ready to push into her sweet body. Holding off on doing this when they first arrived had been torture. But it was worth it.

She arched her back again, trying to ride his finger, but for this he wanted to be inside her. He wanted her coming around his cock as he pierced her neck, took her in the way shifters did—bonded them together for eternity.

For dragons, as with all shifters, mating was sacred. And for dragons, it would link them together forever, even in death. It was the one true way dragons were different than other shifters. When a mated dragon died, so did their partner. It was strange—he wasn't even afraid of dying. Not when he knew he'd be going with Fiona.

"You're such a tease," she murmured, rolling her hips against him.

Pulling back, he looked down at her, drank in every inch of her. Her dark hair spilled all around the red and white blanket underneath them. The smoke of his mating manifestation combined with her blue fire, which flickered over every surface he could see. "Tease?"

"Mm hmm." Sitting up, she reached for his cock, gripped it hard while keeping her eyes locked on his. "I want this in me right now. We've waited long enough."

He growled low in his throat. Yeah, he could do that. He covered her body with his, crushing his mouth to hers with a desperation he never felt except when he was with her. She always made him feel like this: savage and wild. Somehow he pulled back, breathing hard as he stared down at her. "On your knees," he murmured.

Her eyes flashed bright, mirroring the blue fire flickering around them as she rolled over, her long, lithe body a work of art.

Her long dark hair fell down her back in soft waves. He wrapped his hand around the length, tugged gently once. She arched into his grip and let out a throaty moan that went straight to his cock.

With his free hand, he ran his palm over her smooth ass. He wanted to lean down and nip at it—so he did, just a little bite on each cheek. God, she was perfection.

She jerked once but couldn't move because of the hold on her hair. "Come on. Don't make me beg." The wild ocean scent of her desire wrapped around him, invaded his every pore. She was his life, his everything.

"Tell me what you want," he murmured, sitting back up and moving in behind her. He rubbed his hard length along her folds, but didn't penetrate, just teased. She was so damn slick. It wouldn't take long for him to push over the edge—to push *her* over the edge. He remembered how much she liked this position—and it was the perfect position for him to claim her.

"Inside me now," she demanded, her fingers digging into the blanket beneath them.

His control was completely shredded. Oh so slowly, he pushed inside her. He sucked in a sharp breath as he thrust all the way into her, as her inner walls tightened around him.

She let out a garbled moan, a shudder racking her body as he buried himself as far as he could. Oh yeah, she was his heaven. Pure and simple as that.

He remained still inside her, his balls pulled up tight as he reached around her and cupped her mound. He couldn't wait to feel her pulsing around him, to feel her coming around his cock. Fifty-two years he'd been missing her, wanting her, needing her. All the pain of living without her faded away, as if it had been a mere blink in time.

His canines had already descended and he was holding his instincts at bay. For now. Both sides of his supernatural nature demanded he mate by piercing her with his teeth. Soon enough, he told himself. *Soon enough.*

He teased her clit, rubbing her in a small, circular motion he'd learned long ago drove her crazy, pushing her to the edge incredibly fast.

Holding tight to her hair, he kept rubbing and her inner walls kept clenching around him faster and faster. It wouldn't be long now.

"Oh, God, Oh... I'm so close already," she rasped out, her body jerking slightly beneath him.

"Let go." He barely gritted the words out, his jaw was clenched so tight. "Come for me." He needed her to, needed to bring her pleasure. To finally bond them.

He knew the second before she was about to come. Her inner walls started convulsing rapidly, little flutters around his cock that drove him crazy.

On a cry, she did as he'd ordered and let go, her climax punching through her as she gasped out his name.

In that instant, he let go of his own control, let the darkness in him take over. The orgasm that had been building inside him ripped free as he emptied himself inside her. He embraced every primal instinct inside him, every part of his nature as he bent and bit down on the sensitive skin between Fiona's neck and shoulder, piercing her deeply with his canines.

Claiming her. Mating her. Linking them together for as long as they had left. One day, two, it didn't matter.

"Ian!" she screamed in anger even as her climax continued thrumming through her.

His own orgasm consumed him as he tasted her blood, felt the power of their bond click into place with a certainty, a solidity he'd never imagined. They were linked until death now.

As he came down from the high of his climax, he loosened his grip on her hair. Just like that, before he'd even managed to pull out of her, she swiveled to face him.

Her blue eyes blazed fire, the rage in her expression cutting as she slammed her fist against his chest. "You promised me!" she yelled at him. "You swore you wouldn't mate with me!"

In the blink of an eye, he had her flat on her back, pinned beneath him. She shoved at his chest, writhing and wriggling and trying to buck him off, her anger a live thing, but he was immovable. And he'd stay right where he was until they'd had this out. He'd thought he'd feel weaker once they bonded since he was fully linked to her, but he felt the same. Better, even. "Yeah, I lied." His voice was eerily calm. "I'm a half-demon. I don't feel any guilt either. You're mine, forever. If that's one day from now, so be it."

Tears tracked down her smooth cheeks as her body started trembling. "I don't want you to die," she whispered, her face stricken. "You swore." Her voice broke on the last word.

His heart cracked open, but he didn't regret his decision. Cupping one of her cheeks, he swiped at the wetness. "Would you want to live without me?"

Tears flowing freely, she shook her head.

"Then don't expect me to live without you. You're mine, Fiona. Have been from the moment I laid eyes on you, from the moment you tried to warn me off fighting your brother because you were worried I'd get hurt. Don't you dare expect me to live a life without you! You go into the afterlife? So do I. Simple as that. If we have a day left, I want to enjoy every second of it with you."

Sobs racked her at his words, and okay, guilt wormed its way through his veins, shredding him up. He still didn't regret his actions. Sitting up, he pulled her into his lap, wrapping his arms around her as she buried her face against his neck. "Oh, Ian, I don't deserve you."

She was wrong about that, but he just continued rocking her and rubbing his hand along her spine. "If the roles were reversed, what would you have done?"

"The same thing," she murmured against his neck, not even pausing in her response. The scent of her truth filled the room, potent and all-consuming.

"That's what I thought." He shifted slightly so he could wipe the rest of her tears away. He'd known she'd be upset but they still had a little time left. And so far he still felt energized. He wanted to take advantage. "Let's spend our time together with only joy. No more tears."

"No more tears," she whispered, cupping his face in her own hands. He leaned in to brush his lips over hers when she went preternaturally still in the way only supernaturals could.

Instantly he went on alert, sliding her off his lap and standing. He couldn't scent a threat but that didn't mean there wasn't one. "What is it?" he asked, holding out a hand to help her stand.

"Will you turn off the alarm?" Her voice had an odd quality to it, but she didn't seem afraid so he nodded.

After turning it off, he returned to find her standing at the sliding glass door that led to the back porch. She'd pushed the curtain back and opened the door. Though it was early in the morning, an almost full moon hung in the sky, illuminating the thick green trees for miles and miles.

Completely naked, she walked out onto the porch, bypassing the covered hot tub until she stood at the ledge that overlooked the mountainside stretching out before them.

"Hold on," he murmured, stepping back to grab a blanket for her. She'd been so cold earlier—

She jumped onto the ledge, and in a move that would forever give him nightmares, she dove off the edge—and shifted into the most beautiful dragon he'd ever seen.

Her pale silver and white scales glittered under the moonlight as she swooped toward the tops of the trees, her wings flapping sharp and steady. She rolled midflight, showing off her skills, before twisting and shooting straight up in the air in a move that showcased her raw strength. Then she disappeared from sight, her camouflage falling into place.

Happiness swelled inside him as a burst of laughter erupted. He wasn't even sure why he was laughing. It was either that or cry. She was whole and appeared healthy all of a sudden. And he realized that he'd never felt weak, not even for a second, after mating with her. He'd expected her sickness to infect him, to take over since they were bonded. He'd heard of other dragons who'd felt wounded when their mates were and had assumed it would be the same for him.

It was almost too much to hope that mating had healed her, but...his dragon and demon nature were damn strong. And what else could this be?

Less than five minutes later he heard Fiona land somewhere in front of his cabin so he raced back through the house. He yanked the door open to find her standing on the porch two feet in front of him, in human form, completely naked with a big smile on her face. Her entire being pulsed with health and strength.

"My dragon's back!" With a laugh of pure delight, she threw her arms around his neck.

Joy like he'd never known surged through him as he lifted her off her feet and hauled her back inside. While he might not be a hundred percent certain that the mating bite had counteracted the poison, he was certain that he loved this female with everything he had.

And he was going to spend the rest of their lives, however long that might be, showing her exactly how much.

CHAPTER TWENTY-FIVE

B o set his cell phone on the countertop of his kitchen island, stunned at what he'd just heard.

"I told you everything would be fine," Arya said, taking a sip of coffee, eyeing him over the rim of it. She watched him with the eyes of a predator. Of course, she watched everything that way.

After returning from New Orleans early this morning with no luck from the magic man who lived there, his mate had finally crashed. But Bo hadn't been able to sleep. He'd known that Arya was on her way and he wanted to wait up for her.

"How did you know?" His brother Ian had just told him that while they weren't completely certain that Fiona was cured, her dragon was back and they both felt completely fine. Not sick or tired. Definitely not dying.

She lifted a shoulder. "Because I'm very ancient and I've seen almost everything."

Arya had told Bo that all Ian had to do was mate with the female and the strength of the mating bond would destroy the poison—specifically the demon blood. Bo hadn't been able to contact his brother and he had no idea where the cabin was either. So he'd been stalking him for hours only to receive a call a few minutes ago.

"No, how'd you know he'd mate with her? What if it had been too late?"

Now Arya snorted. "I knew Ian would mate with her, because he was desperate to follow her into the afterlife. Because I would have done the same thing for my Dragos."

Shit. He'd never considered that his brother would do that, but he should have. Dragons mated in the most intense way. And the truth was, if Bo lost Nyx... He wouldn't want to stick around this plane for one second longer either.

He shoved that thought away, refusing to even think of something happening to his perfect mate. "Well, they're on their way back. Ian wants Fiona to see Ophelia again, to do some tests just to make sure. He asked that you stay for an extra day, said he has something he wants to talk to you about." And Bo was pretty sure he knew exactly what it was.

"Of course. Dragos and I are heading to New Orleans tonight to catch a show. I've heard Cirque de Soleil is quite good. But we'll be back tomorrow." She slid off her chair and somehow managed to look deadly while doing it. To his surprise, she patted his cheek in a way only his mother had ever done. "You're a good brother." And at that, she left his kitchen, off in search of her mate who was somewhere on Bo's property doing who the hell knew what.

In the last year his life had changed so drastically. Before, he'd valued his privacy and hadn't had any siblings except Cynara that he'd known about. And he'd never had an actual relationship until Nyx. He'd also never allowed other supernatural beings onto his property, that was certain.

Now…it was like his life had exploded with friends and family, and he wasn't even sure how many people were at his house right now. All his siblings except Ian, and Bo's mate, some shifters from the Stavros pack and Arya and Dragos were on the grounds. Maybe more.

And he wouldn't have it any other way. Now that he knew Ian's mate was going to be okay, he needed to find the others and tell them. Because they were all still reaching out to their contacts, trying to find someone who could help Fiona.

Then, he knew that Nyx and Liberty would start planning a party to welcome Fiona to the family. She'd get to see how half-demons and wolves liked to have a good time. And at that thought, he laughed. She'd either be amused or horrified. Probably a bit of both.

CHAPTER TWENTY-SIX

Out of respect, Ian stood as Finn strode into the little French coffee shop. The bell jingled again as the door shut behind the Alpha.

Pushing his sunglasses back on his head, the male nodded once at him and stepped farther inside. "Why here and not Bo's bar?" Finn asked as he reached the small round table.

Ian picked up his coffee. "Figured we'd have more privacy here. Just humans," he murmured even though there was no one around except a young human female in the storeroom grabbing the pie he'd ordered. "Plus I'm picking up a key lime pie for Arya." He and Fiona were headed over there later and he knew the ancient dragon liked them.

Finn just snorted and glanced around the matchbook-sized place. Located in Ocean Springs, it was across the Bay Bridge from Biloxi so not too far from where they lived, but far enough away from that it wasn't likely any wolves would be here.

The display cases had rows and rows of confectionary art—at least that's what Lyra had told Ian. "You know your mate's the one who suggested this place to me."

Finn didn't show surprise even as he said, "Never heard of it."

Ian lifted a shoulder. "Shit's good here."

The Alpha started to respond when the girl with long, blond hair came out from the back, a big smile on her face. She didn't even bat an eye at Finn in his biker jacket and perpetual scowl looking out of place in the ultra-feminine shop.

"As soon as I'm done ringing him up I'll grab your order." Her smile was wide and shopkeeper friendly as she placed the box on the counter next to the cash register.

"He'll take a latte and a dozen of the little tiramisus. Plus another dozen cannoli. Just add it to my bill," Ian said before Finn could respond. He glanced at the Alpha to find the male watching him with a mix of annoyance and humor.

Once he'd paid for everything and they had their boxes, they headed outside and sat at one of the faux wrought iron tables. He was afraid he'd break the chair under his weight it was so damn delicate looking. But it held.

"You order me a fucking latte?" Finn muttered, picking up his drink nonetheless.

"First, I know you drink lattes. Vega told me. Second, the food is for your ladies so you're welcome." That got him a half-smile from the Alpha even as Finn shook his head. "And third, me ordering for you is an example of exactly why I can never be part of your pack. My dragon and demon side—and okay, my human side—are dicks. I don't do well with orders. I guarantee I'll always have your back. Unless it puts my family in danger, you can always call on me. Always. I owe you a debt—"

"No you don't."

Ian lifted a shoulder. "Whatever. I owe you and you'll take my gratitude."

Finn snorted but didn't respond, just watched the passing traffic on the quiet street of downtown Ocean Springs.

"I know you never officially offered to have me as a packmate—"

Finn's ice blue gaze snapped back to him. "I was going to."

Ian nodded once. "Yeah, I figured. And I'm truly honored." In a way he couldn't ever put into words. He'd been so damn alone for so long. Now to be wanted by a pack and a clan? It was a lot to process. "But you know it would never work. You'd have to come down hard on me eventually." It was simply his nature to buck orders.

Finn nodded again, then let out a sigh filled with relief. "Yep. You're a worthy male. Hell, more than worthy. I'd be honored to call you a packmate. But I'm glad you're going to take Arya's offer. It'll make my life a hell of a lot easier."

Ian wasn't surprised the male knew about the offer. "Fiona and I are meeting with her later."

"Good. And I'm glad your female's okay."

His throat tightened once. "Thank you. Like I said, you need anything, just ask. If the Petronilla clan is amenable, we'll be staying in the South for now." He knew Fiona didn't want to move and he'd live anywhere she was. "Especially with Vega going to college. If you need me to check in on her once in a while, just let me know."

Finn blinked, the first true sign of surprise Ian had ever seen from the male, before his careful mask fell back into place. "Thank you."

Ian held out a hand, shook the male's hand once before they went their separate ways. He knew he'd be seeing the male soon and more often than not, considering one of his brothers was part of his pack and the other lived in his direct territory.

Inhaling the crisp, salt-tinged air, he headed down the sidewalk to his truck, half-smiling at the sight of beads leftover from a parade hanging in the oak trees lining the street. Humans and their weird traditions were a mystery to him. He had a feeling today was going to be a good day.

* * *

"I'm kind of nervous," Fiona whispered to Ian as they strode up the steps of the beach house. She'd let Ophelia take multiple samples of her blood and everything had come back clean. Not only that, but Ophelia had scanned her using her healer's magic and assured Fiona that she was completely fine. And she felt more than fine—incredible, now that she was mated to the man she loved more than anything. It was like nothing she'd ever imagined. Because no one would be able to truly understand what it was to be mated unless they were. It was unique, special.

She'd been so angry at him for mating with her, but it was hard to be mad when he'd saved her life, and loved her enough to leave this plane with her. And she'd have done the same thing.

"After everything we've been through, now you're nervous?" Ian laughed lightly and gave her hand a gentle squeeze as he easily balanced his pie box in another hand.

"When I mentioned to Ophelia that we were going to meet with Arya, she seemed to be nervous for me." And Ophelia wasn't afraid of anything.

"Nah, Arya's great. She can be a little eccentric, but she and her mate were in hibernation for...centuries. I think they're still adjusting to this time period."

She glanced up at the three-story raised beach house painted a periwinkle blue. "Let's do this, then."

Before Ian could knock on the door, it swung open to reveal an attractive couple—definitely dragons, given their scent and size. The male was at least six feet five inches, broad with dark hair and silvery gray eyes. The female was tall, even taller than Fiona, with blond hair pulled back into a twist at her nape, showing off stunning cheekbones. She looked like a supermodel. They both wore cargo pants and T-shirts and the female had...a machete strapped to her thigh. *What. The. Hell.* Well, Ian had said that she was eccentric.

"Ian, welcome." The female stepped back, motioning them inside.

"Arya, Dragos, this is Fiona O'Riley—now Fiona McCabe. My mate."

Warmth spread through Fiona to hear him call her Fiona McCabe.

Arya gave her a warm, genuine smile as she clasped one of Fiona's hands between both of hers. "You're originally part of the Ó Raghaillaigh clan."

Fiona blinked in surprise, but nodded. "That's right."

"We've got breakfast and coffee in the kitchen," Dragos said, clapping Ian on the back and nodding politely at Fiona as he took the pie box.

Once they were settled inside, Fiona's nerves skyrocketed again. Ian wanted to officially accept the Petronilla clan's offer to make him a member. But only if they could continue to live down south and she didn't have to give up her job. Those were his requirements.

The truth was that if they denied her request, she would still join the clan because she knew how much it meant to Ian. She could do her job anywhere and he deserved to be a member of a clan.

"I think I know why you're here, and my son Conall has given me permission to speak on his behalf as Alpha."

Something told Fiona that no one gave Arya permission to do anything.

Ian nodded once. "I want to officially accept your offer to become a member of the Petronilla clan. As long as we are accepted as a couple and Fiona and I can remain living here, we'd like to become contributing members."

Arya and Dragos both nodded, almost in unison. "Accepted," she said.

Fiona blinked, then looked at Ian, who appeared just as surprised as she was. "That's it? Don't you want to know more about me?" she blurted before she realized how ungrateful she sounded. She winced, tried to backtrack.

But Arya simply laughed. "We've wanted Ian as part of our clan for months. If he chose you as a mate, you must be worthy. That said, I've already done research into you, and since you were smart enough to leave your tiresome, draconian clan, and you've done a lot of good over the past fifty years... We don't need to know any more. You're both permitted to remain living where you are, but you'll always have a home in Montana should you ever choose. In fact, I think I'll have to insist you spend at least a month out of the year up there with us." At the last part, she looked at Ian, her expression filled with a maternal sort of adoration as she spoke.

Which just melted Fiona's heart. She wouldn't mind spending time with this female one bit. "Thank you. That's incredibly generous," Fiona said, squeezing Ian's hand once. This was more than she'd hoped for.

"Thank you," Ian said quietly, and Fiona was under the impression that he was fighting a wave of emotion. He'd been alone for so long and even though he'd found family in the last year, now he was being accepted into a clan who didn't care about his dual nature.

Arya pulled first Ian then Fiona into a tight hug before standing back. Dragos cleared his throat loudly, making the female roll her eyes.

"Tell them," the big male murmured, power vibrating through his words.

She gritted her teeth once, then sighed. "I was going to wait, but...Dragos and I might have had a few words with your former clan."

Dragos cleared his throat again.

"Fine. *I* might have had a few words with them." In a flash, her eyes flicked to dragon, the predator looking out at them holding centuries of terrifying secrets and power. "Their sons wreaked a lot of havoc on a pack my own clan considers allies. Not only do I know their reputation for treating women like servants, I know how they kept the two of you apart for so long. They won't be bothering either of you ever again." The promise that reverberated in the female's words shook Fiona to her core.

After everything she and Ian had been through, the truth was, she hadn't been worried about her former clan members coming after them. But to know without a doubt that she and Ian were now part of a new clan, one who protected their own, gave her a sense of peace.

When she looked at Ian she saw the same relief in his amber eyes as well. Without thinking Fiona launched herself at Arya, pulling the powerful female into a tight hug. "Thank you," she rasped out, wishing she had more than the two words to convey her gratitude.

The female patted her gently on the back then stepped back, looking as if she felt a little awkward before she turned away to the display of food. Moments later foodstuff was piled high on two plates and practically shoved in front of them.

Since all Fiona and Ian had been doing the last few days was making love, she wasn't going to say no to a plate of bacon, eggs and fruit.

Before they dove in, she leaned over, brushed her lips against Ian's stubbly cheek. He turned to her, caught her mouth in a quick, breath-stealing kiss.

Oh yeah, she loved this male and couldn't wait to see what adventures lay in store for them. As long as they were together, they could face anything. For the first time in a long time, she didn't feel alone—and she knew he didn't either.

They had family, a clan, and even wolves they could count on. It was a bright new world, and a future stretching out before them that she'd never dared hope for. The only thing she knew for certain was that she'd never be separated from him again.

Thank you for reading Saved by Darkness. If you don't want to miss any future releases, please feel free to join my newsletter. I only send out a newsletter for new releases or sales news. Find the signup link on my website: http://www.katiereus.com

ACKNOWLEDGMENTS

I've said this before and I'll hopefully say it many more times. Getting a book to where it's ready to be published is a team effort and I have a great team to be thankful for. In no particular order; Kari Walker & Carolyn Crane, thank you guys for your insightful thoughts into this story! Julia Ganis, thank you for being such a thorough editor. Thank you to Jaycee of Sweet 'N Spicy Designs for another beautiful cover. Sarah, thank you for all the behind the scenes things you do that save my sanity. As always thank you to my readers! To my family, thank you for feeding my caffeine addiction. Last but not least (as always), I'm grateful to God for so many opportunities.

COMPLETE BOOKLIST

Red Stone Security Series
No One to Trust
Danger Next Door
Fatal Deception
Miami, Mistletoe & Murder
His to Protect
Breaking Her Rules
Protecting His Witness
Sinful Seduction
Under His Protection
Deadly Fallout
Sworn to Protect
Secret Obsession
Love Thy Enemy
Dangerous Protector
Lethal Game

Deadly Ops Series
Targeted
Bound to Danger
Chasing Danger (novella)
Shattered Duty
Edge of Danger
A Covert Affair

The Serafina: Sin City Series
First Surrender
Sensual Surrender
Sweetest Surrender
Dangerous Surrender

Non-series Romantic Suspense
Running From the Past
Dangerous Secrets
Killer Secrets
Deadly Obsession
Danger in Paradise
His Secret Past
Retribution
Merry Christmas, Baby

Paranormal Romance
Destined Mate
Protector's Mate
A Jaguar's Kiss
Tempting the Jaguar
Enemy Mine
Heart of the Jaguar

Moon Shifter Series
Alpha Instinct
Lover's Instinct (novella)
Primal Possession
Mating Instinct
His Untamed Desire (novella)
Avenger's Heat
Hunter Reborn
Protective Instinct (novella)
Dark Protector
A Mate for Christmas (novella)

Darkness Series
Darkness Awakened
Taste of Darkness
Beyond the Darkness
Hunted by Darkness
Into the Darkness
Saved by Darkness

ABOUT THE AUTHOR

Katie Reus is the *New York Times* and *USA Today* bestselling author of the Red Stone Security series, the Moon Shifter series and the Deadly Ops series. She fell in love with romance at a young age thanks to books she pilfered from her mom's stash. Years later she loves reading romance almost as much as she loves writing it.

However, she didn't always know she wanted to be a writer. After changing majors many times, she finally graduated summa cum laude with a degree in psychology. Not long after that she discovered a new love. Writing. She now spends her days writing dark paranormal romance and sexy romantic suspense.

For more information on Katie please visit her website: www.katiereus.com. Also find her on twitter @katiereus or visit her on facebook at: www.facebook.com/katie-reusauthor.

Printed in Great Britain
by Amazon